Rutland Library Services

www.rutland.gov.uk/libraries

Rutland
County Council

Charges may be payable on books overdue at public libraries. This book is due for return by the last date shown, but if not required by another reader may be renewed – ask at the library, telephone, write or email, quoting your library service number, or the barcode (below), and the last date shown above, or visit our website.

THE SONG OF THE NIGHTINGALE

A Hawkenlye Mystery

Alys Clare

severn
House

This first world edition published 2012
in Great Britain and in the USA by
SEVERN HOUSE PUBLISHERS LTD of
9–15 High Street, Sutton, Surrey, England, SM1 1DF.
Trade paperback edition first published
in Great Britain and the USA 2013 by
SEVERN HOUSE PUBLISHERS LTD.

British Library Cataloguing in Publication Data

Clare, Alys.
  The song of the nightingale.
  1. D'Acquin, Josse (Fictitious character)–Fiction.
  2. Helewise, Abbess (Fictitious character)–Fiction.
  3. England–Social life and customs–1066-1485–Fiction.
  4. Detective and mystery stories.
  I. Title
  823.9'2-dc23

ISBN-13: 978-0-7278-8194-6 (cased)
ISBN-13: 978-1-84751-447-9 (trade paper)

All Severn House titles are printed on acid-free paper.

Severn House Publishers support The Forest Stewardship Council [FSC], the
leading international forest certification organisation. All our titles that are printed
on Greenpeace-approved FSC-certified paper carry the FSC logo.

MIX
Paper from
responsible sources
FSC
www.fsc.org   FSC® C018575

Typeset by Palimpsest Book Production Ltd.,
Falkirk, Stirlingshire, Scotland.
Printed and bound in Great Britain by
MPG Books Ltd., Bodmin, Cornwall.

For Jon, Hannah and Imogen,
who know what it's like for families to be apart

Cytharizat cantico
Dulcis philomena,
Flore rident vario
Prata iam serena.

Like a lyre sings
The sweet nightingale,
Full of laughing flowers
Are the joyful meadows.

From *Carmina Burana*,
Cantiones profanae

PROLOGUE
Early in 1211

The three men were homeless and starving. Driven from their previous sporadic employment by the new poverty of their former masters, driven from their homes because they could not pay the meagre rent, they had, like so many others in King John's England, been reduced to roaming the countryside begging for handouts from people almost as hard-pressed as themselves.

They were not alone in their hunger and their desperation. What set them apart was their brutality.

All three were natural bullies, although one – a dark-countenanced, broad-shouldered man named Wat – was the worst. The other two, accepting instinctively that his cruelty was considerably more ruthless their own, deferred to him as the natural leader. Sometimes – increasingly – they feared that he would take them into dark places where they would probably not have gone without him. But the pair had the weakness of character that so often typifies the bully: it was easier to continue throwing in their lot with a tough, strong man like Wat than to go their own way. It never occurred to either of them that they might remonstrate with him and try to bring him back from the worst excesses of his savagery.

Over the months, they had roamed far from their former homes, in the west of England, at first travelling steadily towards London and then turning south. There were quite a lot of towns and villages where, because of some act of theft, violation or casual cruelty, the various forces of law and order were after them. They could not safely retrace their steps. Going ever on, in time they found themselves on the fringes of the great forest that stretched across the south-east corner of the land. There was a big abbey nearby; the trio heard people refer to it as a place where you could find care, kindness and a bite to eat. Not even the promise of food tempted the three men to approach the abbey, however. They had no time for priests and monks; and nuns, as Wat remarked with a leer, were only good for slaking a man's lust, and then only if they were young and pretty.

The trio made themselves a rudimentary camp a few hundred paces inside the perimeter of the forest. Even when they had been in work, they had always been lazy and shiftless, needing the threat of someone else's boot up their arses to make them pull their weight. Resentful of command, they were at the same time not capable of working for themselves, being to a man unimaginative and without any idea that dedicated effort might better their lot. Hence the camp was poorly made and totally lacking in comfort. The roughly-made roof leaked; there was no deep bed of branches, twigs and dead bracken to stop the damp from the ground penetrating their thin blankets; they did not know how to hunt nor which wild plants were safe to eat, and so were constantly hungry; and they quarrelled so violently and so frequently over whose turn it was to fetch firewood and tend the hearth that the fire was always going out.

Not one of them had the least modicum of sensitivity in his nature. If they had, they would have felt the forest's deep unease at their presence within its borders.

And their fate would have been quite different.

It was late one January afternoon, when since daybreak a fierce east wind had blown without ceasing, frequently hurling brief but angry sleet showers against the three men's chilled flesh. They had reached the depths of their miserable discomfort. Everything in the camp was wet; every garment they possessed was torn and filthy; nobody had scavenged for food, water or firewood; they were close to starving and shivering with cold. One – the youngest and least robust – had a persistent sniff and a harsh, barking cough. They looked at each other and silently came to the conclusion that they had to venture further afield in their search for plunder. For three or four weeks, they had made do with the isolated cottages and lonely hovels that hunched under the forest fringes, always spying out the land first to make sure that no big, strong husband or son lived within. They kept away from tough men, preferring the softer targets of feeble widows or the helpless, querulous elderly. Now, however, they were uncomfortably aware that they had robbed these local dwellings of everything there was to rob. Their victims were now as empty-handed as the three men.

Wat said they must go back towards the town on the river which they had passed – giving it a wide berth – on their way south to the forest. They would not go too close; as soon as they found a likely household, they would break in, grab what they could and then melt away back to the forest.

As soon as the short, bleak day came to its end, they set out. Wat carried a sword, in a worn leather scabbard, and his short, thick staff. The other two were armed simply with lengths of wood.

The sword was old and beautifully crafted. It had seen service in Outremer, where its carefully-forged Spanish steel blade had flashed and scythed its way through many infidel necks. Handed down solemnly from father to son through the generations, it was a family heirloom.

Not Wat's family; he had stolen it from its hiding place beneath a straw mattress on a low, meagre cot in a cheap lodging house in a small town south-west of London. The lodging house had been run by an elderly woman and her widowed daughter, and Wat had thrashed the former and raped the latter, leaving them bleeding and traumatized. He had ransacked the lowly dwelling's dark, dank rooms; the sword was the sole item worth stealing, and Wat had got away with it only because its owner was sleeping like a dead man.

Wat had his left hand on the sword's hilt as he led the way, and such was the confidence in his braggart step that the other two fell in meekly behind. He had a vague idea of where he was heading, recalling having seen a small but reasonably prosperous-looking dwelling set by itself down a track winding away off the road that led from the valley up to the forest. He wasn't quite as sure of himself as his demeanour suggested, but, nevertheless, his luck was in and he found the place after only one wrong turning.

Soft-footed as a cat for all his size, Wat crept up to the house. It was stoutly built, and even in the dim moonlight Wat could see that whoever lived within kept the place in good repair. He went up to peer through the tiny window. Inside, sitting snugly beside a small fire, he saw a frail old man, a plump woman who had a bad cough, and a sweet-faced younger woman.

Wat's hungry eyes fixed first on the pot of gruel that was suspended over the fire. His stomach gave a long rumble, and saliva filled his mouth. As he watched, the young woman leaned forward to give the pot a stir. Such was his position that, for a moment, he could see right down the front of her gown to where the rounded, creamy breasts swelled. As hunger of another sort flooded his veins and made him hard with desire, he took in the rest of her. The smooth curve of her hips. The long legs. The slim ankles and tiny feet.

Very little could have stopped Wat then. The family's fate was already set in stone.

He glanced briefly at the other two, gave a curt nod and then put his shoulder to the door. At first it did not yield; the old man, very aware of how alone they were out there, had recently fixed a stout bar that rested on brackets either side of the door. But Wat's blood was hot and, maddened by the delay, he renewed his efforts, his two companions coming to help. There was a splintering crash, and the door broke apart.

The old man had managed to rise, shaking, to his feet. He had a long knife in his hands. Wat, grinning, stepped swiftly forward and wrenched it out of the old man's grasp even as he tried to summon the strength to swing it.

'I'll have that,' Wat remarked, giving the knife a few experimental swishes. 'You might hurt yourself, Grandad.' He ran his thumb along the knife's edge. 'Might be useful, once I've found a whetstone.'

One of the other two men was bending over the pot of gruel, grabbing the heel of bread that stood ready and dunking it deeply into the savoury-smelling gravy. The plump woman gave a heartfelt cry – 'Oh no, please, no, it's all we've got, and the first hot food we've had in days!' – but the man elbowed her roughly aside. She fell, hard, to the floor, banging her head. She tried to get up again, and the man kicked her. With a low moan, she collapsed.

Now the young girl stood in front of the hearth, a wooden ladle in her hand. Wat barked out a laugh, echoed by the others. He reached out and grabbed her by the hand that held her makeshift weapon, twisting her arm up behind her back and making her cry out in pain.

'Tuck in, lads,' Wat said.

For a short while there were no sounds in the small room except for the slurping, animal sounds of the three men wolfing down the little family's supper. The plump woman lay still on the floor; the old man sat gasping to breathe, clutching convulsively at his left arm, and the young girl bit her lip to stop herself crying out from the pain Wat was so thoughtlessly inflicting. When the pot was empty, Wat looked round the room and, catching the old man's terrified gaze, said, 'Now, what else have you got hidden away?'

'*Nothing!*' The single word emerged as a sort of squeak.

Wat spat out an oath. 'Don't try to fool me, Grandad. Snug little place like this, stands to reason you'll have some treasures tucked away to tide you through the bad times.'

'No, no!' the old man wailed. 'Everything's gone, every last coin and silver spoon! It's these incessant demands for taxes, you see,' he added, attempting an ingratiating smile.

Wat sniffed. Taxes, yes. People had to pay taxes; even he knew that.

The girl moved fractionally in his grip, trying to ease the pain in her arm and shoulder. With food in his belly, Wat's other hunger flooded through him again. 'No treasure, you say, Grandad?' he said with a sneer. He twisted the girl round so that he could look into her face. 'Now I call that downright impolite, don't you, sweetheart? Looks like your old dad can't see what's right in front of him, eh?'

In one single, violent movement, he thrust his hand inside the neck of her gown and dragged downwards. The material was clean but worn, and gave instantly. The girl threw up her hands across the front of her white chemise, but Wat pushed them away and ripped that from her as well. He flung her down on to the floor, pushed her legs apart and drove into her. After a few thrusts he was done. Kneeling back, he stared down at her. She lay still, eyes closed, lips clamped together. Wat looked up at his two companions. 'Who's next?'

When, after an eternity, they went away, the girl slowly got to her feet. Before she did anything else – even before she

wrapped the ruined garments around her – she staggered to
the water barrel behind the screen in a corner of the room and
washed herself, forcing the cold water inside her sore and
aching body, trying to remove every trace that her assailants
had left. Then, when she was at last blessedly numb, she
picked up her shift and gown and tied them round her as best
she could. She straightened her hair and put on her coif. Then,
trying to walk erect, she went to look at her parents.

Her father was dead. For years his heart had pained him;
he had stayed alive thanks to the special medicine made from
the foxglove plant that he regularly took. Now, his damaged
heart seemed to have given out under the horror and the shock.
She went over to crouch beside her mother. Would there be
comfort there?

No. Her mother was still alive, but she was beyond giving
comfort to anyone, even her own daughter. Her eyes were
wide and unfocused, her body shaking with repeated tremors.
From time to time she gave an eerie chuckle.

Her mind had gone.

The girl looked dispassionately around the room, noting
what was missing. The men had taken everything they could
carry: a thick woollen blanket; the neat pile of three wooden
platters which the little family had been about to use to eat
their supper; several cooking implements; her father's worn
old boots, with the mud still clinging to them from the last
time he had ventured outside. The room was now all but bare.

With a sigh, she looked at her dead father. She would have
to see to him, first thing tomorrow. The country was still under
the pope's interdict, forbidding the clergy of England to carry
out their normal duties, which, among other privations, meant
that nobody was laid to rest in the graveyard and prayed over
by their priest; people disposed of their dead themselves. Not
having much belief in priests and prayers, the girl was not all
that bothered by the prospect, except that, with the ground so
hard, it would be a long, arduous job to dig the grave.

She stood in the still, silent room for some time. Anger began
to stir, burning up through her and paining her as forcefully as
the rapes had done. She opened the broken door and slipped
quietly out of the house. She walked the few paces to the edge
of the forest, moving in under the deep shadow of the trees.

She knew the forest: she had lived close by it all the years of her life.

She made herself go on until she emerged into the glade she sought; it was not very far. There she stopped, drew a deep breath and, with all her might, gave a great cry. 'My father is dead and my mother driven out of her mind!' she shouted. 'I have been raped, and that which was mine to give to the man of my choice has been torn from me!' She paused, listening to the echoes of her voice die away. Then, drawing another breath: '*Avenge me!*'

In time, she turned, walked out of her clearing and went home. The gesture had been one of defiance; she had no hope that anything would come of it. Who, after all, was there to hear her? She knew she was on her own.

She was mistaken. The forest had a spirit, and that spirit knew a grave wrong had been done.

Vengeance was already on its way.

ONE

Helewise, daughter of Leofgar Warin and his wife Rohaise, and known in the family as Little Helewise to distinguish her from the grandmother for whom she had been named, stood by the window of her chamber staring out at the bare landscape. The February weather was bitter, and as yet there had been few signs that spring would ever come. The previous autumn had been very wet, and the winter had been hard; stored grain had rotted, animals had died and food was scarce everywhere. There had been barely enough to eat, even in the Warin household. In addition, her parents were constantly nagging at their daughter and the servants not to waste fuel, so that the main hall of the old house, where they all spent most of their time, was barely ever warm enough. Everyone was miserable, their hard lives made harder by the incessant demands of the king's inspectors. If they weren't enough to put up with, constantly coming up with new ways of taxing the suffering populace, there were also the men sent out by the church, demanding that everyone give tithes to help the poor. Help the poor, indeed, Little Helewise thought with a quiet snort of disgust. Everyone knew that many, if not most, of the tithes went anywhere but to the most needy. It was rumoured that, all over the land, members of the clergy were making themselves rich as the interminable interdict wore wearily on, which was even more unfair when many priests, using the excuse of being commanded by the pope himself, were apparently sitting back and doing absolutely nothing to help the people.

It was quite different at Hawkenlye Abbey, Little Helewise reflected. Abbess Caliste was, presumably, as honour bound as any other nun, monk or priest to obey the pope's dictates, yet somehow she and her loyal team were managing to succour all the desperate people who came asking. Little Helewise knew – or suspected – that men such as her father, her uncle Dominic and her grandmother's dear friend, Sir Josse d'Acquin, were helping to the best of their ability, and quietly sending as much as they could spare for the abbey to distribute. It made Little Helewise proud, even if sometimes, if she was honest, she might wish her own household kept back just a bit more for their own use. It was a selfish thought, perhaps, but she was only sixteen and life was dark and frightening.

The reality of her bleak, miserable situation broke out all at once from the corner of her mind in which she had tried to pen it. She suffered the ensuing wave of distress, then, when it had passed, straightened her spine and raised her head. Had anyone been there to witness, they might have thought she was steeling herself to go into battle.

She sighed, trying to find something to be cheerful about. Feeling suddenly exhausted, she crossed the cold stone floor and sat down on her bed, swinging her legs up and lying back on the soft pillows. She pulled up the wool blankets and the thick fur cover, snuggling down and making a warm nest. Gazing out across the chamber, she caught sight of a silver box resting on the low table beside the bed. It had been a gift from her father. He had brought it back from a recent trip to London, hoping, she guessed, to cheer her up.

If only it were that simple.

The box was a pretty thing. It was rectangular in shape, about the size of her hand, and, although the sides were decorated with a swirling pattern of leaves, the top was plain. She reached out for it, holding it up so that she could see herself reflected in the bright metal.

She saw her own wide eyes staring back at her, light in colour like her grandmother's. Her thick, dark hair was drawn back severely, leaving her pale face mercilessly exposed. She read knowledge in her eyes; the lids were puffy from weeping, and the dark circles that were etched deeply around them bore witness to sleepless nights.

She was pining. She was listless, miserable, and her customary high spirits appeared to have quite deserted her. Anxiety rode her constantly. Hardest to endure was the enforced imprisonment within the house. Not that she was alone in having to bear it; every young woman of her acquaintance was in the same position. The harsh winter was to blame: that, and the widespread, desperate poverty of the people of England. Bands of the homeless and the dispossessed lived – existed – out in the wilds of the countryside, and even the ones who had begun as honest men eventually became desperate. Cold to their very bones, often sick or wounded, hunger drove them to violence, and terrible tales were whispered of their crimes. Men such as Little Helewise's father no longer considered it safe to permit their womenfolk to travel the roads and the tracks unless they were accompanied by at least one strong, stoutly-armed man to act as guard, and the trouble with *that* was that most strong men in the employ of those such as Leofgar Warin were far too busy on essential tasks to have any spare time to escort a young woman while she went off visiting.

Little Helewise was lonely, longing more than almost anything to be allowed to go and visit family or friends. One member of the family in particular . . .

It was no use asking. Her mother Rohaise, frowning, always tense and anxious, preoccupied with running a home on increasingly tight rations, had no time for such queries. Had Little Helewise pleaded again, she knew she would get exactly the same answer: *if you have time on your hands and are bored and at a loose end, I will find you something to do.* The *something to do* would invariably be a dreary, repetitive, dull task such as helping mend the household linen, or chopping endless cabbages and root vegetables for the soups that seemed to have become the household's sole food. To make matters worse, the task would have to be done beneath the stern, eagle-eyed scrutiny of her mother, who had a way of making it perfectly clear that she considered her daughter far too prone to daydreaming, time-wasting and generally failing to *drive* herself, whatever that meant. Working in her mother's company was, Little Helewise reflected, uncomfortable at the best of times. Now, it would be—

No. She must not think of that.

She lay back on the bed and hunched the blanket and the soft fur more tightly around her ears. She stroked the fine wool of the blanket with her fingertips. Her family were growing wealthy because of wool and, despite the increasingly severe demands of the king's incessant taxes, this wealth appeared to keep steadily growing. Not that it was doing them much good at the moment, when the terrible winter meant that food of every kind was in such short supply. But the flocks were surviving, despite the snow that refused to go away and the cold wind that went on blowing out of the north-east. The thick wool that now insulated the ewes against the elements would be shorn in the spring, as it was every year, and sent over to the Low Countries, where it would be turned into the fine, highly prized cloth that fetched the highest prices.

Money.

Yes, it was good to know it was there, shoring up her family and keeping them safe from the sort of lives endured by the tramps, vagabonds and brigands who paced the lanes and the tracks and somehow existed out in the woods. She would never take it for granted; never underestimate its importance.

But, oh, *oh*, it couldn't buy happiness, and it couldn't solve the sort of misery she was facing now.

She was on her own, and sometimes her heart hurt so much that it felt as if it would break.

Of all the extended family, it was Little Helewise who pined most for the absentee: Ninian, the adopted son of Josse d'Acquin, had been forced to flee England late the previous October – over three months ago now – and not a word had come to say where he had gone, how he was, whether he was managing to eke out an existence, or even if he was still alive.

He is still alive, Little Helewise said silently to herself. *If it were not so, I would know.* She repeated the same phrases most days. Sometimes she managed to convince herself.

Her grandmother and Josse had gone after him, once he was no longer suspected of murder and it was safe for him to come home. Little Helewise's hopes had ridden high, so sure had she been that they would find him. Sir Josse was a legend – strong, determined, capable and resourceful – and Grandmother Helewise had the reputation of never giving up on a task until it was completed to her own and, more importantly, God's satisfaction. Grandmother Helewise used to be abbess of Hawkenlye Abbey; the habit of command, and the ability to inspire awed respect from lesser beings, was still draped around her like a rich and elegant cloak, or so it seemed to her granddaughter.

Not that such considerations had held Little Helewise back when her grandmother and Josse had returned alone. She remembered now, deeply ashamed of herself, how she had railed at the pair of them for their failure, not seeing until it was too late the shame in Josse's brown eyes and the pain in her grandmother's face.

'*You should have tried harder and ridden further!*' Little Helewise had screeched, beside herself with bitter disappointment and the agony of her loss. 'How could you let him go?' Then she had rounded on Josse. 'You claim you look on him as a son!' she shouted. 'How could you just give up? *I thought you loved him!*'

Even in her distress, she had seen the tenderness of the deeply sympathetic glance her grandmother bestowed on Josse. 'There are reasons, Granddaughter,' Helewise said quietly. Josse made as if to stop her, but she shook her head. Then she said, 'Little Helewise, you must be very brave.'

And she told her where Ninian had gone.

Of course, Little Helewise had understood then, or at least she had begun to, once the storm of fierce, furious, angry, helpless tears had passed and she was herself again. Ninian, her beloved man, her one true love whom she had loved as long as she could remember, appeared to have wandered into the middle of a vicious, terrible war; one in which – according to Josse, who had patiently and lovingly tried to explain – the pope and the king of France had joined forces in order, each for their own reasons, to eradicate a heretical sect who lived somewhere far to the south in a land called Languedoc. Ninian had been making for a specific address – that of an elderly woman who was the sheriff of Tonbridge's mother – but apparently this distant land was in uproar, and the town where the old woman lived had been razed to the ground by the crusading knights and their armies. Nobody had any idea where Ninian might now be.

If, indeed, he was still alive.

Nobody had said that out loud, but Little Helewise had been quite sure they were all thinking it. She had vowed then and there not to give in to such negativity, replacing it with her constant silent assurance to herself: *he is alive, and he will return to me.*

She had quickly made her peace with her grandmother and Josse, offering a sincere and heartfelt apology even before her mother had time to order her to. Both the older people had understood. She thought she had seen tears in Josse's eyes, and her grandmother had given her a hard, bracing hug and murmured, 'Chin up. Have courage, dear heart, and we shall pray that all will be well.'

Over the slow winter months, Little Helewise had discovered painfully that having courage and keeping one's chin up were easier said than done. Praying might be all right for her grandmother, who had after all long been a nun, but, as far as Little Helewise was concerned, it made a poor substitute for a real-life, handsome young man whose brilliant blue eyes danced with laughter and who loved her as fervently as she loved him.

Enough, she now told herself firmly. She could feel tears pricking behind her eyelids, and all of a sudden she despised herself for being so weak. Yes, she was faced with an ongoing, miserable anxiety which nothing she could do would lessen, but she was not improving matters by lying alone in her chamber weeping about it. She sat up, threw back the covers and stood up, automatically reaching down to straighten the bed and leave it tidy; her mother was fussy about things like that.

Her mother . . .

Suddenly, Little Helewise knew what she wanted to do. Living under her parents' roof was not helping her. On the contrary, Rohaise's attitude – that Little Helewise should count her blessings and start doing a great deal more to help the management of the household, and that it would probably be better for everyone concerned if she put all thoughts of Ninian behind her and got on with her life – was, Little Helewise now realized, one of the most disturbing and hurtful elements of the whole situation. It would, she reflected ruefully, have been so nice to curl up beside her mother on the bench beside the hearth, open her heart and reveal all her worries and anxieties. She pictured her mother's face, the expression tight, anxious; the sharp eyes on the lookout for any behaviour requiring a reprimand. Slowly, Little Helewise shook her head.

There wasn't going to be a tender fireside scene, because her mother just wasn't the type you went to for comfort.

But, Little Helewise thought, *I know someone who is.*

Moreover, if only she could get herself to that welcoming household where suddenly she so longed to be, maybe there might be some way of organizing another search party to go and look for him. The people there missed Ninian almost as much as she did; of that she was convinced. And, when all was said and done, if there *was* going to be another attempt to find him and bring him home – and how urgently she wanted him! – then it certainly wasn't going to set out from her parents' home.

She rearranged her hair, drew on a clean coif and straightened her gown. She was going to seek out her father and ask quite a big favour; one, moreover, about which her mother would undoubtedly have a lot to say. It would be as well to present herself looking neat and tidy, and it would certainly help if she volunteered to do a few useful tasks to help out during what remained of the hours of thin daylight.

Feeling considerably better, as even sad and anxious people usually do if they can find a purpose, Little Helewise left the chamber and, stitching on a smile, went to find her father.

TWO

In the House in the Woods, Josse d'Acquin was finding it increasingly impossible to cope with the varying degrees of depression, irritation, resentment and flashes of fierce, hot temper displayed on a daily basis by almost every one of his household.

I am a reasonable man, he reminded himself one morning as, frustrated and hurt, he strode away from Hawkenlye Manor and off down his favourite track into the forest. Still fuming, he went over the recent scene: his son hadn't appeared for breakfast, so his portion had gone cold and stale, and you just shouldn't waste food, especially now when times were so tough; his daughter had leapt to her absent brother's defence, using the incident to issue a not very subtle reminder to her father that she, too, might like to have a similar freedom to absent herself from the house; his faithful young servant's elder boy had timidly edged the bowl of porridge towards him and dipped the end of his spoon into it, upon which his mother, face flushing in embarrassment, had lost her temper and screeched at her son that he should count his blessings, go on his knees to thank God that he and his family had a safe home with Sir Josse, and shouldn't even *dream* of stealing food put out for someone else, even if that someone was not actually eating it himself.

At that point Josse had pushed his chair away from the table – rather roughly, for him – and strode out of the hall, not pausing even to pick up his warm cloak, something he was now regretting, as it was colder out of doors than he had anticipated.

As he paced along, his bad temper cooling as swiftly as his hands and feet, his mind filled with images of his household, of those dear people – kin, loved ones, faithful servants – who made up his world. He had known loneliness before they all came here to the House in the Woods. It was the fulfilment of a deeply personal dream, to live here with the people he loved; to need them and, more crucially, to be needed by them.

Restored to good humour – even if not quite ready to go home – Josse thought about them all in turn, bringing each to mind in the way a devout man might handle the beads of his rosary, pausing at each one to think, to pray, to wish them well. To tell them silently, perhaps, what they meant to him.

His longest association was with his servant Will; with a smile, Josse thought back to the day Will and his withdrawn and silent woman, Ella, had first come into his life. They had proved their worth so many times over the years, and Josse didn't know what he would do without them. Will, in particular, he regarded as a friend rather than a servant, and would have said as much to Will had he not been very aware that such sentiments would be all but incomprehensible to Will and hence deeply upsetting. Will had a firm and unshakeable belief in a man knowing his place; moreover, Josse was aware that Will was content with his lot. It was not every man who could say that.

Will and Ella were not Josse's only servants, for in addition there was Gus, formerly a lay brother at Hawkenlye and now happily married to Tilly, who had begun life as the lowest, lowliest kitchen maid in a Tonbridge inn. Gus, the child of gypsies, had filled out from the skinny boy he used to be and was in his prime, broad shouldered and starting to look a little stout; although of late he, like everyone else, often left the table hungry and had drawn his belt in a few notches. Tilly had developed into an excellent cook, managing small daily miracles by turning meagre amounts of unappetizing food into meals that the household fell on; it was only rarely now that Josse caught a glimpse of the shy little tavern girl of old.

Both Gus and Tilly had bloomed in their new life at the House in the Woods, and the three lively children Tilly had borne her cheerful, amiable husband were the living proof. The eldest boy was quiet, like his mother, but capable; with a grin, Josse reflected that in truth he did not begrudge the lad a bowl of unwanted porridge. The younger pair – a girl and a boy – tended to quarrel rather more than Josse would have liked, but he hoped it was just a phase.

Thinking about Gus and Tilly's children turned Josse's mind to his own. Meggie, oh, Meggie! She was suffering badly because of being penned up at home; very obviously, she missed the freedom of going to the little hut in the woods – where once she had lived with her mother, Joanna – whenever and for as long as she liked. But Josse had made a rule: nobody was to leave the house alone, especially the womenfolk. Meggie, bless her loving heart, abided by the dictate, although sometimes she looked so sad, and he wished he knew how to take the frown away from between her delicate brows. It was, he realized, weeks – months – since he'd heard her laugh, and nowadays she rarely even smiled.

But I have no choice! he thought bitterly. The countryside was full of brigands, robbers, and vagabonds, homeless men who preyed on others not quite so unfortunate, who did not hesitate to attack the vulnerable for little more than a piece of bread. Rumours flew around all the time of travellers robbed and beaten; of lonely households broken into, the occupants terrorized, raped, beaten, even killed. Josse had no fears for such an assault on the House in the Woods; several strong men lived there, and their leader – Josse himself – was a former soldier. He had drilled his household in what they should do if ever anyone tried to break down the stout door; the women, too, had their own roles to play. Josse, smiling, reflected that, had he been an outlaw, he would rather have faced one or two weedy men than Meggie when her blood was up.

He was aware that he was reluctant to think about the other woman who lived under his roof; the one he loved as much, in a different way, as he loved his daughter. But then thinking about Helewise had never been easy . . .

His mind wandered back to how the two of them had hurried over the narrow seas last autumn, intent on finding Ninian. He had felt then that the argument she used to make him give up the search – that his loved ones were suffering enough with one of the family gone without losing Josse too – had been underhand. He still believed it now, although he knew in his heart that she was right. But then, just because what she said was true, it didn't mean she'd been justified in saying it. He hadn't forgiven her. Sometimes, glancing at her and catching her unawares, he thought that she hadn't forgiven herself.

Josse's anger flared anew, and he kicked out viciously at a dead tree stump. Families always had their problems and upsets, he was sure of that, but, for all of them, even small matters were exaggerated by the conditions under which they were at present forced to live. Alone out there in the dense woodland, unseen, unheard, Josse drew a deep breath and, in words that would have made a nun blush, told King John exactly what he thought of him.

It was the king's fault; the king whose intransigence had led to the interdict placed on his poor suffering country. The man had showed so much promise, Josse mused. He had met the king a few times, had known him as a bright, shining boy. Where had it all turned sour, so that an intelligent, capable man should have reduced his realm to hunger, poverty, uncertainty and danger?

Josse still kept his eyes and ears open to what was happening in the wider world, and he was also deeply worried at what he had heard concerning the serious rift between King John and Llewelyn ap Iorwerth, prince of North Wales. John had married his illegitimate daughter, Joan, to Llewelyn back in 1206, which brought about a truce for a time, but the two powerful men were now in open conflict again. Llewelyn had supported John's favourite-turned-enemy, William de Braose, who, uncomfortably for the king, was one of the few people rumoured to know the truth about what happened between John and his nephew, Arthur of Brittany, vanished these seven years and believed by all but the most innocent and gullible to have been done away with by his Uncle John because he stood between John and the throne. Now, they were saying, the king was planning a spring expedition into Wales. On the basis that *my enemy's enemies are my friends*, the word among the wise was that the king intended to summon the many prominent men who had a grudge against the powerful Llewelyn and make an alliance with them. Campaigns needed money; once again, the relentless, cruel demands were being sent out.

Hawkenlye Manor, tucked away as it was deep in the forest, often missed the random attentions of the king's more lowly officers, since few outside the immediate vicinity knew the house even existed, and those who did know tended to keep their mouths shut. Josse was a generous neighbour and was well known for being free with a handout for those in grave need who came asking for it.

The House in the Woods was a well-run, virtually self-sufficient establishment. Josse, his mood improving again now that he had vented his anger at his king's behaviour, thought about his home with satisfaction. Thanks to the abilities of men such as Will, Gus and, increasingly, Josse's young son Geoffroi, the household made the very most of the acreage, and the family had enough and to spare. Geoffroi's speciality was animals; Josse had no idea how his son had come by his natural touch with any creature from a large bull to a wounded sparrow – perhaps it was a gift from the lad's mother, Joanna – but he was grateful every day for his son's skill. Most of the breeding ewes were in lamb; Josse had watched with fascinated eyes as Geoffroi proudly demonstrated the fact early in this month of February, kneeling down in the snow to gently squeeze a teat so that the waxy fluid came out, an indication, according to Geoffroi, that the ewe was pregnant and her milk was coming in.

The House in the Woods gave all that could be spared to Hawkenlye Abbey, but what they gave was never enough. Josse's thoughts turned to Abbess Caliste, and he ached for her. She was thin, perpetually anxious, haunted by her inability to help all those who came in such need to the abbey's doors, and he knew he was helpless to prevent her gradual and irrevocable change from a beautiful woman into a hollow-eyed skeleton. She ate barely anything, they said at the abbey. There was – or so she would see it – always someone who needed the meagre food more than she did. And, with the king excommunicated and England still under the pope's interdict, there was nothing anyone could do because the abbeys were officially under the king's control and he dictated how much of their own produce and goods they were allowed to keep. In Hawkenlye's case, the amount was pitifully small.

And, Josse thought miserably, above and beyond all these anxieties and problems – as if they were not enough – there was the ongoing, overriding hurt that each member of the household suffered: Ninian's absence. He was so far away, somewhere in that war-torn land in the south, and neither Josse nor anyone else had the least idea when he might be back. It was safe now for him to return, but how on earth were they to get that message to him when nobody knew exactly where he was?

Josse had been marching through the woods with little thought as to where he was going, and it was with faint surprise that he looked up now, as a different quality of light permeated his faraway thoughts, to find himself once more approaching his own house. He paused for a moment to simply stand and look, for the sight of his home always gladdened his heart.

Stone steps led up from the cobbled courtyard to the stout door, and beneath the main hall was an undercroft, its two tiny windows looking out like narrowed eyes. The roof swept down low, giving the impression of sheltering arms, and the house stood firm and solid on its stone foundations. To the left, still within the circle of the trees that protected the house, was the stable block, where, from the sense of activity and the sound of voices that Josse could hear floating out towards him, it appeared visitors were even now leaving their horses.

Shaking off the last of his depressing reflections, Josse hurried to see who they might be.

'. . . couldn't say when he'll be back, sir,' Gus was saying as Josse strode inside the stable building. Gus, turning, gave him a relieved smile. 'Here he is!' he exclaimed, standing aside to reveal a tall, slim, well-dressed man who wore a sword at his side, a young woman in a heavy and costly riding cloak, and a second man, clearly an attendant, who was powerful-looking and armed with a cudgel and a long knife.

Josse hurried forward and took hold of the tall man by the shoulders. 'Leofgar, dear man, it's too long since we've seen you!' he said happily, embracing him. 'And Little Helewise!' He hugged the girl to him, for he was very fond of her. He had noticed in one quick glance that she was pale, and his heart went out to her in her sorrow; she must miss Ninian all the time. 'Your grandmother will be delighted to see you, as indeed will we all,' he added, trying to raise a smile from her.

Valiantly, she did her best, returning Josse's hug warmly. 'I'd rather hoped you would say that,' she murmured, disengaging herself and looking up into his face. 'May I stay for a while?'

Taken aback, Josse shot a swift look at Leofgar. 'Well, I—' he began. But, realizing that did not sound very welcoming, he started again. 'I should like nothing better, nor, I imagine, would the rest of my household, for time drags heavily and it seems winter will never end. But can your own family spare you?' Again, he met Leofgar's eyes, and the younger man gave a swift nod.

'My daughter could do with a change of scene, Josse, if you're willing to put her up,' Leofgar said. 'As you say,' he added, 'we're all sick and tired of being cooped up within our own four walls, and it is hardest for our womenfolk.' There was no need for him to elaborate. Josse, glancing across to the silent, burly attendant, reflected that Leofgar hadn't even trusted that he himself would be sufficient guard for his daughter. *What times we live in*, he thought sadly.

'Dear girl,' he said, taking Little Helewise's hand, 'you may stay as long as you like, as I hope you know without my

telling you. Come in, both of you – we'll break the news that
Little Helewise is to stay, and I hope, Leofgar, that you will
eat and drink with us before you return home? I will arrange
for something to be sent out to your man here, and—'

'A kind offer, Josse, but no,' Leofgar interrupted. 'I would
prefer to set off homewards immediately. Rohaise worries,' he
added quietly.

Josse nodded his understanding. All the family knew that
Rohaise worried.

Little Helewise was reaching up to take the paired leather
panniers off her horse's back, and Josse hurried to help her.
Thinking she might like a moment to say a private farewell
to her father, he said to her, 'I'll take these into the house;
come in when you're ready, we'll be eagerly waiting for you.'
He took Leofgar's hand in a quick, firm grip, muttered, 'Don't
worry, we'll take good care of her,' nodded to the burly attendant and set off across the yard to the house.

The members of Josse's household were as delighted with
their guest as he had predicted; it was as if, he thought as the
afternoon wore on and they all went on sitting round the big
dining table long after the meal was finished, chatting
cheerfully, they hadn't seen anyone from the world outside
the House in the Woods for weeks and weeks. Which, when
he came to think of it, they hadn't.

He could happily have stayed there for the rest of the
afternoon, watching the welcome return of Meggie's smile and
the expression of quiet happiness on Helewise's face. But,
as the sun put in a brief appearance before beginning its slide
down into the west, Will appeared silently at his side and
muttered that someone wanted to see him.

'Who is it, Will?' Josse asked as, getting to his feet, he
walked with Will towards the door.

'It's him that's sheriff of Tonbridge, that Sir Gervase de
Gifford,' Will replied, keeping his voice low.

'Then you should have invited him to come inside and join
us!' Josse exclaimed.

Will looked affronted. 'I did, only he wasn't having it. Said
he needed to speak to you private, like.'

Josse was instantly contrite. Of course Will would have

asked Gervase to come in! He knew the rules of hospitality as well as anyone, and abided by them. 'Sorry, Will.'

Will gave a sort of snort, which Josse took to signify his apology had been accepted.

Gervase was waiting for Josse in the stables. Like Leofgar earlier, he too had a guard with him. Also like Leofgar, he gave the impression of being a man in a hurry.

An impression which was borne out by his opening words: 'Josse, I can't stay – I've other outlying manors to visit yet, and it'll be getting dark soon.'

He had spoken softly, as if he didn't want to be overheard. Josse, going to stand close beside him, said, 'What is it, Gervase?'

The sheriff looked around him quickly, then, observing that nobody could overhear, said, 'Three bodies have been found, all male, in a shallow grave up on the forest fringes over towards Hawkenlye Abbey. Not a place much frequented, and I imagine they'd have stayed buried, only some wretch sneaking out to do a bit of poaching with a highly illegal hound came across them, or rather the hound did. It smelt the rotting flesh, and no doubt it was as hungry as every other living creature in this benighted land.'

Noting, but not commenting on, his friend's uncharacteristically bitter tone, Josse said, 'Rotting flesh? The bodies have lain there some time, then?'

Gervase gave a grim smile. 'Apart from informing you about the discovery – you'll understand the implications without my telling you – that's why I'm here. You know about bodies, Josse.'

The implications, Josse thought; meaning, no doubt, that Gervase had come to warn him there was a murderer, or murderers, about. The dead did not bury themselves in graves, shallow or otherwise. As to the other reason for Gervase's presence, Josse was all too afraid he understood that, too.

'You have helped me many times over the puzzles posed by death, old friend,' Gervase was saying, 'death by violence in particular. Will you help me again?'

'Of course,' Josse said. Then: 'There was violence done to the bodies?'

'Hard to be sure, from a quick preliminary look, just how they died, but it appears one of them had been tortured.' Gervase paused, then said, 'He has cuts incised into his chest. If you didn't know, you'd almost think they were letters, but if so, they belong to no language or letter system that I am acquainted with.'

Josse felt a surge of pity for the victim. It was bad enough to suffer being killed by another's hands, but how much worse to be forced to endure such agony before death released him. 'You said the bodies were found near to Hawkenlye Abbey, so presumably that is where they have been taken?' he asked.

'Yes,' Gervase said. 'They're – it was thought that the patients in the infirmary ought not to be subjected to such sights and – er – smells, so Abbess Caliste found a room in the undercroft beneath the nuns' dormitory, and the bodies lie there.'

Better and better, Josse thought ruefully. Not only was he to be torn away from hearth, home and a pretty new guest to inspect three dead men, but in addition the bodies were putrid and stinking. He suppressed a sigh. 'I'll go over to the abbey tomorrow,' he said.

Gervase grasped his hand. 'Thank you, Josse. I'll get up there myself, as soon as I can. Until tomorrow.'

'Aye, until the morning,' Josse replied.

He watched as Gervase mounted his horse and went out of the stable, joining his guard out in the yard. With a final wave, Gervase put spurs to his horse and hastened away.

THREE

Meggie was awake before the dawn. Living in the House in the Woods was good, in every respect save one: she never seemed to have any time by herself. Until now she had at least had a tiny sleeping cell to call her own – it was situated between Helewise's room, set apart in one corner of the house, and the passage leading to the main hall – but yesterday Little Helewise had arrived, apparently for an indefinite stay, and the obvious place to make up a bed for her had been in with Meggie.

Not that Meggie disliked Little Helewise: far from it. The girl loved Meggie's beloved half-brother as much as Meggie did herself, and, but for the interdict, Little Helewise and Meggie would surely by now have been sisters-in-law. No – it was simply that early morning and late evening alone in her cosy room had been the times Meggie could retreat into the solace of her own thoughts, and now, because of her new companion, she couldn't.

She glanced across at Little Helewise. One of the things she most wanted to do now was to put herself into the light trance state that allowed her to discover things beyond the reach of her waking senses; there was something about Little Helewise that sent out a clear, light, warning note, and Meggie did not know what it was. *I do not know YET*, she corrected herself with a smile.

She knew that the girl was deeply unhappy, and that was perfectly understandable, with the man she loved so far away, out of reach, out of touch and, apparently, in grave danger. It was enough to make anyone miserable, and Meggie, too, had to work hard to keep depressing, negative thoughts at bay. Little Helewise and Ninian, Meggie suspected, had only just been discovering the depths and the truth of their feelings for each other when he was so abruptly torn away, which would have made the pain of the rift that much worse.

Was that it? Meggie wondered. Was it enough to account for the different emanations that she sensed coming from the girl? Tentatively, delicately, Meggie sent out a feeler into Little Helewise's mind.

The girl was dreaming. Effortlessly, Meggie slipped into the dream with her. Ninian was there, laughing, teasing, his bright eyes shining with love. He had his arms around Little Helewise, squeezing her in a tight hug. Meggie sensed where the dream was leading to and prepared to detach herself – such things were private. She would just give it a few more moments . . .

Two things happened simultaneously, combining to send out a jolt of power that pushed Meggie's questing thought right back inside her own head: she picked up something else – although in that alarming instant she had no time to evaluate what it might be – and Ninian bent his dark head to close his mouth on Little Helewise's, sending out a shaft of sexual energy as powerful as a lightning strike.

Well, thought Meggie, rubbing ruefully at her aching head, *that serves me right for being nosy.*

She lay back on the pillows, drawing up the covers against the cold. Nobody would be up yet, and the fire in the hall would be lifeless. There might still be some glowing embers in the kitchen hearth, but it was some time still before Tilly, or perhaps Ella, would rise and get a proper blaze going. Everyone was asleep except Meggie.

She wished, *wished* that she could bring herself to disobey Josse and do what she so longed to do: set out, all by herself, and spend some precious days of solitude in her mother's little hut in the forest. From there, too, situated as it was, she would be free to slip away to visit the precious, powerful Black Madonna figure, hidden in her secret niche in the crypt beneath St Edmund's Chapel, close by Hawkenlye Abbey.

But Josse had forbidden them all to travel unaccompanied in these dangerous times, when hungry villains and outcasts roamed the woods and the deep, lonely places. For Meggie, who had lived in the Great Forest all her life, it was especially hard to face the fact that an environment she knew and loved like a mother could present danger, especially to one like her, but she knew there was a grain of truth in her father's fears. People had indeed been attacked in isolated houses; households had been robbed, vandalized; girls and women had been assaulted, or so the darkest rumours whispered. Meggie was utterly confident that she would be perfectly safe in the little hut, for, apart from other skills she possessed, such as how to wield a sword and how to detect when an attack was coming even before the attacker was aware of it, she knew how to hide the hut so that even those who were familiar with its location could not find it.

It was a skill she had learned from her mother. It pained Meggie to remember, but sometimes Joanna had felt compelled to disguise the hut's location when Josse came looking for her.

Oh, Meggie thought, oh, but there were things about her mysterious mother that she would never understand.

Now, of all times, she really needed the peace and privacy of the little hut. Of late she had been beset with both dreams and waking visions of her brother Ninian, and the overriding message that they left in their wake was the urgent, driving need to get in touch with him and tell him he must come home.

Why? she wondered as she curled deeper inside her blankets. Why now, and not before? As soon as he had gone, for example, or when her father and Helewise had returned last autumn after their unsuccessful attempt to find him? There had to be something else; something over and above the fact that his family all missed him so acutely; that they worried about him so much more now that they knew the place he had been sent to by Gervase de Gifford – his mother's address in Béziers – was in the middle of a ferocious war.

Why do I feel so compelled to send word to him?

What she needed, she knew, was to open herself in deep meditation so that her mother could get through to her, for Joanna had been a silent presence in Meggie's dreams, unseen but constantly sensed. Meggie knew – although she didn't know how she knew – that Joanna wanted to be involved; was offering her help, if only Meggie would accept it.

I do not understand how she can help, Meggie thought, her distress growing. Joanna was dead; gone from the world these twelve years, disappearing in some sort of vision in Chartres Cathedral, which Josse seemed to know something about but of which he was so very reluctant to speak that Meggie could not bring herself to press him.

But the fact remained, even if Meggie didn't understand: she desperately needed to reach her half-brother, via some sort of mental communication that was also beyond her comprehension, and somehow her mother – his mother too – was telling her urgently that she had the means to bring this about. What Meggie had to do was to isolate herself, bring about a trance state – that bit was easy enough – and wait.

The problem was that she could not do this in the House in the Woods. Apart from the difficulty of finding a time and a space to be alone, she had long schooled herself to close herself off from her mother when she was under her father's roof. Josse had loved Joanna very deeply; Meggie suspected

that he still did. He had worked so hard at learning to live
without her, and Meggie knew perfectly well that, one day,
he hoped he and Helewise might become more than the good,
true friends they had been for so long.

He doesn't need the reminder of his earlier love, Meggie
thought. *It wouldn't be fair*. He was working so hard at learning
to live without her, and Meggie would not countenance
anything that would interrupt the process.

Just at that moment, as the thin dawn light at last began to
penetrate the gaps in the shutters, Meggie did not know what
she was going to do. It was still early; nobody would be awake
for ages. She might as well go back to sleep . . .

Little Helewise opened her eyes and looked across at her
sleeping room-mate. Meggie was snoring softly; not enough
to have disturbed Little Helewise, and, now she was awake,
the sound was rather friendly and companionable.

For a while she just lay comfortably in her warm bed and
stared across at Meggie. It was such a relief to be here; even
better to be sharing a room with the person she so much
wanted to talk to. She was tempted to reach across and nudge
Meggie awake. She didn't think Meggie would mind, and
Little Helewise was bursting to speak to her.

No. She tucked her hand back beneath the bedclothes. She
would let Meggie sleep on. Now that she'd got here, and
Josse and his lovely family had made her feel so welcome
and let her know without any doubt that she could stay as
long as she wanted, there really wasn't any hurry. It would
just be a matter of finding a moment when – Little Helewise
yawned hugely – she and Meggie could be quite alone, with
no fear of interruption. And that was hardly going to be
difficult . . .

Little Helewise curled up like a kitten by the fire and went
back to sleep.

Before they had all retired to bed the previous evening, Josse
had sought out Helewise and repeated quietly to her what
Gervase de Gifford had told him. He had said he would set
out for Hawkenlye Abbey early the next morning.

Helewise had been thinking about that for much of the night.

Now, rising early and making her preparations, she knew that she must speak to Josse as soon as he was up.

It was a pity that she must act now, when her beloved granddaughter had only just come to stay, but that couldn't be helped. Helewise felt she was a driven woman: everything else – even love and obligations to family – came second. Now, using the quiet time before the rest of the household was up and about, she sat down on her narrow bed and reflected over what had led her to her decision.

Helewise knew how much her successor, Abbess Caliste, must be suffering as she tried to maintain Hawkenlye Abbey's great reputation as a refuge, a place of help, healing and comfort, under the harsh conditions of the interdict. Although Helewise had long made up her mind that she would not risk stirring up memories of her own regime at Hawkenlye by returning to the abbey, nevertheless, as the weeks and months had passed, she had felt increasingly uncomfortable doing nothing to help. Yes, sometimes the hungry, the sick and the desperate made their way into the depths of the forest and sought her out in her small room in the House in the Woods, but so few knew that either she or the house were there, and the total number she had managed to comfort in some way remained pitifully few. And so many were in need!

The idea had come to her late one night as she finished her prayers and got wearily into bed. The abbey itself might be unavailable to her, but what about the little cell beside St Edmund's Chapel? She had lived there for many years between standing down as abbess and coming to live in Josse's household. Putting aside false modesty, she admitted to herself that she knew she had done good there. And now, when the abbey church's huge doors were firmly closed against the populace, the little chapel, overlooked as it was, could surely be a place of true solace. Helewise could return to her little cell – winter would surely soon be easing its grip at last – and maybe other like-minded women could join her there. Helewise could pray with people, provide a kindly ear as they poured out their troubles and, hopefully, offer sound advice. While she was competent enough to deal with minor wounds and the more common ailments, she was, however, no healer and knew little about herbs. Perhaps

Tiphaine, formerly the herbalist of Hawkenlye Abbey, might
be persuaded to join her and add her unique skills to
Helewise's enterprise? Perhaps even Meggie would consider
helping? Both women were healers, in their way; both were
exceptionally good at their craft. Until recently, the idea had
been just a dream; now, Helewise had made up her mind that
the dream was going to come true.

Josse overslept and had to be roused by Will. He came
reluctantly out of deep sleep, yelled at Will and had to
apologize; he upset the bowl of water Will had provided for
him to wash and shave his face and was forced to complete
the task with icy water straight from the butt outside; he fell
over as he tried to ram a cold foot into his boot and banged
his head on the end of his bed.

All in all, it was not a great start to the day.

The rest of the household had finished breakfast by the time
he sat down to eat his. He chewed mechanically on dry bread
and a rather stale piece of cheese, thinking about the mission
he was about to set off on and reflecting that going to
Hawkenlye Abbey was not quite the same now that Abbess
Caliste was in charge. Not that Josse had anything against
Abbess Caliste, except that she wasn't Helewise. Josse had
always so enjoyed attempting to puzzle out even the most
gruesome mysteries of violent death when he was doing it
with Helewise.

As if she had sensed he was thinking about her, Helewise
glided into the hall and came to stand at his shoulder. He
smiled a greeting, patting the bench beside him in invitation.
She sat down and he said, 'Would you like to share my herbal
infusion? Meggie made it to fortify me for my journey, and
there's plenty here.'

She hesitated, and it seemed to him that she was looking
at him strangely.

'What is it?' he asked. Anxiety grasped his heart. 'Oh,
Helewise, you are not unwell?'

'No! Oh, no, Josse, I am perfectly all right.' Briefly, she
touched his hand with her fingertips. 'Only, there is something
I must say.'

He realized he was holding his breath. 'What is it?' A dozen terrible answers ran through his head, and he tried to dismiss them all.

She must have appreciated what he was feeling, for instantly she began to speak. 'Josse dear, I cannot reconcile my conscience if I remain here doing so little, when out in the wider world there are so many in such dire need. I have to do something to help. I cannot go back to the abbey, for reasons you and I have discussed before, but I intend to ask Abbess Caliste's leave to return to the cell by St Edmund's Chapel, where I lived before I came here, and from there offer aid and support as I once did.'

He felt his heart race. He tried to speak, but his mouth was dry. He swallowed and tried again. 'For ever?' he whispered.

He did not think she understood, at first. Then she did, and her face went pink. She had been looking into his eyes, but now hers dropped. She stared down at her hands, the fingers twisting together, and said, very softly, 'I don't know.'

He didn't stop to think. The idea of her leaving, going back to the tiny dwelling beside the chapel and living there all alone, without him, was intolerable.

'You would not be safe there on your own,' he said harshly, pushing back the bench and pacing to and fro across the hall. 'I cannot let you do it, Helewise.'

'Dear Josse, I am not asking your permission,' she said gently. 'Since you are bound for the abbey this morning, I'm asking if you will escort me there and, once inside, ask Abbess Caliste if she will come out to speak to me. It is *her* permission I need,' she added softly.

He stopped his pacing, pausing to stand right in front of her. Was this it, then? he wondered. Was this the end of his dream to change his relationship with this beloved woman, so that at long last they might be to one another what he had always hoped they would one day be?

He studied her calm, resolute face.

It seemed it probably was.

'You'd better prepare your pack,' he said roughly. 'I'm leaving as soon as I've finished my breakfast.'

But he found his appetite had vanished. Turning on his heel, he muttered that he was going to see about the horses, and hurried out of the hall without looking back.

Had he done so, a swift look at Helewise's face might have given him pause for thought.

Josse had barely finished asking Will to prepare Helewise's mare when Meggie came running into the stables. Without preamble she took hold of his hand and said, 'Father, Helewise has told me she's going back to the cell by the chapel, and I want to go too.' He made as if to speak but she wouldn't let him. 'No, no, please hear me out! I know you'll say it isn't safe and we'll all get attacked and robbed and raped, but Helewise is going to get Tiphaine to join us, and Abbess Caliste will probably send one of the younger lay brothers to look after us at night, and we'll be as safe there as here, Father, I know we will!'

He shook his head, quite bemused. Why would Meggie want to go and live in the tiny cell? She didn't—

Then he knew. St Edmund's Chapel was the closest building to the hut in the forest where Joanna had lived; where, indeed, Meggie had lived all her life until she came to the House in the Woods.

For perhaps the first time ever, he looked at his daughter with an emotion other than solely love. 'I would prefer it if you were honest about your motives, Meggie,' he said, his tone chilly. 'It is your hut, rather than helping Helewise tend the needy at the chapel, that draws you, I think.'

Anger stirred amid the bright lights in her brown eyes. 'You malign me, Father,' she said, equally coldly. 'I admit I am desperate to return to the hut, and I've made no secret of the fact. I shall indeed try to visit it, but it is not the reason I want to go with Helewise.' Before he could ask her to explain, she ploughed on. 'Helewise said she'll need healers, and I am a healer. I'm *useless* here,' she said with sudden vehemence, 'and not being able to do what I know I can do well makes life all the harder and Ninian's absence more painful to bear.'

'Don't you think we all feel that way?' he demanded.

'About Ninian, yes, of course,' she said hurriedly. 'But, Father, you, Geoffroi, Will and Gus are busy from dawn to dusk, as are Ella and Tilly, for the work you all do is right here. What is there left for me? I cannot do what I excel at, and everyone else is so efficient that there is very little left for me to do!'

Her words echoed faithfully Helewise's of a short while earlier. Had he not known both women better, he might have suspected them of collusion.

He raked through his mind, trying desperately to come up with something with which he might appeal to her, even though he was all but certain it was useless. Then he had an idea. 'What about Little Helewise?' he demanded. 'She's come here to stay with us, undoubtedly because she wants to be with her grandmother and with you, a young woman close to her own age who also loves Ninian dearly, and yet here you are, you and Helewise, planning to run out on her the moment she's arrived. Is that kind, Meggie?'

Meggie's face filled with such love and tenderness that he gasped. 'Oh, dearest Father, I'm so sorry, but that is no reason to stay!' she cried, and he saw tears in her eyes. 'You see, Helewise had the same thought. She's talked it over with Little Helewise, and she's coming with us.' Again, he started to protest, and again she didn't let him. 'I know, I know, the little cell by the chapel is hardly suitable for a girl like her, used to considerable luxury, but we've thought of that. She can stay down at the abbey if she'd rather, where without doubt the nuns will find her plenty to do to take her mind off worrying about Ninian.'

Josse felt the passion and the anger flow out of him. Suddenly feeling very tired, he sank down on a straw bale and dropped his head in his hands. 'You seem to have it all worked out,' he said from behind them. 'If you won't listen to me when I express fears for your safety, if you won't pause to consider that I might worry about you, miss you, then who am I to stand in your way?' His voice had risen, and he made himself stop and draw a deep breath. 'Go and pack a bag,' he said wearily. 'I despair of you all.'

He heard a sound break from her – perhaps a sob? – and then her hurrying footsteps running out across the yard. When he looked up, she had disappeared round the corner.

The journey through the forest from the House in the Woods to Hawkenlye Abbey was usually a pleasant one, whatever the season or the weather. Today, despite what he knew awaited him, Josse couldn't wait for it to be over. He had

asked Gus to come with them, fearing that he was in no
state to protect three women if his worst fears were realized
and they were attacked, and Gus was the only one who had
a smile. Even his did not survive the first couple of miles,
by which time the prevailing mood seemed to have affected
him too.

They reached the chapel, and Helewise turned to him.
'Perhaps Little Helewise and Meggie might ride down with
you while you ask Abbess Caliste if we may take up residence
in the cell,' she suggested. 'They could then return here to
give me the reply, leaving you free to proceed with your own
business at the abbey.'

It made sense. 'Very well,' he said curtly. 'Gus, will you
stay with Helewise?'

'Aye, Sir Josse,' Gus agreed. He was looking around him,
interested, and Helewise, apparently noticing, dismounted.

'Come, Gus, I'll show you inside the chapel, and then we
might have a look inside the cell and see what sort of a state
it's in,' she said.

Josse could bear to watch no more. He put his heels to his
horse's sides, and Alfred set off at a canter down the long slope
to the abbey. There was no need to turn round to see if Meggie
and Little Helewise were following; he could hear them.

If he had been holding out secret hopes that Abbess Caliste
would refuse even to think of her predecessor and the two
young women taking up residence in the cell by the chapel,
Josse was doomed to disappointment. She pounced on the idea
with delight, saying she'd been thinking along the same lines
herself but, unable to spare any of the Hawkenlye nuns, monks
or lay brethren, had let the matter rest.

'But how perfect to have Helewise back!' she exclaimed.
'Oh, Sir Josse, word will soon spread, and everyone will
remember how very much they depended on her presence
when she was there before. And she'll have Meggie and her
own granddaughter with her, so she won't be alone, and we
shall make quite sure that the cell is guarded at night. I'll get
some of our handier brethren to put up a shelter,' she went
on, apparently thinking aloud, 'and finding volunteers to watch
over three such courageous and good women will not present

a problem.' Suddenly, she looked up at Josse. 'Do they need anything from us?' she asked. 'We have very little, but I would not like to think of them cold or hungry.'

'They anticipated your agreement to the suggestion, my lady abbess,' Josse said wryly. 'They have brought with them from Hawkenlye Manor all that could be spared of food supplies, medicaments and blankets, as well as a small bag each of personal belongings. They will be as comfortable as the small space allows, I believe.'

Abbess Caliste nodded. 'Very well, Sir Josse. I shall go and see them myself once they have had a chance to settle in.'

'I'll go outside and tell the young women what you've said, my lady—' Josse went over to the door of the abbess's room – 'and then I will proceed with my own mission here today.'

'The dead men, yes.' She came round from behind her table to join him. 'I will summon our infirmarer, and we will take you to where they have been laid out.'

It amounted to something, Josse thought a little later as Abbess Caliste and Sister Liese led the way down to the rooms below the nuns' dormitory, when a man actually looked forward to inspecting dead, putrid bodies. But such was his present mood that anything which took his mind off his own pressing sadness was welcome just then.

Sister Liese opened the door of a dark, windowless little room, pausing to light a lamp with the candle she held in her hand. Inside, she moved calmly around what lay on the trestle tables to light three further lamps. Then she turned to Josse and said, 'Come and look, Sir Josse. We did brush off the earth that clung to them from their interment, but their clothing has not been disturbed by us, and so you see them much as they were when they were in the ground.'

Josse was grateful for the forethought of whoever had directed the recovery of the bodies. It was always useful if you could view your victims as their murderer left them. He was even more grateful to whoever had been burning incense; the smell from the bodies was still very much in evidence, but at least the incense masked it a little.

Then, putting all else aside, he stepped forward and began his inspection of the three dead men.

FOUR

They lay side by side on rough trestle tables, each body covered with a strip of worn, patched but clean linen. Sister Liese met Josse's eyes and, at his quick nod, folded back the sheet covering the first body.

It was that of a man in early middle age. He had been small and wiry, narrow in the chest and shoulders; the sort of body a man developed when he had been hungry most of his life. He was dressed in a ragged tunic over a thin shirt; patched and darned hose; worn, down-at-heel boots that had not been cleaned for a very long time; a heavy, hooded cloak, very soiled. Standing out amid this dowdy collection, like a gaudy finch in a flock of sparrows, was a very fine belt made of soft, supple leather, rich dark-red in colour. It had a buckle that appeared, to Josse's eyes, to be gold. He pointed to it, then looked at the abbess and the infirmarer.

'Gold?' whispered Sister Liese.

Abbess Caliste leaned closer, gently scraping the buckle with a fingernail. 'Solid gold, I do believe.' Straightening, she said, 'I do not wish to make false accusations, especially when this poor man cannot defend himself, yet I do wonder how he came by such a treasure.'

Josse didn't wonder; he was pretty sure he knew.

He looked at the face of the corpse. Narrow, eyes close together, the mouth open and what flesh there was on the scrawny cheeks already falling in, giving him a rat-like expression.

How had he died? As if Sister Liese read Josse's thought, silently she indicated a darker patch on the man's rusty brown tunic. Carefully loosening the strings that closed the garment and drawing the fabric aside, he saw a small patch of dried blood, right over the heart.

He studied the wound, gently pulling the flesh this way and that. 'It's a deep, straight cut, made with a slim blade,' he said quietly. He pressed the chest on both sides of the wound, and a little clotted blood appeared. 'He did not bleed much, to judge by the body and the clothes that he wore. I would say the stab went straight into the heart, killing him instantly.'

'He would not have suffered, then,' Sister Liese observed.

'Very little,' Josse agreed.

He moved to the next table. Sister Liese, having deftly covered the first man once more, now folded back the sheet that was spread over the second body.

This man was bigger, taller, broader and far more muscular than the first. He was clothed in similarly worn and dirty garments, and, in his case, the one outstanding item was a soft woollen muffler wound round his neck. It was, incongruously on such a masculine body, soft pink. In a well-used scabbard on his belt, he carried a sword. Josse drew it out and inspected the blade, which was stained with what looked like blood.

It was a fine weapon. He looked around for something with which to wipe it and the infirmarer, correctly guessing, reached inside her sleeve and handed him a square of linen. 'There is water in the bucket by the door,' she murmured.

Josse nodded his thanks, then dipped the cloth in the water, saturating it, and proceeded to clean the sword. As the layers of dried mud, blood and general dirt slowly came away – *this was no way to treat such a blade*, he thought as he worked – he could make out a compelling design of intertwined curves and circles etched into the bright metal. He held the sword up for the two nuns' inspection. They looked at it, then back at him, their expressions enquiring.

Josse smiled to himself; it had been foolish to expect nuns to know about swords. 'This is a fine weapon,' he said. 'It is, if I'm not mistaken, Toledo steel, and it was made by a man who excelled at his craft.'

'Indeed?' said Abbess Caliste politely. Her glance then slid away to the dead man, and Josse took the hint. He returned the sword to its scabbard and resumed his inspection.

The man's face was brutal, even given the unflattering effects of violent death. The lips were coarse, and barely covered the misshapen, discoloured teeth. The nose was broad and fleshy, and the eyes gave an impression of having secrets to keep, set deep as they were beneath heavy brows.

Abbess Caliste, sensing Josse's first careful study was

complete, said, 'This is the man whom we believed was tortured. Shall I bare his chest to show you, Sir Josse?'

Josse drew a steadying breath. If the two nuns were prepared to look on whatever terrible wounds had been inflicted on the man, then he must not flinch. 'Aye.'

The abbess leaned over the corpse and unfastened the tunic and the chemise, from the neck to the navel, folding them back on themselves and leaving the throat, chest and abdomen bare. Sister Liese and Josse both leaned forward together, bumping heads.

'I am sorry, Sir Josse.' Sister Liese instantly stepped back. 'It is the first time I have seen the wounds.'

Professional curiosity, Josse assumed. 'Let us look together, Sister,' he said.

As well as the same small mark right over the heart, the chest had been carved with what looked like a big letter H. Josse was not very familiar with letters, but it seemed, even to him, that this one had rather too many extra lines, as if someone had been doodling and adding embellishments; vaguely, he pictured an illuminated initial letter in a big Bible. He might not have been much good with letters but he was, however, very used to wounds; he looked up, met Sister Liese's blue-green eyes and raised his brows in query. She gave a quick nod.

Turning to the abbess, Josse said, 'My lady, you may set your mind at rest regarding this man's suffering. His death would have been as swift as that of the first man, caused by one deft stab into the heart. The cuts to the chest were done after death.'

'After—' Abbess Caliste put a hand to her mouth. 'How can you be so sure, Sir Josse?'

'Sister Liese, I believe, agrees,' he said. The infirmarer muttered her affirmation. 'Had the cuts been made into living flesh, there would have been massive loss of blood. The heart had ceased to beat before the damage was done.'

'I see,' said the abbess. Leaning close to Josse the better to see, she shook her head in puzzlement. 'I feel I ought to know what those marks are, for in some way they seem familiar to me . . .'

It was easy to forget, Josse reflected, that Abbess Caliste

had quite an unusual past: left, as a child, on the doorstep of poor but kind and decent people, she had entered Hawkenlye as a girl and become one of its youngest ever fully professed nuns. Her origins, it had gradually emerged, were with the strange, mysterious folk who from time to time spent a few weeks or months in the Hawkenlye forest. Was it possible, Josse now wondered, that she was remembering some arcane symbol that she had once known in another life?

'Perhaps we should show the marks to others who might recognize them?' Sister Liese suggested. 'My lady, should I fetch parchment and writing materials, so that we might copy them?'

'Yes, please do that,' the abbess said. 'You will find pieces of scrap vellum on my table, Sister, and also a quill; and my ink horn.'

Sister Liese hurried away, leaving Josse to uncover the third corpse. Apart from the fact that this man had been considerably younger than his two companions in death, other elements of his clothing and appearance were similar. All three looked as if they hadn't eaten a decent meal in weeks.

This man, too, had died from a single stab through the heart.

Whoever killed them, Josse thought, assuming they had died by the same hand, had known exactly what he was doing. To kill one man thus could have been a lucky thrust that just happened to reach into the body and stop the heart; to dispatch three in the same way suggested a killer with a rare skill.

Which was, he acknowledged, a frightening thought.

He drew up the covering sheet, and he and Abbess Caliste stood either side of the third body. Neither spoke. He thought she was probably praying. After a short time, Sister Liese reappeared, carrying a small, rough-edged piece of parchment, a long, graceful quill, carefully sharpened, and a horn of ink.

'Shall I copy the marks?' the abbess asked Josse, taking the quill in her hand and dipping the tip into the ink.

'Aye, my lady, if you will,' Josse replied.

Sister Liese turned and bent over slightly, offering her back as a writing slope, and the abbess spread out the parchment. She leaned over the body on the central table, studying the symbols, and then, very carefully, she reproduced them. 'Thank you, Sister,' she murmured when she had finished, and the infirmarer straightened up. The abbess waved the parchment around to dry the ink, then handed it to Josse. 'What do you think, Sir Josse? Have I made an accurate enough copy?'

He studied her work, looking repeatedly from it to the wounds on the chest and back again. As far as he could see, her reproduction was perfect. 'A fine job, my lady,' he said with a smile. He rolled up the parchment and tucked it away.

She nodded. 'Have you any further need of the bodies?' she asked. 'Only, they had been properly buried and now have been exhumed; I think we should rebury them as soon as we can.'

'I agree, my lady. I would ask only that we wait until Sir Gervase de Gifford has had a chance to view the dead men, but, since he said he would try to meet me here this morning, that should not mean too much delay.'

The abbess nodded again. 'Very well. I will send word to Father Sebastian and ask if the burial may be performed as soon as he can spare the time.'

Josse was impatient to leave, for he had already decided to whom he would show the strange symbols. He touched a hand to the breast of his tunic, where the rolled-up piece of parchment crackled softly. But Abbess Caliste had offered to send for refreshments for him and, since he had undertaken to see Gervase this morning, there was little option but to accept.

They sat together in the abbess's little room where, presently, Gervase joined them. Josse took him down to the room in the undercroft, where he viewed each body in turn, listening without response, other than the occasional nod, while Josse related his findings and conclusions. Back up in the abbess's room, he and Josse downed mugs of spiced wine – very thin, quite acid wine, light on the honey and the spices, but then times were hard – and Gervase then turned to Josse.

'Were the men buried immediately after they were killed?' he demanded.

'Aye, I'd say so, although it's more difficult to be certain in winter, when there are no egg-laying insects around. But there was no sign of animal predation.'

Gervase gave a wry smile. 'You mean, they'd probably been put in the ground before any hungry badger, fox or wolf had a chance to gnaw at them?' As if belatedly remembering the abbess's presence, he turned to her with a courteous bow and said, 'I am sorry, my lady. I did not mean to be flippant.'

'I know, Sir Gervase,' she replied calmly.

He bowed again, then turned back to Josse. 'And can you say how long they'd been in the ground?'

Josse knotted his brows in an intense frown. 'There was some putrefaction, but not as much as I had expected. It's been cold, of course, and that appears to slow the process down.' He came to a decision. 'The really harsh weather began after Christmas, and, had the men been killed and buried before that, the decomposition would be further advanced. I cannot be sure, Gervase, but my guess is that they were murdered and buried no more than a month or six weeks ago.'

'We are now in mid-February,' Gervase muttered, 'so six weeks takes us back to the start of January.' He was silent for a moment, clearly thinking.

'Has that date some meaning for you, Sir Gervase?' asked the abbess as the silence continued.

He looked at her. 'Perhaps, my lady.' He hesitated, then went on: 'For some weeks in the final quarter of last year, there had been reports of a series of robberies and assaults on isolated houses. It seemed that whoever was perpetrating the crimes had been steadily moving southwards, reaching the area around Tonbridge – my jurisdiction – some time in December.' He paused, frowning. 'The assaults were all too often brutal, I am afraid to say. Old people attacked, battered and beaten, to persuade them to reveal where they had hidden their money and their valuables. One elderly widow, living alone, was forced to see her guard dog killed before her eyes, and then she was hit over the head repeatedly, until she was blinded in one eye. And all she had hidden away was half a mouldy cheese and a clipped penny.'

There was silence in the room. Then Josse said, 'The assaults have now stopped?'

Gervase sighed. 'No reports have reached me of anything since January. Either the perpetrators have moved on, or else—'

'Or else they now lie dead in our undercroft,' the abbess

finished for him. Abruptly, she stood up, and Josse, noticing how the power in the room shifted as she did so from the sheriff to her, thought anew what a quietly strong and authoritative woman she had become . . .

But she was speaking, and he made himself listen.

'. . . any real likelihood we shall discover the identities of the three men, Sir Gervase?' she was asking.

'Very little, my lady, if they are indeed who we believe them to be, for they are not local,' he said. 'You wish, of course, to have them taken away for burial, I know, and—'

'They can be buried in the Hawkenlye graveyard,' she interrupted. 'Sir Gervase,' she went on, her tone softening, 'in the absence of certainty in this matter, we should leave judgement to a higher authority. I will ensure that such details of the men that we have are recorded, in case anyone should ever come looking for them. Then our priest will bury them, and we shall all pray that the Lord has mercy on them.'

'It is highly likely that they are all three guilty of grave crimes, my lady abbess,' Gervase said, his face stiff.

'If so, then they have already paid by their deaths,' she replied implacably. 'If they are innocent, then they deserve our compassion and our prayers.'

She appeared, Josse reflected, to have covered either possibility more than adequately. Amused, despite himself, at Gervase's obvious discomfiture, he suppressed a smile.

The sheriff was bowing again to the abbess, taking his leave. 'If there is anything further I can do for you in this matter, my lady, or, indeed, in any other, you have only to summon me,' he said.

She bowed in return. 'Thank you, Sir Gervase.'

He nodded briefly to Josse, muttered his thanks, and then swept out of the room. Josse could hear his footsteps pacing quickly away.

'Have I offended him, Sir Josse?' the abbess asked softly. 'Would he have had me judge and condemn those three men, refusing them Christian burial and the hope of resurrection, even though we cannot be certain they are guilty of the crimes Sir Gervase described?'

'If he is offended, then the fault is his and not yours,' Josse replied. He went over to her and took her cold hands in his;

he had known Caliste a long time, and he hoped she would not mind the small intimacy. 'You are quite right, my lady—' he let go of her hands – 'and it is not for us to judge.'

She nodded, her expression relieved. 'Thank you,' she said simply. 'What a friend you are.' Then she stood on tiptoe and placed a soft kiss on his cheek.

Riding back up to St Edmund's Chapel on its rise above the abbey, Josse could still feel the imprint of that kiss. Reflecting how nice – how unusual – it was to have a woman be tender to him, resolutely he put Abbess Caliste out of his mind and turned his attention to what lay ahead.

He tethered Alfred to a tree and strode over to the little cell. The low door had been propped open and a thorough washdown of the ceiling, walls and floor had obviously been carried out. Now, Gus was busy erecting three simple, narrow cots against the far wall of the cell, while Helewise, her granddaughter and Meggie, sleeves rolled up and their gowns covered by voluminous white aprons, busied themselves organizing the stores they had brought on to the set of shelves inside the door. Three neat piles of bedding sat on a mat on the grass, waiting until Gus had finished.

All four greeted Josse with happy faces. He noticed that Little Helewise already had more colour in her cheeks and, for the first time since she had arrived at the House in the Woods, she was smiling.

He decided it was time to swallow his hurt and resentment, and wish them well. 'The weather looks set to improve,' he said, standing back to observe their handiwork, 'which must surely indicate that your endeavours are blessed.'

Meggie came up to him and linked her arm through his. 'We'll set the hearth stones back in place as soon as the floor's dry,' she said, 'and I've already collected kindling and firewood enough for today. We'll be snug as fleas in a blanket by nightfall!'

He laughed. Then, anxiously, he said, 'What of the lay brothers who will watch over you? Will they be—?'

'Don't worry, Father,' she said, squeezing his arm. 'There are two of them, both strong, brave young men, and even as we speak they are in the forest, foraging for dead wood to

build their shelter. We really will be quite all right,' she added
in a whisper.

He prayed, silently and intently, that she was right.

Then, deliberately turning his thoughts away from his fears,
he said, 'Meggie, I have something here I'd like you to look
at, if you are willing.' He withdrew his arm from hers and
reached inside his tunic, bringing out the parchment. He
unrolled it and handed it to her.

She studied it in silence for some time. Then she said,
'Where did you get this?'

He hesitated, then said, 'It is a copy of the symbols that
were scratched on to the chest of a dead man.' *Scratched* did
not really describe the manner in which the symbols had been
etched, but any more accurate word would sound too brutal.

She nodded. There was another period of silence – he sensed
she was deep in thought – and finally she said, 'This is, I
think, what is called a bind rune. It's a combination of three
runes blended together, so that the meaning of all three merges
together to make an ultimate message.'

'Runes . . .?' He was familiar with the word, but was not
sure if his scant knowledge was enough.

She smiled. 'They are ancient symbols, Father, used in
magic writing for spells and talismans. They can form charms
for protection and defence – warding off evil – and, in addition, those who have studied them are able to use them as an
aid to prediction. Or so it's said,' she added hastily.

He smiled to himself. Did his beloved daughter still think
he was unaware of her strange powers and her wide knowledge
of the secret world she had shared with her mother? 'Can you
interpret what this symbol means?' he asked.

She frowned. 'Yes, I *think* so . . .' She hesitated, and he could
tell that she was still thinking even as she spoke. 'It's – you
have to sort of hold the three individual meanings in your mind
and let them mix together, so that each one contributes to a
bigger meaning . . .' She fell silent again, her frown deepening,
her lips moving as she muttered under her breath.

Then, abruptly, she turned to him, her face shining with
triumph. 'I've got it!' He returned her grin. 'This man, was
he a bad man? Had he done something wrong?'

'Er – he might have done, aye.'

She was nodding again. 'He did. Or, at least, whoever carved this symbol in his chest believed he did, and he – or someone – killed the man because of what he'd done.' Holding the parchment in one hand, she pointed with the forefinger of the other. 'This rune is Haegl—' she outlined the letter Josse had thought was H, two uprights with a connecting bar that sloped down from left to right – 'and it means disruption, or hurting, bad damage. This one is Eoh—' her finger drew over the right-hand upright of the H, which had a mark from the top end sloping down to the right and one going up from the bottom and to the left – 'and it means prevention, or a weapon – maybe deflecting harm. Then finally this one is Tir—' her finger moved to the left-hand upright, which terminated in two downward-pointing lines forming an arrow head – 'and it stands for battle. Taken together, you have Tir-Eoh-Haegl, which has so many meanings and levels of meaning that I can't begin to explain them all, but the overriding one is a battle to prevent damaging forces; against evil, if you like.' Her eyes turned to him, wide with awe. 'Father, this is a very powerful bind rune.' He noticed that her hands holding the parchment were shaking. 'Whoever cast it, whoever cut it into that man, he was telling the spirits that the man had been killed in order to exact vengeance.'

FIVE

In the isolated village high up in the Pyrenees that had become his home, Ninian had thrown himself so whole-heartedly into life with his new friends that at times he almost forgot he did not belong there. The winter was harsh, with snow so deep around the village that getting in or out was all but impossible. Food was scant, and apparently nobody was tempted to relieve their hunger by slaughtering a sheep and tucking in to a good meat meal. There wasn't much to do, but there was lots of praying. Despite all this, the overall impression Ninian received was that everyone was happy and would not have exchanged their lot even for a king's palace.

The villagers lived in small cottages, huddled close together and sometimes interconnecting, and communal living was the norm. Kin or friendship groups selected one house, where everyone crammed in together, both during the working day and for the short hours of leisure. Weaving was the main occupation; men, women and the older children were busy all day, as long as the light lasted, at the small, simply-constructed looms which they made themselves. Ninian had studied the people as they worked and had been encouraged to learn the technique. His teacher, a jolly, round-cheeked girl of about fifteen called Corba, explained the method: 'We have so little room that we have to weave the way they did in ancient times, using these frames that are propped against the wall, you see, because they do not take up so much floor space. The warp threads hang from this crossbar, and they're kept taut by being tied to the loom weights. Then we weave from the top, moving to and fro across the width of the cloth, winding the finished cloth around the frame's top beam and adding warp threads that we unwind from the weights, like this, so that a piece of cloth can be as long as you like.'

It had both sounded and appeared simple when Corba did it. Ninian's first attempt had his friends hooting with laughter, and he too could not suppress his grin at the sight of the wobbly, uneven length of fabric. Nevertheless, he kept it, announcing that he would wear it as a scarf, a constant reminder not to underrate the inherent difficulties of a task.

When he had first arrived late the previous autumn, before the snows, Ninian had lived with Alazaïs de Saint Gilles, the woman he had been sent to find. Later he moved out – kind though she was, it was clear she preferred to be alone in her tiny house – and now he lived in a household of two young men and their elderly grandfather. The youths were among the group that Ninian was training; a task for which he was far better suited than weaving. Consequently, he was as busy as anyone else in the short hours of daylight, dedicated to his self-appointed task of passing on everything he knew about fighting. Considering that he had spent many years learning the skills you needed to become a knight, he knew quite a lot. His pupils had become his friends, and he had grown close to many of them.

The men did not want to fight. They believed it was wrong

to kill, and their ways were paths of peace. But what were they to do if others attacked? *Simply lie down and die*, the elders said, *for that way we shall be reunited all the sooner with our true spiritual selves, from which we were torn away to this earthly existence.*

Some of the younger men felt the same; quite a lot more had started quietly turning up whenever Ninian began to instruct. For them, earthly life was still too sweet to wish to give it up.

In those early months of 1211, everyone knew that the vicious, unrelenting crusade against the Cathars would not stop. But nobody fought in the winter; certainly not in the Pyrenees, anyway, for the snow was a more effective ban on hostilities than any truce made by kings or priests. In the village, the ice-bound months passed slowly but peacefully. The villagers tended their sheep, worked at their looms, said their prayers, met in the enfolding darkness after the day's work to talk animatedly about their faith.

With nothing else to occupy him in the evenings, Ninian had taken to sitting quietly in the corner of whatever room the elders had gathered in, and listening. He learned a great deal. He learned of the basic conundrum which, it seemed, lay at the heart of the Cathar faith: how can an all-powerful, good and merciful god permit the monstrous evil that undoubtedly existed in the world? The answer was that there had to be two equally powerful gods, one all good and the other all evil.

Many of the conversations that roamed freely all around him in the course of those long evenings in tiny, smoky rooms, with inadequate heating and one feeble tallow lamp for illumination, were so far above Ninian's understanding that he did not even try to follow them. Some things, however, stuck in his mind: *Cathars* was what the outside world called his new friends; it was a term coined by their enemies. Their own name for themselves was *good men* or *good women*; or, as they would say, *bonshommes*. Those who loved and supported them, but who were not ready to take the ultimate vow that would admit them into the rarefied circle of the bonshommes, were simply called *credentes*: believers. And the term *perfect*, which appeared to

apply to the extremely devout men and women who led the
rest – people who lived lives of such austere purity that it was
hard to see how they managed to look so happy all the time
– was a word used by the enemy not in admiration but with a
sarcastic irony. Like Cathar, it also meant *pure one*, but as a
constant, sarcastic insult, as if to say, *you lot think you're so
pure, too good to be true!*

The leaders themselves had no special rank or title. They
did not need one, for their promise to live a perfect life was
between themselves and God. Everyone and everything else
was irrelevant.

They read the bible. This, Ninian perceived, was the worst
sin in the eyes of the Catholic Church, for whose priests the
idea of letting a layman anywhere near the Word of God was
anathema. St John's Gospel was the important book for the
bonshommes. Ninian's knowledge of the scriptures was
sketchy to the point of being virtually non-existent, and to
begin with he had paid attention when one of the elders read
aloud from the bible only because it was such a novelty to
hear and understand, since the words were not in the Church's
language, Latin, but in the vernacular of the people. The
bonshommes had not only translated the bible into the *langue
d'oc*, they had also set up paper mills in the region so that
they could copy out as many copies as the people desired.

Mary Magdalene turned out not to be a sinner and a
prostitute, as she was in Ninian's vague memory. On the
contrary, she was held in great esteem by the bonshommes as
the close and beloved companion of Jesus. She was honoured
and worshipped throughout the Languedoc, for the people
believed she had lived the last years of her life there. One of
Ninian's new friends came from the village on the Mediterranean
coast where they claimed Mary Magdalene had arrived in an
open boat in which she'd travelled all the way from the Holy
Land, in the company of Martha, Lazarus and a dark-skinned
Egyptian maid called Sarah Kali. So beloved was the Magdalene
in the south that it seemed to Ninian she was virtually the
region's patron saint.

The bonshommes were diligent and thorough teachers,
painstaking and patient. When they encountered credentes who
could not read and who found it difficult to understand the

central tenets of the faith, they used a series of images to help comprehension. Many of the good men and good women carried their own set of images, some beautifully painted and printed on thick card; some more crude and on thin, flimsy paper that showed signs of long handling. The paper mills must have been busy, Ninian reflected, and somewhere there must be rooms full of artistically-gifted bonshommes and credentes, patiently copying out the images.

He was reminded of the precious manuscript that he had unwittingly taken with him on his long journey from southern England to the Midi. The same life thrummed through the little cards as in the vibrant paintings in the manuscript. The manuscript he knew to be so holy, so inherently powerful, that it was virtually magic. It contained, amongst other treasures, a notation of the celestial music that the good men and women tried so desperately to recall from their days in the spirit realm. Just once, Ninian had heard human voices reproduce the music. Shaken to his core, he'd felt as if the solid earth had tilted beneath him. He knew he would never be the same again.

Curious about the images that the bonshommes used as teaching aids, Ninian had asked Alazaïs. The images, she explained after a moment to gather her thoughts, were symbolic. The idea was that a glimpse of an image would bring to mind what lay at the heart of the illustration: 'They stand for much more than they are,' she added.

Ninian was none the wiser. He would have liked to ask if he might examine a set, but somehow he understood that his request would politely and kindly be turned down. Perhaps he just wasn't ready . . .

The weeks passed and turned into months. In time there came the first signs that the iron grip of the ice and snow was starting to relent; the drip-drip of melting icicles was a constant music to the day's work; snowdrops pierced the snow; both humans and animals were restless.

Everybody knew, although it was not spoken aloud, that the crusade would start again as soon as the roads up into the mountains were clear of snow. And now, increasingly, well-meaning people with anxiety in their eyes would hint to Ninian that it was time he began to think about going home.

Home. The word seemed to echo round inside his head. He wished there were some way to get word to England that he was safe and well, but he could not think how to do it, and nobody in the village volunteered a suggestion. Perhaps they feared that any such attempt would somehow reveal information to the enemy. He did not know.

Home. The House in the Woods, Josse, Meggie, Geoffroi, all the others in that close, affectionate household. Little Helewise: his beloved Eloise, as he had come to think of her. Creamy skin, so soft under his fingers. Thick, dark-brown hair, that he used to take in his hands and wind into a long rope to wrap around his own throat, binding her to him, binding himself to her . . . Except that it hadn't, because men had died – important men – and Ninian had been accused of their murder.

I cannot go home, he thought.

His friends' gentle suggestions turned gradually to worried urgency. 'It is not your battle, Ninian,' an ancient, serene-faced elder told him, one claw-like hand clutching at his wrist. It was February, a morning of hesitant sunshine, and they had climbed up to sit on a rock in a sheltered spot overlooking the village.

'You're my friends, Guillaume,' Ninian protested. 'I have lived and worked alongside you all these weeks and months of winter. I can't just leave you. Besides,' he hurried on, as Guillaume began to speak, 'you need me. Who'll carry on with instructing your fighting men if I'm not here?'

Guillaume gave a faint shrug. 'We should not fight,' he murmured.

Ninian bit back his protest. It was all right for Guillaume, for he was old, he'd had his life, and, as a perfect, he was probably longing for the release from earthly existence that would allow his soul to fly joyfully back to heaven. But Ninian knew, because they had told him, that many of the younger people were not ready to die.

'Some of the villagers don't share your strong convictions,' he said quietly.

Guillaume waved a thin hand. 'I know, I know.' His fine face creased in a frown. 'I understand,' he added in a whisper. He glanced up at Ninian. 'Nevertheless, you should prepare to leave. Give your pupils a few more lessons, then you must put your pack on your fine horse's back and ride away, before—' He did not go on.

Before the snows melt and the passes into the mountains open again, Ninian finished for him. Trained in the ways of fighting knights as he was, he well knew what would happen then. They would come thundering down from the north, hungry for plunder, hungry for the sweet, sun-warmed lands of the south, ready to kill in the name of their god, their pope and their king, most of them not overly concerned with the cause when the prizes were so seductive.

Guillaume had fallen silent beside him, and Ninian sat wondering what de Montfort would do once he had sufficient men under his command. Swiftly he went over what he had learned of the final months of the previous autumn's campaigning. De Montfort had appeared unstoppable, winning a series of victories culminating in the fall of Termes, a mountain-top town in the Corbières that was said to be out of reach to anything but the goats. The lord of Termes was now in a Carcassonne dungeon.

The elation of de Montfort's armies in the wake of their success had led to a wave of hangings and burnings, so terrible and so widespread that many southern lords had chosen surrender over death. More and more rebel strongholds had gone, and the threat of war hung over all of Languedoc. In January, Pedro, king of Aragon, deeply worried at the convulsion in these lands so close to his own, had reputedly approached the men of power within the Church. He undertook to recognize Simon de Montfort as his vassal, thus legitimizing his conquest of the lands already taken, but in return Pedro demanded that Raymond of Toulouse – who happened to be his brother-in-law – should assume once more his rightful position as the most important lord of Languedoc. The Church agreed, but only under conditions that amounted to the Languedoc lords meekly giving up and walking away, leaving their homes, their lands and everything they possessed to the vicious, avaricious, ever-hungry and ruthless crusaders.

The lords of Languedoc elected to go on fighting.

Where would the blow fall next? Ninian went over in his mind what he knew of de Montfort's tactics, trying to work out where he would turn his attention once he was ready. Last autumn, the crusaders had been pressing further and further into the territory of the great St Gilles family, northwards across the ridges and valleys to the east of Toulouse. Which town should now be preparing to defend itself? If only there were a way of knowing what was in de Montfort's mind.

Very slowly, the beginnings of an idea began to crystallize . . .

He became aware of Guillaume, stirring restlessly beside him, and realized with a stab of guilt that the poor old man must be getting very cold. 'We should go back to the village,' he said, leaping up and holding out his hands to Guillaume. 'Come on, let me help you.'

With a wince and a groan, Guillaume got to his feet. Clinging tightly to Ninian, he made his careful way down the steeply-sloping, rocky path. 'You are a good man,' he said, squeezing Ninian's hand. He added softly, 'You undoubtedly have many who love you and miss you, back in your faraway home.' The squeeze intensified. 'You should go back to them, Ninian. They must surely need you.'

Equally gently, Ninian reminded Guillaume why it was that he was there. 'I'm a wanted man,' he murmured. 'Remember? I told you that back in England they think I'm a killer, and they'd hang me if they caught me.'

Guillaume gave a dismissive snort. 'Ah, they'll have forgotten all about that by now,' he said briskly. 'Men have short memories.'

No they don't, Ninian thought, picturing the furious face of King John. *Not this man, anyway*.

But then a strange thing happened. For all those months since the fight in the glade beside St Edmund's Chapel, so far away in the Hawkenlye forest, he had believed without a shadow of a doubt that what he had just said to Guillaume was true: if he went home, he would, although innocent, be arrested and hanged for murder.

Now the thought came to him: what if it *wasn't* true?

What if, somehow, the king's men had discovered what had really happened and everyone else also knew that Ninian was no murderer?

He seemed to experience a sudden flash of bright light

within his head, and he thought he heard his sister's voice. It wasn't the first time; quite often – more frequently, recently – he'd experienced the odd sensation that she was calling him, trying to tell him something, but he'd convinced himself it was nothing more than his imagination and his yearning for a glimpse of home.

Now, as he came to a halt at the foot of the path, aware of Guillaume's worried eyes on his face, he realized that, if Meggie really was trying to communicate with him, she had suddenly got a lot more urgent . . .

He didn't tell Guillaume. He didn't tell anyone. Using as an excuse the need to go out to the stables on the edge of the village and tend to his horse – let them think he was taking their advice and starting his preparations for departure – he went off by himself to think.

What could Meggie be trying to tell him? Could it be that Guillaume was right? Against all expectations, could those at home who loved Ninian and believed in him have somehow managed to prove his innocence? Oh, but if that were true, then he could indeed return to England.

Home. The family, the House in the Woods, Hawkenlye.

Little Helewise. His Eloise.

With a shock of horror, he realized he could no longer bring her face to mind.

In despair, he crouched down, his head in his hands. *I love her, I truly love her! The hundreds of miles between us, the months since we've been together, don't matter, for nothing can change our love!*

He raised his head, a smile beginning.

So why, came the cruel question, instantly wiping away the smile, *can't you recall her face?*

He did not know, but, back in the village, he was the subject of a concerned conversation between Guillaume, Alazaïs, and four of the other elders.

'He is young, he is passionate, he has become deeply involved with his new friends and the rest of us here,' Alazaïs said, 'and they have taken the place of his family. It is quite clear that he is a loving man, and, having given his affection to us, he does not want to leave us. Especially,' she added with a soft sigh, 'when he knows as well as we do that danger will return soon.'

'We have no claim on his loyalty,' one of the other elders said. 'Coming here as he did, bearing our precious manuscript all the way from its hiding place in England, he has already done us a great service.'

'His flight here was not entirely selfless,' a tall, slim woman pointed out. 'He was accused of murder, and he needed a place in which to hide.'

'He could have found one a great deal closer to home,' Alazaïs pointed out. 'It was my son who suggested he came here to the Midi, and my son, I am certain, was primarily concerned with getting the manuscript to us. He *used* Ninian,' she said in a low voice.

There was a short silence.

'You should not feel the need to share your son's guilt over this,' Guillaume said gently; he knew Alazaïs very well.

She gave him a quick smile. 'Thank you, my dear.' She turned to look at the others, huddled close in the dim light within the cottage, and her smile disappeared. 'I have indeed felt guilty, but I have put the guilt to good use. I have, I believe, come up with a way in which we can persuade Ninian that, if he agrees to leave, he will actually be helping us.'

The five old people leaned closer and, in a very quiet voice, she told them her plan.

SIX

Vengeance.

Riding back down the long slope to Hawkenlye Abbey, Josse thought about what Meggie had just told him. So the three dead men had been killed in revenge for something they had done, and, to make quite sure that the world knew, the appropriate runes had been carved into the biggest man's chest. If Gervase was right in his assumption that the dead trio were the same men who had been performing the many acts of assault, robbery and violence throughout several counties, then there must be any number of people crying out for vengeance.

One of them – or possibly a group – must have followed the brigands to the Hawkenlye Forest and extracted that vengeance.

Josse had decided that his first act should be to ask the nuns and monks at the abbey if any of them remembered a stranger, or group of strangers, who had arrived some five or six weeks ago. Normally, such an enquiry would be fairly pointless, since the abbey's widespread reputation as a place of succour and healing meant that it was always full of strangers. But now the abbey church was closed, there were no services, the king's commissioners doled out that meagre part of its own money that the abbey was allowed to spend on charity and, it seemed, most would-be pilgrims had decided it wasn't worth making the trek and so they stayed at home.

Thinking guiltily that the major cause of Abbess Caliste's distress was possibly about to help him in his quest, Josse left his horse in the care of a lay brother in the abbey stables and went to find her.

'Vengeance,' Abbess Caliste murmured. 'Three runes merged together into a bind rune.' She looked up at Josse. 'A very powerful symbol.'

Again he had to remind himself that she had not always been a nun. She had not always been called Caliste, either; the name given to her by the plain but good people who cared for her for the first fourteen years of her life was Peg.[1] Helewise had once told Josse that Caliste had known what her true name was because it had been carved on a piece of wood that she had worn round her neck on a leather thong. Not that anyone else would have been able to make it out, since it was written in the strange script of the forest people.

If the young Caliste had been able to read the symbols carefully written on her pendant, it was little surprise that the adult abbess was familiar with the concept of bind runes . . .

Forcing his mind back to the present, he said, 'I'm wondering, my lady, if perhaps the person responsible for the

---

[1] See *The Ashes of the Elements*

deaths of the three men could have visited the abbey. It would have been early in January, and, although I agree it's unlikely that a man intent on murder would deliberately go among the company of people who might later recall him, we have to remember that he could have come from far away and reckoned on being back home again when the bodies were discovered.'

The abbess was nodding. 'Quite so.' She paused, clearly thinking, then said, 'Besides, the killings were committed for revenge. Possibly that emotion overrode the fear of being caught.'

'Aye, possibly.'

'So, you wish to ask my nuns, monks and lay brothers if they recall any visitors who turned up here at the time of the deaths,' she said briskly. 'Please do.'

'I would ask you too, my lady,' he said with a smile. Busy as she always was, preoccupied with the huge problems of running a big abbey on barely any money, still he knew very well that she managed to keep an eye on almost everything that went on within the walls, and probably within a mile radius outside them as well.

She sat for a while, a slight frown on her face. Then she said, 'We were very quiet then. Few people were about, strangers or otherwise. We—' Then the frown cleared and, her face suddenly animated, she said, 'There *was* a man . . . yes, I remember now.'

'What—?'

She held up her hand. 'Sir Josse, I did not meet him myself, so I can tell you little. I only knew about him because Sister Estella was troubled by her encounter with him and sought me out to ask what she should do.'

'What happened, that she should be troubled?' Josse asked.

Abbess Caliste paused, and he guessed she was putting her thoughts in order so that she would be able to tell her tale quickly and efficiently. It was something Helewise had always done. 'Sister Estella is one of our novices,' Caliste began, 'and she is a light-hearted, happy soul who loves to chat.' Perhaps thinking this did not sound very nunlike, she added, 'She lifts our hearts in these hard, sad times, and we value her simple, optimistic spirit. She often goes down to the vale, where she shines her cheery light on those few pilgrims who still come to Hawkenlye to take the water, and on the day in question, she saw a man standing beside the little chapel down there. She—' Abbess Caliste frowned. 'No, this will not do, for you need the exact details and I do not know them.'

She rose to her feet, swiftly crossed to the door and, opening it, hurried outside. The sound of her voice briefly floated back, then she returned.

'I have sent for Sister Estella,' she said, resuming her seat. 'Best that you hear what she has to say in her own words.'

Sister Estella must have been nearby, for very soon there was a timid tap on the door. The abbess admitted her, swiftly introduced Josse and told her what he wanted to know. She seemed somewhat overawed, Josse noticed, the cheerful, round face a little pale as she stood before her abbess biting her lips.

'The abbess tells me that in January you were worried by a man you saw by the chapel in the vale,' he said, giving her what he hoped was a reassuring smile. 'Could you tell me about him? It would be really helpful if you would,' he added.

She returned his smile, and he saw that she was a young woman made for happiness. She was very pretty, her wide blue eyes fringed with long lashes. 'I'll try, sir.' She turned back to the abbess, who nodded encouragingly. Then she said, 'He looked so anxious, and I reckon that's why I went over to him. Since he was standing outside the chapel – actually leaning on the door – and it was, of course, locked, I wondered if he wanted to go inside and pray or something, so I asked him. He seemed to come out of a deep reverie, and when he actually managed to focus his eyes on me, he said, "I have need to speak to a priest, but priests are not here."

'I said, no, they weren't, but if he needed a friendly ear, I could provide one, then he gave a sort of laugh, but it sounded as if he was hurting, and he said, "There is a deed I must do, but it is wrong, and I need to know that I will be forgiven."

'I told him that only God can forgive, but that he always does if someone sincerely repents.' She turned to the abbess. 'That's right, my lady, isn't it? I said the right thing, didn't I?'

'Yes, Sister Estella, you did,' the abbess agreed.

'What happened then?' Josse asked. 'Did he – I don't suppose he gave you any idea of whether he was going to go ahead with this deed?'

Sister Estella frowned in thought. 'He – oh, I don't know! It's hard to describe, and I may mislead you if I don't explain properly.' Her worried frown deepened, and Josse felt he'd do anything to bring back her happy equanimity. On the other hand, it appeared she had some information that it would be very useful to know.

'Tell us about this man,' he said. Trying to keep his tone pleasant and free of the stress he could feel within himself, he added, 'Can you describe him? What did he look like?' If he asked her something simple to begin with, perhaps she would find it easier to proceed to whatever was worrying her.

Sister Estella's expression relaxed and, not stopping to think, she said, 'He was brown.'

'*Brown?*' Josse and the abbess said together.

Sister Estella gave a chuckle. 'Yes. His skin was the colour of a chestnut just out of the shell, as if he'd been stained. It was a lovely colour,' she added, 'and his flesh looked very smooth. His eyes were so dark they were almost black, and he had a neatly-trimmed beard. I couldn't see his hair, because he wore a long bit of cloth wound round and round his head. He was dressed in a dark-brown robe that swept right down to the ground, and he had a cloak thrown back over his shoulders. Oh, and he had a gold ring in his left ear. He was very handsome.' Blushing suddenly, as if realizing that such a flowing description of a man was perhaps not fitting in a woman vowed to chastity, she lowered her eyes and stared down at her feet.

'That's very good, Sister Estella,' Josse said encouragingly. 'I can almost see him!' She risked a look at him from under her eyelashes, and he thought he saw a swift grin. 'How old would you say he was?'

'He wasn't a lad, but he wasn't all that old either.' She bit at her lip. 'I'm not very good with ages. Sorry, sir.'

'Never mind. Was there anything else about him that struck you? How did he sound?' She looked puzzled, so he rephrased the question. 'Did he speak like people round here?'

Her face cleared. 'No, he didn't. When I said how he'd asked about priests, those were the exact words. That's when I noticed he didn't sound like a local.'

'Tell us again, if you would.'

'"I have need to speak to a priest, but priests are not here."'

'Could you detect any particular accent?' Abbess Caliste asked.

Estella shook her head. 'I don't really know about accents,' she said. 'I don't come across many strangers.' Josse thought she had finished, but then she added, 'He sounded as if he was unused to speech. His voice was sort of rusty, as if he didn't use it much.'

Josse nodded. Then he said very gently, 'Sister Estella, you've been most helpful and I'm very grateful. Now, a few moments ago you wanted to tell us something, but you weren't sure quite how to. Can you now say what it was?'

She looked as if she was plucking up her courage. Then she said, 'I had the feeling that he was a man who would do what he felt he had to. He'd come seeking a priest, and that made me think he knew very well that what he intended to do was wrong. But I reckoned that, even if he didn't find a priest, he'd go ahead anyway. He was . . .' She paused, clearly searching for the right word. 'Driven.'

Abbess Caliste caught Josse's eye. 'A man who would perhaps carry out his intended task and afterwards pray for forgiveness,' she murmured.

'Aye.' Josse sighed. What a pity, he reflected, the confessional was sacrosanct; even if this dark stranger had managed to find some priest to hear his confession for murder, nobody was ever going to know.

Both women, he noticed, were watching him; Sister Estella looked apprehensive. 'My lady abbess, Sister Estella, thank you for your time,' he said with a bow. 'I shall go now and seek out Gervase de Gifford. It may be that others have come across your brown stranger, Sister—' he turned to the novice with a smile – 'and perhaps one of Gervase's men will know where he is.'

He turned to go, but there was a quick movement, and suddenly Sister Estella was right beside him, a hand on his arm. 'Sir Josse?'

'What is it, child?' he asked kindly.

She seemed to struggle for words. 'He's – oh, I know I said
he was handsome, and went on about how he looked as I've
no right to do, but it's not his looks that were important, not
really. He—'

'Go on.'

'He was a *good* man!' she burst out. 'Yes, he said he needed
forgiveness for a bad deed, but I reckon it was something bad
done for a good cause, and that's not really terrible, is it?'
She turned to the abbess and then rapidly back to Josse. '*Is*
it?' she demanded.

Josse sighed. He knew what she meant and, if indeed it had
been this mysterious stranger who killed the three brigands,
and the deed was done in vengeance, then it was exactly as
Estella had said: *something bad done for a good cause.*

Quite how he was going to persuade Gervase of that, if and
when they ever caught this man, he didn't know.

As the day drew on, Meggie grew increasingly desperate to
evade the company of Helewise and her granddaughter, not
because she did not enjoy being with them but because the
compulsion to get away to her mother's little hut was becoming
unendurable.

The intensity of her need to escape made her feel guilty
because the three of them had spent such a happy day together.
Little Helewise seemed quite different from the pale, hollow-
eyed, sorrowful and anxious young woman who had arrived
at the House in the Woods with her father the previous day.
Now she had colour in her cheeks and her ready smile had
frequently turned to laughter. Having feared at first that Little
Helewise might have been sick, Meggie had been watching
her closely. She had concluded that, whatever had ailed the
girl, a day of very hard work, largely spent in the invigorating
open air, had put it right. Perhaps it had been no more than a
sudden intolerance of the endless weeks shut up inside the
walls of her father's house. Plus, of course, pining for Ninian.

Perhaps, though, it was something else entirely . . .

Now, as Meggie sat with Helewise and her granddaughter
beside the fire – set in a small circle of hearthstones inside
the cell that was to be their home – she cast a surreptitious
glance at the young woman.

She thought hard for a few moments.

Then she smiled.

The three women ate their simple supper, and as the other two cleared up, Meggie got to her feet.

'I'd better go and see if our two guardian angels are all right,' she said, heading for the door. 'They were having a job getting their fire going, and it'll be cold out there tonight.'

Helewise looked up with a smile. 'They'll be used to cold nights,' she said. 'Their usual accommodation down in the vale is very basic, you know. But it's a kind thought,' she added.

Meggie returned the smile. 'I thought, since they're out there for our sake, it would be nice to show we appreciate it.'

She slipped outside. Her face felt red-hot; guilt was flowing through her again. It was very hard, she was discovering, not to be truthful with someone who trusted you implicitly. It was so easy to fool them that it hurt.

She hurried across to the crude but sturdy shelter that the lay brothers had put up and pushed aside the heavy piece of leather which served for a door. The two young men lay either side of the fire, which was now burning brightly. They were wrapped snugly in sheepskins, their eyes shining with excitement.

'I'm sorry to disturb you,' Meggie said. 'I just wanted to check that you were all right.'

The elder of the two laughed. 'Reckon that's our job, miss,' he said. He glanced at his companion. 'We were about to come to make sure you and the others were tucked up snug for the night.'

'We are,' Meggie assured him. 'We'll be settling down to sleep soon, so you can too.'

The younger monk gave a huge yawn. 'Sorry,' he said with a grin. 'S'been a busy day.'

'Sleep well,' Meggie said.

She stayed outside for a while longer. Then she went back to the cell and closed the door.

She did not have long to wait. She lay on her back, warm under the covers and not bothered by the hardness of the plank bed. She strained to hear her companions' breathing: *slow, steady*, she said silently to them, *yes, that's the way. Sleep. Sleep.*

When she was sure both women were asleep, she got out of bed, took her heavy cloak off her bed and, making barely a sound, quietly left the hut. She tiptoed past the lay brothers' shelter – she could see the glow of the fire but there was no sound other than the soft, rhythmic snoring of one of them – and hurried off across the clearing and into the forest.

There were a few clouds in the sky, occasionally covering the waxing moon, but Meggie knew her way so well that she could have done the journey with no light at all. The sky, however, had all but cleared by the time she reached the hut, and the moonlight enabled her to see that the rope knot with which door was secured had been retied.

Someone had been inside.

Not one of the family; she was sure of that. Only Ninian and Josse ever came to the hut. Ninian was far away, and Meggie knew that her father never came from choice. She was almost certain, moreover, that he would not go inside the hut without an invitation. He never spoke of it, but Meggie knew without being told that his memories of Joanna's hut were bitter-sweet.

So, a stranger had used the place. Meggie walked slowly all around the hut and its surrounding clearing, stopping to inspect the herb garden and going down to the stream, behind which the tall, ancient trees of the forest stood in silent protection. Eventually, she went back to the hut and, unfastening the rope, went inside.

She got up on to the sleeping platform and wrapped herself in her cloak, unfolding the heavy wool blankets and draping them over the top. She was warm from walking and wanted to preserve her body's heat. She thought about what she had just seen.

There were signs that a horse had been tethered under the shelter of the skeletal willows down by the little stream. She had noticed some droppings, covered with a scrape of earth. She had fetched a spade and removed the dung to the herb bed, bare in that end of winter season. The unknown visitor, she realized, had covered his – or her – tracks pretty well, considering what an out-of-the-way spot it was, but Meggie's thorough search had uncovered some hoof prints and a scatter of oat husks. The visitor had clearly taken good care of the horse; Meggie had found a wisp of horse hair from where the animal had been groomed. The hair was reddish-brown. Now she held it in her fingers, absently plaiting it into a neat braid.

She raised herself on one elbow, looking around the hut. She had left the door open, and the blueish moonlight streamed in. The interior of the hut looked almost exactly as she had left it, and anyone but Meggie would not have noticed the tiny differences. Whoever had used the hut – and she knew without a doubt someone had – had been careful and respectful.

It was just as she had thought. She gave a small private smile of satisfaction, pleased that again she had trusted her instincts and again they hadn't let her down. She'd known even before she saw the retied knot that someone had been there. She had tested her reaction to this alien presence and, as extra protection, sent up a swift thought to Joanna's guardian spirit. Her mother's and her own response had been the same: there was no danger.

She settled back on the platform. Her mother felt very close. Whoever had been inside the hut had not disturbed the sense of Joanna's presence; this in itself told Meggie that the visitor meant no harm.

She felt herself relax. Soon, oh, soon, she would sink down into the light trance state in which she so urgently needed to be. There, with any luck, she might begin to understand why she kept having the strong sense that her mother was calling out to her. *I'm here*, she said silently to Joanna. *Tell me what it is you want me to do.*

Her breathing slowed and deepened as the trance took her.

Within Hawkenlye Abbey, the three dead men lay like statues on the trestles in the undercroft beneath the nuns' dormitories. Sister Liese had left incense burning, and the air within the stone-walled crypt was very cold, but still the stench of death was slowly and steadily permeating the room. It was rumoured that the men were to be buried within the next couple of days, and many among the Hawkenlye community considered that it would not be a moment too soon.

No priest was meant to bury the dead. Under the pope's interdict, funerals were not permitted. Abbess Caliste and her priest did not believe that a king's quarrel with a pope should mean men went to their graves with nobody to pray for their souls, and the abbess had murmured to Father Sebastian that such prayers were even more vital when the bodies in question belonged to men who had in all probability been violent criminals.

Not that the indistinct figure creeping along in the deep shadow of the dormitory walls was aware of any of that. He was there to do one task only, and all his thoughts were bent towards its completion.

He reached the low door that led to the undercroft. It was locked, but locks did not present a problem. Reaching into a pouch that hung from his belt, he extracted a set of narrow, delicate tools fixed on to a ring, careful not to let the pieces of metal clink together. With a quick look around him – there was nobody in sight; the abbey seemed to be fast asleep behind the security of its stout gates – he put the first of the tools into the lock. He used two more in swift succession, then the lock gave and, opening the door a crack, he went inside. He took a candle stub from a fold of his tunic, striking his flint to light it. Then, unhurriedly, he went on down the passage.

The door to the room where the three men lay was not locked. He raised the latch and went inside. He stood for a moment looking down at the corpses, the light held up over each in turn as he folded back the covering sheets.

He saw what he was looking for. He reached out his free hand, muttering a prayer as he did so. He replaced the covers and then, without another look at the dead men, he spun round, left the room and paced swiftly back up the passage. Outside, he locked the door again – if those within the abbey chose to lock up the dead at night, he would not argue with it – and then he slipped back into the shadows.

A few moments later, anyone watching the section of wall behind the herb garden would have seen a dark shape quickly climb over and disappear into the night.

SEVEN

Josse had been persuaded by Sabine de Gifford to stay the night at the sheriff's house. By the time he had finished explaining to Gervase about the implications of the strange marks on the dead man's chest, it was late. Having experienced before the delights of Sabine's cooking – even in straitened times, her flair meant that her family still enjoyed variety in their meals – Josse had readily accepted the invitation. Gervase had provided wine, of so good a quality that it too was a treat.

Josse took breakfast with the family the next morning. Gervase and Sabine's two sons were big boys now – too grown-up to be petted – and both they and their parents tended to spoil the eight-year-old Alazaïs. The cheerful meal was disturbed by the arrival of one of Gervase's deputies, urgently demanding his attention. With a muttered curse, Gervase got up from the table and went outside. There was murmuring – a quick question from the sheriff and a quiet reply – and more conversation, then the sound of footsteps hurrying away.

Gervase stood in the doorway and beckoned to Josse; whatever he had to say, clearly he did not want his daughter to overhear. Josse got up and followed him back outside into the courtyard.

'One of the king's agents has been attacked,' Gervase said. He frowned. 'He's a—' But whatever he had been about to say concerning the man was bitten back; to judge by Gervase's expression, it had been derogatory. 'His name's Matthew and he works for Benedict de Vitré.' Josse raised his eyebrows at the name, and Gervase nodded. 'I see you know of Lord Benedict,' he murmured.

'Who doesn't?' Josse replied. Lord Benedict de Vitré was said to be a very close friend of the king, a position he chose to interpret as meaning he could do exactly what he liked as long as he did his job. Since his job was extracting money from everyone in his manor and forwarding it to the king, he was universally loathed. His habits of callous ruthlessness had been adopted by his underlings, and Josse had heard rumours that Lord Benedict turned a willingly blind eye to assault and rape.

'It seems Lord Benedict had sent Matthew and his gang of thugs sniffing around the outlying hamlets and villages down to the south-east of Tonbridge,' Gervase went on. 'After money, of course. Lord Benedict clearly hopes to impress his friend the king by dispatching a few more bags of gold in order to help finance this new expedition into Wales.'

'No doubt creaming off a decent portion of the bounty for himself first,' Josse said quietly. Gervase glanced swiftly at him but did not comment. 'What happened?'

'Matthew arrived at an isolated farm just to the north of the forest,' Gervase said. 'An all too familiar tale, I fear: the man of the house said he'd already given everything he could spare, Matthew refused to believe him and set his men ransacking the place, the man protested and Matthew got his men to take him outside and tie him to a tree so that Matthew could flog him.'

'Matthew is *wicked*!' Josse hissed. 'He—' With difficulty, he stopped. 'And now you say he too has been assaulted?'

'Yes. He didn't turn up at Lord Benedict's house yesterday, and Benedict sent his men out to look for him. They found him early this morning. He'd been tied to a tree and flogged.'

'He's still alive?'

'Yes, although he won't sleep on his back for a week or two.' Gervase paused. 'He was given exactly the same number of strokes as he meted out to the farmer.'

Josse couldn't help the small cheer that seemed to sound inside his head. 'An eye for an eye,' he said.

'Vengeance again,' Gervase said tersely. 'If we are right in our thinking, those three men who lie dead up at the abbey were murderers, and hence were killed. Lord Benedict's man Matthew abuses his position and does not hesitate to flog a man for no reason, and he in his turn has been given the same treatment.'

'Is that not justice?' Josse demanded. 'Matthew is a vicious man and has got what he deserves, and—'

'*Hush*, Josse!' Gervase looked quickly around, but there was nobody in earshot. 'Whatever else he may be, Matthew is acting for the king.'

'Even so, you should be—'

'*Enough.*' The single word was barked out. Leaning close to Josse, Gervase said, 'These are dangerous times, Josse. Do not be provoked into speaking words that may land you in trouble.'

'I'll speak my mind!'

'Not in my presence.'

Stung, Josse stared at his old friend. Gervase whispered, 'I know, Josse. But what would you have me do?' He paused, then went on, 'Lord Benedict will be howling out in fury at this assault on one of his men. We shall have to redouble our efforts to find who is behind these attacks, and, moreover, make sure that we are *seen* to be redoubling them.'

'And what will you do with the perpetrator if and when he is caught?' Josse asked coldly.

Gervase turned away. 'What I must do.'

Then he went back up the steps into the hall.

Helewise woke in the morning following the first night back in the little cell beside St Edmund's Chapel and wondered at first where she was. When she remembered, she gave a smile of happiness. *I can do some good here*, she thought. *I know I can.*

Little Helewise was still asleep, curled up under her covers, but Meggie's bed was empty. Helewise got up, arranged her gown and her simple headdress, then went outside. Meggie was emerging from the forest, her arms full of firewood.

'You're up early!' Helewise said, going to help her with her burden. 'And how busy you've been!'

'I thought our supply needed replenishing,' Meggie replied, 'and we shouldn't rely on our sturdy lay brothers for everything.'

'No, indeed, and they'll have their own duties down in the vale today,' Helewise agreed. Lowering her voice, she added, 'Do you think we need to tell your dear father that we're only going to be guarded during the hours of darkness?'

Meggie gave her a quick smile. 'No, I don't. It'll only worry him.'

'We are, after all, in sight of the abbey,' Helewise said. She stopped, looking down the long slope to the familiar outline of the abbey buildings. It was odd, but she was discovering that she had no desire whatsoever to venture inside . . .

'I wonder when we'll have our first pilgrims?' Meggie said as she followed Helewise on towards the hut. 'I'm sure word is already spreading that you're here.'

'And you,' Helewise said. 'You, I'm sure, are the greater attraction, healer that you are.'

'I can only heal bodies,' Meggie replied. 'You heal souls.'

'Only God does that.' The protest came automatically. Then, thinking Meggie might have read the remark as a snub, Helewise added, 'Meggie, if St Edmund's Chapel isn't locked, do you think we could go up and visit it? Just the two of us, now, before Little Helewise wakes up?'

Meggie put down her firewood beside the door of the cell. 'Yes,' she said. 'It isn't locked – I just checked.' Her eyes met Helewise's. 'It's high time we went to see her, isn't it?'

They stood side by side in the crypt beneath St Edmund's Chapel, staring at the statue of the Black Madonna in her secret niche. Helewise was only vaguely aware of Meggie beside her; almost all her attention was on the small, dark figure. The Madonna had been fashioned sitting on a low, simple throne, and she wore a headdress like the crescent moon turned on its back. She was heavily pregnant, her precious boy child swelling in her womb.

For Helewise, she was the Virgin Mary.

For Meggie, Helewise suspected, she was someone – something – else entirely.

Helewise began to pray. Silently, she asked for help and support in this new venture. *Let those who are in need know we are here*, she begged, *and bestow on us the strength, the wisdom and the compassion to give to each one whatever it is that will help them best.*

After quite a long time, the two women left the crypt, carefully replaced the trapdoor disguised as a flagstone, and returned to the cell.

People began arriving later that morning. Little Helewise, who stressed that she could neither heal the sick nor offer help to those who were troubled but knew how to stir a pot, had volunteered to work at the hearth. She busied herself keeping the fire going and tending the restorative broth that Meggie had prepared, doling it out to the visitors. Observing her, Helewise thought that the sweet smile and the gentle words of welcome probably did almost as much good as the broth.

Meggie was much in demand, and by noon her supply of herbal remedies was considerably diminished. Helewise had prayed with three different family groups, all of whom had called her my lady abbess and all of whom expressed their delight at seeing her in the little cell once more. She reminded them that she was no longer Abbess Helewise, but she wasn't sure they took any notice.

When the daylight began to fade, she could hardly believe that the day was ending. Little Helewise was tidying up the cell, washing out the little wooden bowls in which she had dished out the broth, and then she was going to begin preparing another batch for the following day. Meggie had gone down to the abbey to visit the herb shed, where she was hoping to find more supplies. The two guardian lay brothers had not yet arrived.

Helewise, then, was alone outside the cell when the last visitor of the day arrived. It was a young woman, pale faced, thin, ill-looking. Grieving, Helewise guessed. The girl was dressed in a worn gown that had been neatly mended; over it was what looked like a man's rough work jerkin.

She stopped a few paces away from Helewise, as if unsure whether to advance. Helewise approached her, holding out her hands. 'May I help you?' she asked. 'There is a little broth left, if you are hungry.'

The woman shook her head. Helewise thought she paled slightly at the mention of food. 'I'm not hungry.'

Helewise waited.

'Are you—?' The young woman stopped. 'They said there's a healer here,' she said instead. 'Someone that knows about herbs.'

'Yes, that's right,' Helewise said with a smile.

She had been about to say that Meggie was down at the abbey but would soon be back, but the girl interrupted. Coming right up to Helewise, she whispered, 'I need your help.'

Then she told Helewise what was wrong with her and what she wanted Helewise to do.

Horrified, Helewise realized the young woman had taken her for the healer; apparently not knowing that Meggie was a generation younger, in her desperation she had blurted out her problem to the first female face she saw.

'But – but that's against God's laws!' she heard herself say. 'You must not ask for that sort of help!'

The girl had shied away. Belatedly appreciating her mistake, she said, 'You're not her, are you? Not the healer?'

'No, I'm—' What am I? Helewise wondered wildly.

The young woman had turned and was running away. Already regretting her hasty response, Helewise started after her, but she was no match for the girl's speed. By the time Helewise reached the first of the trees, the girl had already vanished inside the forest.

Meggie had found some of the materials she needed down at the abbey, grateful for Abbess Caliste's generous response to her request: 'Take whatever you need!' she'd said. The little hut was not, however, the cornucopia of useful herbs that it had once been. Standing there packing up what she had selected, Meggie wished fervently that Tiphaine was still the abbey's herbalist. But Tiphaine seemed to have disappeared, and those who had known her best suspected that she had gone off with the forest people. As Helewise had once sagely remarked, Tiphaine always kept one foot in her pagan past. Whoever acted as herbalist now – if, indeed, anyone did – seemed to be lacking the imagination required for the task. The standard remedies were there, adequately well prepared and tidily stored on the shelves, but standard remedies only got you so far . . .

Meggie realized that she was going to have to make another visit to her mother's hut and raid her own herbal stores. She smiled to herself. She'd been planning to return anyway, but now she had an excuse. The prospect of possibly finding further traces of the mysterious visitor was distinctly thrilling; maybe she would meet the man himself. Always assuming it *was* a man.

Back at the cell, she was greeted by an appetizing smell; Little Helewise had been busy and supper was ready. The mutton and vegetable stew had far more vegetables than mutton, but the girl had been imaginative in her use of herbs and it was delicious.

Wiping her bowl with a piece of bread, Helewise said, 'I feel positively guilty that I enjoyed that so much, especially when we all know quite well that so many will go hungry to their beds tonight.'

There was a brief silence. Little Helewise, her mouth full, looked furtively at her grandmother. Meggie thought how to phrase her reply. 'As you have often observed, Helewise,' she said, 'we can only go on helping the starving, the sick and the desperate if we remain healthy.'

Helewise nodded quickly. 'Yes, Meggie, I know.' She gave her a smile. 'Actually, I was thinking of one person in particular.' She paused, and Meggie thought she looked sheepish.

'Someone who came here today?' Meggie prompted.

'Yes.' Carefully, Helewise put down her empty bowl and then folded her hands in her lap. 'It was late this afternoon. You were down at the abbey fetching your herbs, and a thin, ill-looking young woman arrived. She asked if there was a healer, a herbalist, here, and when I said yes, she thought I meant that it was me. She – er, she told me what she needed.' Helewise stared down at her hands. 'I – er, I was a little hasty, and she turned and hurried away. I tried to go after her – I hurried to the spot where she'd gone back into the forest, but there was no sign of her.' She shook her head, frowning. 'I handled it very badly,' she said angrily. 'I should have offered help, for in retrospect I can see how desperate she was, and now, oh, I'm very afraid of what she might do.'

Meggie had a fair idea of what the young woman had asked for. She had some sympathy for Helewise, who had been thrown into something she could not deal with. She had far more sympathy for the unknown young woman.

Meggie reached out and took hold of Helewise's hand. 'She wanted an abortifacient, didn't she?' she asked quietly. Mutely, Helewise nodded.

Little Helewise whispered, 'What's that?'

Unthinkingly, Meggie said, 'It's a mix of herbs that causes a pregnant woman to slip the unborn child.'

Little Helewise gasped, a soft sound quickly stifled as she

put her hands over her mouth. Amid the larger anxiety, Meggie cursed herself for her tactlessness. *I will speak to her later*, she resolved. Then, turning her full attention to Helewise, she took a steadying breath and said, 'You are right to berate yourself, although I understand why you reacted as you did. I don't think you could have helped yourself, dear Helewise, given who and what you are.'

'I'm no longer either an abbess or a nun,' Helewise muttered.

'Maybe, but you are still a deeply Christian woman, and you have been taught that *thou shalt not kill* applies as much to an unborn infant in the womb as to a man or woman who walks the earth.'

'It does,' Helewise said simply.

Ah, Meggie thought. There seemed no point in battling Helewise head-on, so she said, 'If I might suggest—'

'Oh, please do!' Helewise interrupted beseechingly.

Meggie smiled. 'I think it would have been best to have invited the young woman to sit down by the fire, offer her some broth—'

'I did, and she said she wasn't hungry!'

'—and ask her to tell you a little about herself; how she had come to be pregnant, and why she felt she could not face bearing the child.'

Helewise nodded slowly. 'Ye–es.' Then, a spark in her eyes, she said, 'But, whatever the circumstances, I could never have given her what she asked for, even had it been within my power!'

'Even if to carry a child to term and give birth to it would have taken the mother's own life?' Meggie asked softly. 'Even if the pregnancy was the result of rape?'

Helewise stared at her wide-eyed. 'I – I don't know,' she admitted. Then, rallying: 'If either was the case, then I believe I would suggest that the child be taken away at birth, either to be raised by nuns such as those in the foundlings' home at the abbey, or else given to a family willing to take in another's child.'

Then we shall have to agree to differ, Meggie thought. She wondered if the girl would come back. She hoped so.

But that was for another day. For now there was a more immediate distress to deal with. Getting up, Meggie turned to

Little Helewise. 'I'm going to fetch some more firewood,' she said with a smile. 'Would you come and help me?'

Little Helewise was on her feet before Meggie had finished speaking. With a private smile, Meggie followed her outside.

As soon as they were out of earshot of both the cell and the lay brothers' shelter, Meggie said, 'Due in July, I would guess.'

Little Helewise gasped. 'How did you know?'

'I'm a healer,' Meggie replied. 'I recognize the symptoms.' There was no reply. 'First of all, I should tell you that I am delighted,' she continued. 'I love my half-brother dearly, and I know you do too. I can't wait to be an aunt!'

Again there was no answer. Meggie thought Little Helewise was quietly weeping. She wrapped her arms round the girl, holding her close. 'Don't cry,' she whispered. 'You'll have a beautiful baby, and I'll be there to help you when the time comes.'

'I'm not afraid of the birth,' Little Helewise said. 'But we're not married, and he isn't even *here*!'

Meggie smoothed her hand over Little Helewise's shaking shoulders. 'Nobody's getting married now,' she said lightly. 'You can't, with the interdict. But babies are still being conceived.' Briefly, she thought of the unknown woman who had come looking for help. 'As for Ninian not being here, all I can say is that he will come home, one day.' *He will*, she said with silent fervour. 'In the meantime, you are safe, you have a home, you have a loving family, and—'

'What's my father going to say?' Little Helewise wailed. 'And my *mother*!'

Meggie visualized Leofgar and Rohaise. Yes, Little Helewise was right in being more fearful of her mother's reaction. Illegitimacy was a huge stigma to some people, and unfortunately Rohaise was one of them. Since Meggie herself had been born out of wedlock, as had her brother Geoffroi, and bearing in mind that her half-brother Ninian was not the son of the man to whom Joanna had been wed at the time of his birth, it was a matter of little consequence to her. 'Do you know what I should do?' she asked.

'No.' Little Helewise disengaged herself, wiped a hand across her eyes and pushed back her hair. 'What?'

There was such hopeful trust in her face that Meggie paused for an instant before speaking. This was the moment; she must not waste it. 'I would go back inside the cell and tell your grandmother,' she said firmly. Overriding Little Helewise's gasp of horror, she went on: 'Then the two of you should find an opportunity to tell my father, who is the last person to protest at babies being conceived outside marriage. With him and Helewise on your side – oh, yes, she'll be on your side, I guarantee it – you can then go and face your parents.' She hesitated, then said: 'Your mother will probably lecture you for several days about how wrong it was to let Ninian have his way with you, how he won't respect you any more, how a woman must save herself for the marriage bed, but it's her right as your mother to express her opinion and you'll just have to put up with it.'

Little Helewise's face had softened into a reminiscent smile. 'It was by no means him having his way,' she said. 'If anything, *I* persuaded *him*. There was no immediate prospect of a marriage or a marriage bed, and we weren't prepared to wait. And I don't think respect comes into it really, do you?'

Meggie grinned. 'I don't see it as particularly relevant, no.' She looked at Little Helewise, affection and the beginning of love in her heart. 'Am I right that the baby's due in July?'

'I don't know,' Little Helewise confessed.

'How long had you been lovers before he went away?'

'Not long.'

'Hmm.' She took Little Helewise's hand and set off down the track into the forest. 'We'd better get this firewood, then we'll go back and you can tell your grandmother the news.' Ignoring the muffled groan, she added, 'Tomorrow we'll find a quiet, private moment and I'll examine you and ask you a few pertinent questions. Oh – that is, if you want me to?' *Never assume automatically that someone wants you to treat them* had been one of Joanna's maxims.

'I do,' came the instant reply.

'Very well, then. Tomorrow I'll try to explain everything you need to know, and then, with any luck, tell you when you can look forward to having a baby in your arms.'

As, a little later, Little Helewise and Meggie made their way back to the cell, arms full of foraged firewood, Meggie was thinking hard about Ninian. Was Little Helewise's pregnancy the reason for Meggie's visions and dreams of her brother? Was it what was prompting the urgent need to get through to him? Ever since he had been cleared of the charge of murder last autumn, she had been trying to send him a message via the strange telepathy that sometimes seemed to exist between them, telling him it was safe to return. So far, there was no evidence whatsoever that he had heard her.

Now there was another reason to bring him back: he was going to be a father in a few months' time and in all likelihood he had no idea.

Meggie sent up a swift plea to the friendly spirits, her mother's included, that they might put their ethereal heads together and suggest to her a way to tell Ninian it was time to come home.

EIGHT

As the snows slowly began to melt in the foothills of the Pyrenees, Ninian worked on his plan. His friends were venturing out of the village quite regularly now, for the weeks between the beginning of the spring thaw and the onset of the next season of campaigning were precious and not to be wasted. Once the crusading armies amassed again, Simon de Montfort would tell them where to strike next. Then the brief time of freedom would break up into rumour, fear and the constant, dreadful anticipation that the assault was going to veer their way.

The village was remote, difficult to access and far to the south and the west of de Montfort's steady advance. Ninian knew his way round all the secret tracks and trails leading up and down the mountain on which the village sat, and he recognized that it had been well chosen as a stronghold. He believed it would survive when less easily defended places fell. When he had first been brought there, his guide had blindfolded him; it had been a sensible precaution, and Ninian had not resented it. But now that the time was approaching when he would have to leave the village and find his way back again, he was glad of the local knowledge he had managed to accumulate.

He had kept his ears open and his wits about him all winter, and he believed he knew where de Montfort and his senior commanders were likely to be overwintering. The front line of the crusader assault was sweeping up in a north-westerly direction, and Ninian had a good idea of where it had halted when campaigning had ended in the autumn. Now, he was sure, knights from the north would be setting off for the Midi, weapons of war at their sides and greed for the rich, sunny lands of the Languedoc egging them on. Knowing they were on their way, de Montfort would be making up his mind where to aim them.

With both old campaigners and newcomers arriving all the time, one more northern knight would not stand out. Any man who knew anything of a knight's training would fit in like a tree in a forest. Unobtrusively, Ninian prepared his sword, his gear and his horse; when the moment came, he would be ready.

The opportunity that soon presented itself was so perfect that Ninian could almost have believed some benign spirit had engineered it. The bonshommes had decided that they must contact friends and kin in towns and villages that lay in the likely path of the crusader advance, encouraging them to leave their homes and come to the Pyrenean strongholds while they still could. Listening to the discussions, Ninian heard a familiar name: Utta.

She lived in a small town to the east, where the final convulsions of the Pyrenees began to give way to the plain. Back in the autumn, she had made the difficult journey to Ninian's village because she wanted to meet the son of the woman who, back in England, had once saved her life.[2] She had told Ninian that he was good, like his mother. His impulse to seek her out was genuine, and, fortuitously, it provided him with the excuse he needed to leave the village and come back again.

He knew his friends would not countenance anything as risky as the mission he had set himself, so he didn't tell them. He left the village in the company of a group of four men,

---

[2] See *A Dark Night Hidden*

none of whom he knew well. They each had their appointed task and, when they came to the place at the foot of the mountain where tracks led off in different directions, it was easy to say a quick farewell and head out alone.

At first he was elated, full of pride that he, Ninian de Courtenay, was planning something so hazardous, so brave, purely for the selfless aim of helping the cause of the kind, decent, loving people who had taken him in and helped him when he needed it. After the months of enforced isolation up in the snowbound village, it was a joy simply to be out riding, on an eager horse. Even if the tracks were still icy in places and slushy with melting snow in others, he felt invincible and knew nothing was going to hold him back.

After three days, he was close to the encampment where, it was rumoured, Simon de Montfort was making his plans. Ninian found a sheltered spot in a pine wood from which to observe without being seen, and he thought the rumours were probably true. The camp was extensive and well guarded, and knights were arriving all the time, a few singly or in pairs, many more in rowdy gangs of thirty or forty.

The initial euphoria had long worn off. As Ninian watched the mass of knights, foot soldiers and camp followers, he began to realize the magnitude of the task he had set himself.

The apprehension was only going to get worse the longer he waited. As the sun climbed up towards its zenith, he led his horse, Garnet, out from beneath the pine trees, mounted up and rode down into the camp.

Nobody seemed to question that he was anything other than what he claimed to be: a knight from Brittany eager to carve out a patch of land for himself in the south, and even more eager to shed some heretic blood in order to do so. He encountered a group of Bretons who took him to heart like a long-lost brother, demanding to know where he came from, and when he said Dinan – a town he knew from his childhood – telling him it was a place with a fine reputation for fighting men and he'd better be sure he lived up to it.

He decided that, in view of what he was really there for, it would be best to avoid the Breton contingent in future.

He had been in the camp for only a couple of days when he found out what he wanted to know. That, too, proved risibly easy, for it appeared to be no secret. De Montfort must be very confident, Ninian thought. Perhaps that was what an autumn's successful campaigning did.

The next town to bear the brunt of crusader attack was to be Lavaur, north-east of Toulouse. As word of the decision spread, the encampment got busy with preparations, making repairs to the great siege engines, mending weapons and armour, exercising horses and drilling the foot soldiery. In the midst of the bustle, Ninian slipped away.

He was almost out of the camp when he was accosted by three large, drunken, blond-haired German knights. As they closed ranks and blocked the path, Ninian's heart sank.

'Running out on us, are you?' the first one said, his accent so atrocious that Ninian only just made out the words.

'My business is my own,' he replied shortly.

'You Froggie bastards are all the same,' scoffed the knight. 'First chance of doing a bit of fighting and you run for the hills.'

The remark was so monumentally inaccurate that Ninian didn't even bother to reply.

The big German came closer, looking up at Ninian as he sat on his horse and pointing a wavering finger in the general direction of his face. 'We don't need you lot,' he said, his words punctuated by a drunken hiccup. 'There's an army of our good lads on its way to join us, and they'll be here in time to lay siege to this piss-hole town we're going to attack.' He hiccuped again, then belched noisily and liquidly. 'Oops.'

'I'm sure they'll be a worthy addition,' Ninian said neutrally.

The knight narrowed his eyes, clearly suspecting irony, but Ninian kept his face bland and the big man did not pursue it. '*Ja*, they are fine knights,' he mumbled, 'marching in a long, wide column from their homes in the north, marching to join their brothers here, marching to . . . marching to . . .'

He had apparently lost his thread. He turned to give the other knights a bemused look, then his legs gave way and he sank to the muddy ground. While the man's companions tried to get him to his feet, Ninian put his heels to Garnet's sides and hurried away.

*   *   *

He did not think anybody would come chasing after him. Why would they? In that great encampment of fighting men and camp followers, who was going to miss one man? Ninian had been surprised at the total lack of security, but, on reflection, it was another reminder of de Montfort's invincibility. He didn't care if the enemy knew where he was; didn't even seem to be bothered by the details of his future plans being bandied about by the whole encampment.

He knows he's going to win, Ninian thought.

The concept, once lodged in his mind, seemed to become a certainty.

As he rode along, keeping as much as possible within the sparse cover of the springtime woodlands, always moving in the general direction of the south-west, his resolve hardened. He had an important piece of information, and he was going to make quite sure he put it to good use.

Back in the village, he had heard the young fighters he'd been training speak in awe of the Count of Foix. An Occitan lord in the traditional mould, his support of the bonshommes was as much due to indignation at the crusade against them as belief in their faith; that and the sheer love of a good fight. His ferocity in battle was legendary, and, in his stronghold at the foot of the Pyrenees, he clearly felt himself safe from reprisals when he sent out his wild-eyed knights to besiege an enemy castle or murdered a priest or two.

All in all, Ninian reflected, he was the very man who might make good use of the knowledge that Simon de Montfort was poised to besiege Lavaur and was expecting the arrival of a vast column of German knights, fresh from the north and spoiling for a fight, to support him.

In the hill country half a day's ride from Foix, Ninian stopped by a rushing stream to eat the last of his food. Although the day was sunny, the air was cold, for he was already in the lower reaches of the mountains. As he sat munching his way through dry bread and a rind of pungent cheese, he looked idly around and noticed that what he had taken as rocky outcrops were in fact the ruins of dwellings. Still chewing, he got up to investigate.

It had been a little village of perhaps fifteen or twenty

dwellings; simple stone houses, many linked together in rows on either side of an overgrown cobbled track. He wondered who had lived there, and what had caused them to abandon the place. Unlike so many villages and towns in the region, this was not the site of a recent catastrophe. Nobody could have lived there for decades.

But somebody still came to the place; walking on between the ruins, Ninian discovered a tiny chapel, its wooden door hanging off the hinges and most of the roof gone. He went inside, and the scent of fresh greenery hit him. A garland of spring leaves, beautifully woven, had been placed on the floor in front of a statue.

Ninian went closer. The statue was in shadow and, after the bright light outside, it took his eyes a few moments to adjust.

When he saw what the figure was, he gasped aloud. In an instant, he was back in his own past. Back to a terrifying time when he had almost lost his life and then hurried across France to England, helping to escort an object of great antiquity and immense power to somewhere it – she – would be safe.[3]

That object was a statue depicting a heavily pregnant woman dressed in a sweeping robe and wearing a horned headdress like the crescent moon. She was made of dark wood and was known as a Black Madonna.

She looked exactly like the figure at which Ninian's eyes, wide with wonder, were now staring.

It was as if seeing this figure had opened a locked door in Ninian's mind, for now as he stood there in the little chapel, his head swimming and spinning, he was assaulted by memories, dreams and visions. He saw Josse and a certain tree on the fringe of the Hawkenlye Forest. He saw St Edmund's Chapel and the Black Goddess who reigned there, serene and secure in her secret niche down in the crypt. He saw the hut in the forest, which Meggie had taken over from Joanna. He saw Meggie, whose face was anxious and who was calling out to him, her mouth opening and closing soundlessly, so that he knew she was trying to tell him something but could not make out the words.

Perhaps she was telling him he was no longer wanted for

---

[3] See *The Joys of my Life*

murder and it was safe to come home. Or perhaps that was just wishful thinking.

Briefly, heartbreakingly, he saw his mother. Not as he had last seen her; for he had been only a boy when she had left him in Josse's care and gone to embark on her strange life in the forest; no, she was older now, her long dark hair streaked with grey, her face lined but still beautiful.

He shook his head to try to clear it, for he didn't understand. He was seeing images of home – powerful images, joined now by a vision of Little Helewise laughing up at him, flowers in her hair, love and healthy, eager lust in her eyes – but another, more powerful message was pressing down on him.

It was to do with the Black Goddess. Out of nowhere came the memory that she had been destined for the new cathedral at Chartres, but removed to Hawkenlye because she would be safe there. Chartres . . . It was where his mother had died. Where he and Josse also had almost lost their lives.

'What must I do?' he asked the black figure now. 'I want to stay here and fight with the people who have become my friends. I've got information that's going to help those who stand in opposition to the crusaders, and maybe it'll give us a chance . . .'

It won't.

He wondered where the words came from. He looked around, but there was nobody there.

He felt a wave of dizziness. Had the statue spoken? Or was it just his own good sense, telling him, now that he was in this strange, altered state – he was nearly exhausted and half-starving – what he could not bear to face when he was his normal self?

This battle will not be won, went on the voice, *because the forces ranged against the south are too strong. Church and king together can draw on endless resources and are ultimately invincible.*

'But I can't leave!' he protested, almost weeping. 'They took me in, they've cared for me over the long winter, and I've shared their lives all this time!'

They made use of you, said the voice. *You were sent from danger into greater danger, bearing a treasure which they wanted so badly that they did not care how they got it.*

'But—' He stopped. It was true.

Standing there all alone, weak from hunger, his mind reeling so much from the onslaught that he felt on the verge of delirium, a change began to come over him.

He saw again the images that had so stunned him, one after the other in swift succession: Josse, the forest, the chapel above the abbey, Meggie, the hut.

Little Helewise.

Home.

Then, flashing so fast that he was not sure he'd even seen her, Joanna. And a huge building soaring up into the sky that he recognized as Chartres cathedral, contained within a cone of bright, white light that rose high up into the sky . . .

A stab of pain like a knife thrust hit Ninian between the eyes. With a groan, he slumped to the stone floor. The voice and the visions faded, and he sank into unconsciousness.

NINE

At a very early hour soon after dawn, Abbess Caliste and Father Sebastian stood either side of an open grave. The rain had only just stopped, and the air still had its night chill. Mist obscured the land. It was a good time for committing a forbidden act.

The previous evening, six lay brothers had dug a big hole in the sodden ground, wide and deep enough for three bodies. It was not within the perimeter of Hawkenlye's burial ground; given the present ban on funerals, it would have been foolish to create a large, new grave out in the cemetery for any passer-by to spot. Under the abbess's instructions, the pit was behind the huge compost heap where the straw and horse manure mucked out from the abbey's stables went, together with the scraps and remains from the kitchens. The kitchens were contributing little to the compost at present.

Abbess Caliste watched as the cloth-wrapped bodies were lowered into the ground. She was glad that the three men were so closely covered, for she had no wish to look at them again. She told herself repeatedly that there was no proof they were guilty of the terrible crimes which Gervase and Josse apparently were attributing to them. 'Judge not,' she said firmly, muttering the words under her breath. She forced herself to pray for their souls. They had been dead for five or six weeks, according to Josse. They would, she reflected, already have been judged by the ultimate authority awaiting everyone . . .

Father Sebastian had finished. He nodded to the lay brothers, who picked up their shovels and began filling in the grave. With a final glance in Caliste's direction, he turned and disappeared into the mist.

Hurrying back towards the safety of the cloister, glancing furtively over her shoulder, Caliste wondered if this was what it felt like to be a criminal.

Josse had returned to the House in the Forest the previous day, after his visit to Gervase. The conflicting emotions raised by his conversation with the sheriff had gone on raging in his head. If whoever was extracting eye-for-an-eye vengeance on the cruel and lawless – and Sister Estella's mysterious Brown Man so far seemed the only likely suspect – then Josse for one wasn't going to make any great effort to apprehend and stop him. Gervase, of course, could not afford such an attitude, sworn as he was to uphold the law. Murder, and the flogging of a king's agent going about his duty, were very serious crimes, even when perpetrated against those who richly deserved their fate. Such, Josse was well aware, was Gervase's view.

Josse had found it sweet to return to his own hearth and the company of his household, although with Helewise and Meggie absent, home had not provided its usual restorative. He missed them and, judging by his son's dismal expression, Geoffroi did too.

Which made Josse feel decidedly guilty as he saddled up in the morning and set out for the abbey. Especially since Geoffroi had clamoured to go with him and Josse had said he couldn't. It would have made an exciting change from the day's normal round for the boy to ride out with his father, and Josse was well aware that the reason for his ruling against it was entirely selfish: if Geoffroi was at home with Will, Ella,

Gus and Tilly, then he was perfectly safe and Josse didn't have to worry about him.

The three women at the cell by the chapel had a guest: Tiphaine had arrived. She sat with the others to eat the small meal that passed for breakfast, and Meggie noticed straight away that she was distracted.

'You seem troubled, Tiphaine,' she said, pouring out a cupful of the herbal concoction she had just brewed for them all and watching the older woman sip it. 'May we help?'

Tiphaine looked at her for a long moment. Then she said simply, 'No.'

She did not stay. Beckoning to Meggie, she nodded a quick farewell to Helewise and her granddaughter, then got up and left. Meggie followed her out of the cell and away across the clearing towards the forest. The grass was soaking; it had rained hard during the night.

'You've left those two scratching their heads,' Meggie remarked as they went in under the trees.

'Can't be helped,' Tiphaine replied shortly.

Meggie was puzzled, for Tiphaine normally treated Helewise with respect, as if she regarded her still as abbess of Hawkenlye in all but name. Hoping to take the older woman's mind off whatever was troubling her, Meggie said, 'Helewise had a bit of a shock last night.' Tiphaine didn't respond, so she went on: 'Little Helewise told her she's pregnant.'

A smile twitched Tiphaine's lean features. 'How did she take it?'

'She's delighted. She was anxious to begin with, and said lots of things about Little Helewise and Ninian not being married, but then Little Helewise pointed out that they hadn't really had the opportunity, and wasn't Helewise happy at the thought of being a great-grandmother, and Helewise started to laugh and said she certainly wasn't ready for *that*, and then she put her arms round Little Helewise and said she – all of us – would take care of her till Ninian comes home.'

'She's a good woman,' Tiphaine pronounced. 'Heart's in the right place.'

They had reached the tree line. 'Now,' Meggie said, 'what's the matter?'

'Funny we should just have been talking about a pregnancy,' Tiphaine murmured. Then, abruptly: 'I need your help. I want you to make a draught to rid a woman of an unwanted child.'

Meggie sank down on the mossy trunk of a fallen tree. She guessed who the person in question was and, yes, it was not surprising. The young woman who had spoken to Helewise yesterday had not given up. Somehow, she had managed to seek out one of the few people in the region who would not throw up their hands in horror at her request.

'She came here,' Meggie said after a moment. 'She – er, she had the misfortune to find Helewise alone, and when she said what she wanted, Helewise – well, she reacted as you'd expect.' Meggie was reluctant to criticize; she knew that Helewise had very good reasons for her shocked response, and she also knew that Helewise now regretted that she had been so hasty.

Tiphaine, it appeared, was similarly reluctant. 'Understandable,' she commented. She paused, then added, 'Shame she didn't wait to find out more.'

Coming from Tiphaine, that mild criticism struck like a snake.

'Tell me what you know,' Meggie said.

Tiphaine sat down beside her. For a few moments she sat gazing out through the trees into the sunshine beyond. Then, speaking softly and swiftly, she said, 'Her name's Melania. She lives in a lonely house on the edge of the forest, and in January she and her elderly parents had an unexpected visit from three ruffians. They broke in, took whatever there was to take and two of them raped Melania while her parents looked on. Drove her poor mother out of her mind, seeing her daughter suffer like that and unable to help her. The old father had a bad heart, and the shock and the horror killed him.' She glanced at Meggie. 'Soon as he felt his heart start to pain him, he'd have known he ought to take his medicine, but it looks as if the ruffians wouldn't allow it.'

'Would the medicine have saved him?' Meggie asked.

'It would have got him over that attack,' Tiphaine answered. 'He wasn't going to get well again, but if he'd gone on taking the mixture when he felt his heart stutter, he had a few years left in him. It was foxglove and lily of the valley, mainly, with some borage and birch to help with his rheumatism,' she added, although Meggie hadn't asked.

'You used to prepare it for him?'

'I did.' Tiphaine looked down at her hands. 'They were good people, Melania's parents. Lived there on the edge of the trees, minding their own business, not harming a soul. Unlike others, they accepted the forest people's right to live their own lives and often did them small kindnesses in the years since times became really tough.' She sighed. 'Most of the forest folk have gone,' she said softly. 'They've left the area in search of wilder, more remote places where they'll find some peace.'

Meggie barely heard. She was thinking about a sick old man, begging for the medicine that would help his labouring heart and ease the agonizing pain. Those who refused to give it to him were as guilty of killing him as if they'd slit his throat.

'Stands to reason Melania doesn't want a rapist's child growing inside her,' Tiphaine said bluntly. 'And that's the fact of it, whatever anyone might say about it not being the fault of the unborn child and it having a right to live.'

Slowly, Meggie nodded. All her healer's instincts were to save life, and she had encountered far more pregnant women desperate to save a fragile pregnancy than demanding to have an unwanted one terminated. But what must it have been like for this poor girl, this Melania, to have discovered, as the weeks went by, the outcome of that night of careless brutality? And did Meggie – did anyone – have the right to impose on her the further punishment of bearing, suckling and raising the child of the man who had raped her?

After what felt like a long time, she turned and looked at Tiphaine. 'You asked for my help in making the abortifacient,' she said. 'Why can't you do it yourself?'

'I'm lacking some of the ingredients,' Tiphaine answered gruffly. 'I still use the stores in my old shed down at the abbey – Abbess Caliste knows I do, and she doesn't object, since most of them are my work anyway – but what I need for Melania isn't kept in a place like Hawkenlye Abbey.'

No, Meggie reflected, it wouldn't be.

Abruptly, she made up her mind. 'I've got what you need.

I'll go out to the hut and prepare the potion. You can pick it up there this evening.'

There was a silence. Then Tiphaine said, 'Thank you.'

Meggie studied her. She had imagined that this – Melania's dreadful dilemma – had been what was preoccupying Tiphaine; it was surely enough to make any friend of the poor young woman preoccupied. Yet, as Tiphaine got up and turned to go, she appeared, if anything, even more careworn than before. It was as if, Meggie realized with a flash of understanding, Tiphaine was bearing the weight of a deep and abiding anxiety and knew she could not put it down . . .

There was no point in hurrying after her and pressing her to share her burden. Meggie knew, from long experience, that Tiphaine was her own woman. She only ever shared things when she was good and ready and if there was no other way. Meggie would just have to wait and see.

She stood looking down into the clearing. Helewise and her granddaughter had emerged from the cell and were walking across to the chapel, where the first of the day's pilgrims had gathered in a small, huddled group. It seemed a good time to slip away. Without further thought, Meggie headed off into the forest in the direction of her mother's hut.

Her visitor had been back. This time his attempt to copy her knot in the rope that fastened the door was better; he must have studied hers carefully, and he had almost got it right.

She opened the door and went in. The temperature inside the little room was higher than that outside. She crouched down by the hearth – neatly swept, with kindling and small logs laid ready beside it – and put her hand on the ground. It was warm.

She climbed up the ladder to inspect the sleeping platform. Her own bedding was rolled up and stored at one end, and did not appear to have been disturbed. However, it appeared that a long shape had recently lain there, leaving an impression on the straw-filled mattress. Something caught her eye: at the end where the head would have been – where her own head had rested the night before last – there was a small, shining object.

She reached out and picked it up.

It was a knife, fashioned in the form of a miniature sword. The blade was about the length of her hand, and it was very sharp. The hilt was in the shape of a graceful curve, its ends pointing downwards. Set in the top of the hilt was a tiny, deep-red stone that she guessed was a garnet. The warrior's stone; it was a talisman against injury and death, and was believed to bring victory.

Her unknown visitor appeared to have left her a present, perhaps in thanks for her unwitting hospitality. Thoughtfully, she reached inside the purse she carried at her waist and took out a small coin, putting it exactly where the knife had lain.

Tradition demanded that the gift of a knife must be paid for, otherwise it would cut the friendship.

Although Meggie did not know why, she had the strong sense that whoever had been sharing her hut with her was going to be a friend.

It was with some effort that she dragged herself out of the strange paths of her thoughts and back into the present. She set kindling in the hearth, lighting it with her flint, and, as the flames took hold, built up the fire with the smallest pieces of wood. Soon she had a good blaze going. She went outside to fill her pot with water from the stream and suspended it over the fire. While the water came to the boil, she searched her shelves for the ingredients she wanted.

Then she settled down cross-legged on the floor and, with some reluctance, set about making the potion that Tiphaine had asked for.

Josse had told himself that his purpose in going to the abbey was to find out if there had been developments in the hunt for the three dead men's killer. Assuming him to be the same man who had dealt out retribution to Benedict de Vitré's man Matthew, then he must still be in the vicinity, and maybe someone at Hawkenlye had seen him. If it was indeed Sister Estella's Brown Man who was responsible, perhaps he had come seeking absolution for the flogging he had meted out . . .

However, even as he rode in through the gates, Josse was staring up towards the forest, straining his eyes to see if he could make out any of the three women living in the cell. Were they all right? Had they enough to eat, and were they keeping warm enough at night? Promising himself that he would go and ask them later, he turned his mind to the coming interview with the abbess.

He tapped on the door and went into her room to find Gervase already there. Not pausing for a greeting, Gervase said, 'He's struck again.'

Josse glanced briefly at Abbess Caliste, whose face was pale and drawn. Turning back to Gervase, he said, 'What's happened?'

Gervase passed a hand over his face; before he had uttered another word, Josse knew that what he had to say was going to be bad. 'It's a nasty story, Josse,' Gervase began. 'There's been a family group living down on the wetlands along the river to the east of Tonbridge. There's an old, tumbledown hovel there.'

'I know of it,' Josse replied. He'd had reason to go there, years ago, and it had been in a poor state even then. He was amazed it was still standing.

'I knew the people were there,' Gervase went on, 'and they've been given a bit of help, only nobody's got much to spare. There's sickness in their family.'

'Could they not have been taken to the canons at Tonbridge?' Josse had good memories of Canon Mark.

'No they couldn't,' Gervase said shortly. 'Two of them have a sweating fever, one's already died of it and the remaining three are complaining of headaches and cramps. If they're allowed any nearer to the town, this sickness will run through the whole population.'

'With little to eat, and at the end of a long, hard winter, people succumb all too easily to disease,' Abbess Caliste said. Josse looked at her. 'We should have said the same had Hawkenlye been the nearest point of succour, Sir Josse,' she added gently. 'We would have taken food and medicaments out to them, but we cannot risk the lives of the many for the sake of the few.'

Josse grunted an acknowledgement. 'Go on,' he said to Gervase.

Gervase sighed. 'Some of the townspeople have been

rabble-rousing, one man in particular. I'm ashamed to say he's been employed on occasion by one of my deputies when we've needed men for search parties and guard duties, since he happens to be strong, well built and lacking the imagination to feel fear. He's also a fine shot with a crossbow.'

'I can see that he'd have his uses,' Josse remarked.

'Quite. Anyway, this man – he's called Rufus because of his red hair – decided to take matters into his own hands. He was in the tavern last night, making threats against the family living in the valley. He got a gang together – because he's worked for us, people tend to think he speaks with authority – and, late in the night, he led them out of the town, across the wetlands and along to the hovel. They surrounded it, and Rufus yelled out that the family had to get out and leave the area. "We don't want you filthy rats spreading your foul sickness among decent folks," is apparently what he said. Then he ordered his gang to pile dead wood around the hovel and set light to it. The five people inside tried to flee, running off in all directions, the stronger ones helping and supporting the sick, and Rufus took up his crossbow and ordered them to stop. Then, making sure to keep his distance, he made them line up and marched them away down the river. He and his men escorted them as far as the crossing out to the east of Tonbridge, then they forced them to go over to the north bank. Rufus told them that if they showed their faces again, they'd regret it.'

'He had no authority for this action?' Josse asked.

'Of course not,' Gervase said scornfully.

There had to be more. 'The people came back, didn't they?'

'No, Josse.' Gervase sighed. 'The river was high last night after the rain. The crossing was impassable.'

'So—?'

'The family were caught between the water and Rufus's crossbow. They tried to get across, and one of them slipped on the stones at the edge of the water and fell in. She was little more than a child. One of the adults tried to grab her, but he fell in too. I'm not sure of the exact sequence of events, but they all drowned. Rufus watched as they were swept away.'

'Nobody tried to save them?'

'Apparently not. Rufus commanded his men not to.'

'But that's—'

'I *know* what it is, Josse,' Gervase said tightly. 'One of the gang came to me early this morning, overcome with remorse, or so he says, and I set out with a couple of my deputies straight away to bring Rufus in. He lives at the southern end of the town, in a row that runs along close by the river. Someone beat me to it; we found him lying face down in the water.'

'And I'm sure you're not going to tell me his death was an accident,' Josse said softly.

'No. There was nothing accidental about the knife wound to his heart.'

'Like the other three?'

'Exactly like. Our man, it seems,' Gervase added, 'prefers the quick, clean kill. Rufus was put in the river, I presume, to ram home the message that he'd been killed in retribution for those whose lives he failed to save.'

'*Our man*,' Josse repeated. 'The motive of vengeance appears to be consistent, and so—'

But Gervase held up a hand. 'There's more, Josse.' He paused, as if reluctant to say what he must. 'I know what you feel about this man, and I admit that, in my heart, I have some sympathy with you. But we cannot allow him to continue, for a system under which a man with a grudge – even a genuine one – gets away with taking the law into his own hands is open to the worst possible abuse.'

'This man is acting to avenge deeds that amount to more than *grudges*!' Josse cried angrily. 'He—'

'He must not continue,' Gervase repeated, more forcefully this time. Then, before Josse could protest again, he said, his tone carefully neutral, 'He was unlucky, this time. Someone spotted him as he fled the scene of Rufus's execution. Unfortunately, this person elected not to come straight to me with the information; they went instead to Lord Benedict de Vitré.'

'*Him*!' Josse exclaimed. 'But why? Tonbridge isn't within his jurisdiction, surely?'

'Don't be naive, Josse. Lord Benedict has the favour of the king because, by fair means or foul, he's extremely successful at extracting money for him. Everywhere and anywhere is within Lord Benedict's jurisdiction, if he wants it to be.'

Understanding dawned. 'Lord Benedict, I presume, uses

some of this money to pay for information,' Josse said. 'A fact of which most of the hard-up people of Tonbridge are well aware.'

'I cannot speak for them all,' Gervase murmured, 'but the woman who saw Rufus's killer slip away into the mist knew exactly where to go. Lord Benedict has already sent out a search party,' he went on, 'and, in all likelihood, they'll hunt the killer down, succeeding where I have failed because Lord Benedict has far more men at his disposal, and whereas my men go about on their own two feet, armed, in general, only with clubs and stout sticks, he has the means to provide his supporters with good horses and fine weapons. When his search party find their quarry,' he concluded, 'no doubt they'll extract a little vengeance of their own to pay him back for what he did to their friend Matthew.'

Josse opened his mouth but found he had nothing to say. It was all *wrong*. The man even now being hunted had committed violent crimes – including the ultimate one of murder – but for a very good reason. The prospect of his capture by Lord Benedict's men was utterly repellent, and Josse knew that if it were in his own power to seek out the man and warn him, he would do so. *But how can I*, he thought desperately, *when I do not know who or where he is?*

He looked at Gervase, then at the abbess. 'What can we do?' he asked in a whisper.

Slowly, Abbess Caliste shook her head.

His anger and frustration evident in the single word, Gervase said, '*Nothing.*'

TEN

J osse made his way up to the clearing by St Edmund's Chapel. His heart was sore, and he longed more than anything to share his burden with Helewise.

As he crossed the clearing, he saw her emerge from the chapel. She was facing away from him, and when he called out to her, she spun round. In that first instant, her expression was one of simple delight at seeing him. He hurried across to her, and, even as he ran, it seemed to him that she deliberately straightened her face. Whatever was amiss between them, it certainly hadn't been put right by a couple of days' absence from each other . . .

'Is Meggie here?' he asked coolly, coming to a halt a couple of paces away from her. 'I need to speak to you both.'

'No,' Helewise replied. 'She's gone out to the hut to fetch some supplies that Tiphaine needs. My granddaughter,' she added with a soft smile, 'is down at the abbey, helping out in the infirmary.'

'Tiphaine's here?'

'She was. She's gone again now.'

Josse realized it was some time since he had seen the former herbalist of Hawkenlye Abbey. 'Is she all right?'

Helewise shrugged. 'She looks tired and strained, but who doesn't?' Then in a gentler tone, she added, 'Will you come inside the cell and take a warm drink? You said you need to speak to Meggie and me, but will I do?'

It's you I most want to talk to, he thought. *If only you knew.* 'Aye,' he said shortly.

She led the way inside the small cell. The women had made it very comfortable, and, with a fire glowing gently in the hearth, it was warm and cosy. As if noticing his reaction, Helewise said, 'The one big advantage of living in a tiny stone-walled space is that it's very easy to heat, which is just as well since we're all too busy to spend much time foraging for firewood.'

His heart sank. If they were busy, it meant that pilgrims were finding their way to the clearing. 'You have many visitors, then?'

She gave him a smile, apparently reading his mind. 'Yes, Josse, I'm afraid we do.'

His private little hope that, finding nobody came to seek her out, she would give up this whole venture and come home, quietly faded and died.

She poured out two mugs of a spicy concoction sweetened with honey and handed one to him. She sat down on what he supposed was her own cot, and he sat on the one beside it. He sipped his drink. It was delicious, and he said as much.

'It is rather good, isn't it?' she agreed. 'I must remember to tell my granddaughter.'

'Little Helewise made it?'

'Indeed she did. We are keeping her busy, and she's a very willing pupil. Already, she looks much happier and healthier than when she joined us. She's—' But whatever she had been about to say, she stopped. 'Now, Josse, what did you want to discuss?'

He realized just how long it had been since they had sat down together like this to chew over some puzzle, and how very much he had missed it. There was a lot to tell her: he ordered his thoughts and began.

'So the fact that these acts of revenge are continuing leads you to believe that Sister Estella's Brown Man – if, indeed, it is he who is perpetrating the deeds – is still in the vicinity, and perhaps still looking for a priest to absolve him?' she said when he had finished.

'Aye, that's about it,' he agreed.

'You are sure that he is responsible?' she asked. 'It seems a large conclusion to draw from scanty evidence.'

'I *know*,' he said in frustration. 'But the facts are these: one, the long list of brutal crimes that Gervase knew of came to a halt when the three dead men at Hawkenlye were killed. Two, at around the same time, a stranger told Sister Estella that he needed to talk to a priest because he was about to do something bad. Three, similar acts of vengeance are being carried out again, specifically, the flogging of Lord Benedict's man Matthew and the killing of Gervase's Rufus. In each case, the punishment echoes the crime.'

She was nodding thoughtfully. 'Yes, I do see,' she said. 'And no doubt you are going to tell me that neither Gervase nor you have any other suspects in mind.'

'No, we haven't,' he grunted. 'There's more,' he added, before she could speak. And he told her how the man who killed Rufus had been spotted, and that Lord Benedict's men, their blood up and violence on their minds, were even now out hunting him.

Silence fell when he stopped speaking. After a moment, she reached out and took his hand. 'And you, dear Josse, are suffering deeply because in your heart you do not believe this man is guilty of any crime.'

'Aye, and apparently it's dangerous to say so,' he agreed bitterly. 'Gervase tells me such talk is treason.'

'He's right,' she said quietly. 'I don't know about the dead men down at the abbey, but the other two are officers of the law, even though they are cruel and heartless ones. Anyone who harms them is automatically guilty.'

'It shouldn't be like that!' Josse cried.

'I know, but it is.' She let go of his hand. After a moment, she said, 'What shall we do?'

He appreciated the *we*. 'I've been endlessly asking myself the same thing, and all I can think of is that we try to find him ourselves and warn him,' he said.

She looked taken aback. 'But – you're proposing we should set out for Tonbridge and try to pick up his trail? Wouldn't Lord Benedict's men notice us and realize what we were doing?'

Josse smiled. 'If it's really the Brown Man, then he won't be anywhere near Tonbridge. He's already been to the abbey, or at least to the vale, where he encountered Sister Estella. Unless he's blind and stupid – and I don't believe he's either – he'll have noticed that Hawkenlye Abbey stands on the edge of a very large forest.'

In the hut in the forest, Meggie sat cross-legged by the hearth wondering if she had done the right thing. She had made the potion – she had no doubt that it would work – and Tiphaine had collected it late in the afternoon. Would that poor young woman already have taken it? Meggie wondered. If so, she was in for a rough night. Tiphaine had undertaken to look after her, and Meggie could think of nobody better. Tiphaine was kind, in her own brusque way, and she would make quite sure that the girl – Melania – would understand what was happening to her. Most importantly, Tiphaine would have no doubts that it was up to Melania to make her hard decision, and that nobody had the right to make her feel guilty about it.

The guilt, Meggie thought, *is for me.*

With a sigh, she got to her feet, stretching. The daylight was beginning to fade, and she knew she should get back to the cell. But she wanted more than anything to stay where she was, in the snug safety of her mother's hut. She decided to return to the cell, eat supper with Helewise and her granddaughter and then, once they were asleep, do as she'd done before and slip out again.

The lift to the heart that the decision brought quite surprised her. Smiling, she fetched firewood and laid it ready, then climbed up to the sleeping platform to plump up the pillows and spread out the covers, making sure the shiny coin was visible.

I will be back soon, she said silently as she fastened the door. Then, a spring in her step, she set off for the clearing.

'You missed a visit from your father,' Helewise said to Meggie as they ate the evening meal. 'He was at the abbey and called in to see us.'

Meggie looked up, glancing from Helewise to her granddaughter. 'Did you—?'

'No, he doesn't know yet,' Little Helewise said. She was looking very serene, Meggie thought, and quietly joyful, as if she were communing silently with the new little life inside her. 'I was down at the abbey when he came, and Grandmother felt it was up to me to tell him, not her.' She gave Helewise a sweet smile. 'I think,' she added, 'I'm looking forward to it.'

Meggie wondered if she would be as calm at the prospect of breaking the news to her mother. Out of nowhere she had an image of Ninian's face; it tore at her heart to think of other people knowing he was going to be a father before he did. *Ninian, come home!* Fervently, she sent out the unspoken plea, so familiar now. 'Did Father bring any news?' she asked, to take her mind off worrying about her brother.

'Well, in fact he did,' Helewise said. She told both young women what Josse had told her, and, when she had finished, Meggie had the distinct sense that the solution to a mystery had just presented itself.

She left the hut as soft-footed as the last time and was soon outside and past the lay brothers' shelter, heading out of the clearing and in under the trees. It was a clear night, and she wrapped her shawl round her against the chill.

When she reached the glade where the hut stood, she

stopped. She knew he was there; she could see his horse, in a simple rope head collar and tethered to one of the willows by the stream. The horse was looking at her out of friendly, interested dark eyes. It was a gelding, chestnut in colour, with a long flaxen mane and tail. It shifted a little out of the shadows, and Meggie could see it stood some fifteen or sixteen hands and was stockily built. She sent it a reassuring message, and it gave a very soft whicker.

Meggie stepped closer to the hut. The rope that fastened the latch was undone and hung on a nail. She stopped, closed her eyes and, using all the skill she possessed, sent out feelers to assess what sort of a person was inside the hut.

She could have sworn he was not evil and posed no threat. She sent out a message to her mother and had the clear sense that Joanna was smiling. *Go inside*, her mother said.

Meggie opened the door.

He was sitting facing her, cross-legged beside the cheery fire, exactly where she had sat a few hours earlier.

She saw the glitter of very dark-brown eyes, staring at her as intently as she was staring at him. His skin was smooth and dark – the colour of peaty water with the sun shining on it – and he was lightly bearded. His facial hair was black, like that on his head, which was long, glossy and hung down to his chest. There was a heavy gold ring in his left ear.

Glancing down at the rest of him, she saw that he was bare-chested. A long cloth in some dark colour was wound round his waist, spread across his crossed legs and covering him as far as the ankles. At his side lay a sword in a leather scabbard. His feet, she noticed, were long and graceful. His hands had the same elegant shape, but they were heavily calloused as if from some sort of hard work. He was, she guessed, some seven or eight years older than her.

He smiled, his teeth white and even. 'I have been expecting you,' he said. 'I knew you would come.'

She went to sit down opposite him. 'Who are you?'

'I'm called Jehan Leferronier.'

'You're – a Frenchman?' Did they come as dark as him, she wondered.

'A Breton.' The smile widened. 'I have other ancestry. My grandmother was a woman of Ethiopia.'

'I see.' She didn't see at all. She wondered why she should feel so happy. So relaxed, talking to a stranger in her own hut. He had just told her his name and was smiling at her as if delighted to see her, but was that any reason to lower her guard like this?

Apparently, it was . . .

'My name's Meggie,' she said. 'My father's Sir Josse d'Acquin, and my mother – well, she isn't here any more, but this used to be her hut.'

He made her a low bow. 'I am sorry that I have been staying in it without your permission.'

'That's all right. Thank you for the present.' She touched the slim leather sheath that she had made to keep the knife in, hanging from her belt.

His dark eyes widened. 'You carry it always with you!'

She'd only just acquired it, so *always* was an exaggeration, but she could see what he meant. 'Yes. It's lovely.'

He looked gratified. 'I am happy that it pleases you. Thank *you* for the coin.'

He had found it, then. 'You have to make a token payment when someone gives you a blade, because—'

He put up a hand. 'I understand, Meggie,' he said.

She took her knife out of its sheath and looked at it. 'That's a garnet, isn't it?' She pointed to the red stone.

'*Oui*. It is traditional to put such a stone in a full-sized sword.'

'For protection. Yes, I know.' She paused. 'I've heard it said that, as a gift, a garnet grants affection and loyalty.'

'Yes, I know.' He echoed her words.

Some strong emotion seemed to tremble in the air between them. She could almost see it. With an effort, she recalled why she was there. 'You're – did you pay a visit to the big abbey on the edge of the forest?' she asked. 'Five or six weeks ago?'

Gravely, he nodded. 'I did. I was in search of a priest, but I learned that the priests are forbidden to tend to their flock because his Holiness the Pope has placed England under an interdict.'

'You told one of the nuns that you needed forgiveness for an action you were about to take.' Now his expression became guarded. She pressed on. 'I – we, that is, my father, his close friends and I – know what you did, and also we know of the other things you've done more recently.'

He shook his head, trying to protest, but Meggie did not want to listen to lies.

'You ought to know that someone saw you and there's a manhunt on your trail,' she said, speaking hurriedly, 'but, as far as we're concerned, you've done nothing wrong and we don't think you should be arrested and tried, because they'll undoubtedly find you guilty and hang you. The law isn't very reasonable,' she added.

'Not very reasonable,' he repeated. She could not read his expression. There was quite a long pause. 'You have come to help me?' he asked, and she thought he was suppressing a smile.

'Yes, if you need my help.'

Slowly, he stretched out one long hand and, without even thinking about it, she put up her own hand. Above the hearth, their fingers met and clasped. His touch was extraordinary; she felt as if something had shaken her, deep inside.

'You have already given it, by permitting me to stay in this hut,' he pointed out.

'Until recently I did not know you were here.' How strange it was, she reflected, to think that this man, this stranger with power in his touch and mystery in his eyes, should have been living here in the hut – a place she'd been longing to get to for months – while she was penned up within the safe walls of the House in the Woods. On impulse she said, 'I think my mother knew. She doesn't mind.'

He accepted that without comment.

'You must go,' she urged, although to see him ride away was the last thing she wanted. 'It's not safe for you here.'

He nodded. 'Perhaps not.' He looked rueful. 'I have not completed the task for which I came here.' Were there more revenge killings he was planning? Meggie wondered. 'Now, I think I shall not be able to, because—' He stopped.

Because what? Because the forces of law and order were hunting for him? 'You should go back across the narrow seas,' she said. 'I doubt if they'll follow you.'

Memories were stirring. She'd had a very similar conversation last autumn with Ninian. He'd had to leave England for France, for much the same reason. He hadn't come back, and she missed him all the time.

Jehan Leferronier was watching her as if he was trying to read her thoughts. 'You are sad,' he observed.

'Yes.' She wasn't ready to speak to him about Ninian. 'Where do you come from?' she asked. 'You said you're a Breton?'

'*Oui.* My birthplace was a village in the middle of Brittany. Now, I no longer live in my own land. Along with many other men, I travel to find work. There is a big new cathedral, and the people of the town, wishing perhaps to be remembered for posterity, donate funds so that beautiful things may be included in its fabric.'

A shudder went down her spine. 'Chartres,' she whispered.

'Chartres, *oui.*' He did not ask how she knew. The enigmatic smile was back on his face. 'My horse and I, we set out from home, and for many months I worked in the cathedral. I—'

'I saw your horse,' she interrupted. 'He's very friendly. He didn't object when I appeared out of the forest.'

'Perhaps he knows this is your place,' Jehan suggested. 'But, yes, he is very friendly. His name is Auban.'

'He also looks very strong.'

'Strong, *oui.* He is that blessed creature among horses: one that has a comfortable, steady gait and yet does not protest when his master hitches him to a cart and asks him to haul a heavy load. He is quite capable of carrying two riders, over very many miles,' he added.

Meggie hardly heard, for her mind was reeling. Chartres. He had come from Chartres, and that, presumably, was where he would be returning. Chartres, where her mother had disappeared. Designated resting place for the Black Goddess who now lived in St Edmund's Chapel, brought to England by Ninian. Chartres, Joanna, the Black Goddess, Ninian . . .

I asked my mother for her help in bringing Ninian home, she thought. *I begged her to tell me what she wanted me to do.*

Had she just received the answer?

Suddenly, she realized what he had just said: his horse could carry two. Her fingers were still entwined with his, and now she gripped his hand hard. 'How did you know I'd need to get to Chartres?' she demanded. *How,* she could have added, *when I didn't know myself till this moment?*

He shrugged. 'I do not fully understand,' he admitted. 'I knew of no connection when first I came here to the hut, but since then, during the long, dark nights it seems I have heard a voice, or perhaps she spoke inside my dreams.' He shook his head. 'I would have left weeks ago, but it felt as if someone was telling me, urging me, to wait.' He looked into her eyes. 'For you, I think.'

Her thoughts were flying through her mind, one after the other, so fast that she barely had time to acknowledge each one before the next succeeded it. One outstripped all the others: could she go with him? Was it folly, to set out with a stranger to a foreign land where she would be friendless, helpless?

Not friendless, for he will be with you, a voice seemed to intone inside her head. *Not helpless, for I will be there and so will your brother.*

She knew she had already made up her mind. With a stab of pain in her heart as she thought of what her father's reaction would be, she stood up. 'Wait here for me,' she said. 'I must collect some things that I'll need. I won't be long.'

He nodded. 'I will not leave without you.'

As she set off at a run through the trees, in the direction of the cell, she wondered if there were some way she could leave word to tell Josse what she was doing, where she was going and why. The first two would require few words; regarding the third, she knew there was no way she could tell him, for she didn't know herself.

ELEVEN

Ninian came back to himself to find he was lying in a pile of straw and someone was trying to force water between his lips. At first he pushed the hand away, but then, realizing how thirsty he was, he grasped it by the wrist and held the flask up to his mouth.

'Gently,' said a voice close by as he drank greedily, 'too much all at once will soon reappear.'

He looked up. A man clad in the rough garments of a peasant was crouched over him. They appeared to be in a barn, or outhouse – no, it was a makeshift lean-to, with stone walls and some sort of hanging cloth serving as a door – and, judging by the light, it was evening. Was the man friend or foe? He seemed eager to help, but it was quite possible he had taken Ninian for a crusader, in which case it wouldn't be wise to reveal where his sympathies truly lay.

He struggled to sit up, and waited until the dizziness passed. 'How did I get here?'

'I found you in the chapel.' The man leaned closer. 'It was not safe to leave you there, and so now you are here at my little vineyard, safely hidden, and—'

'*Where's my horse?*'

'He, too, is safely hidden.' The man smiled. 'You did not think I would leave him for others to find and ask about? Besides, I could not have carried you all this way.'

Ninian tried to work it out. From whom would he not have been safe? He studied the man's face, trying to find a clue. He *looked* friendly enough, his tanned, bearded face creased in lines of concern as he tended his patient.

The man, apparently appreciating Ninian's dilemma, leaned closer. 'I know who you are,' he said, so quietly that Ninian barely heard. '*Friends*—' he laid heavy emphasis on the word – 'told me that you were in the area. I have been watching for you. I am Roger of Pépoulie,' he added. Then, in the merest whisper, 'Alazaïs de Saint Gilles is my aunt by marriage.'

'You're one of the bonshommes?' Ninian asked.

'*Shhhh!*' Roger looked anxiously around. Then, with a wry smile: 'I have allegiance to no faith, but I recognize that the bonshommes are exactly what the name implies. I do not approve of their slaughter, especially by an agency as corrupt as the Church of Rome.'

Neither do I, Ninian thought. He took another gulp of water, then said, 'I have to find the Count of Foix. I have some very important information for him, concerning—' He stopped. He only had Roger of Pépoulie's word that he was no friend of the crusaders. The information Ninian had was surely best told first to the count.

Roger of Pépoulie was nodding his approval. 'Quite right to keep it to yourself,' he muttered. 'And, before you ask, I can help you find the count. He will be pleased to meet you, I imagine.' He put the flask of water down beside the sweet-smelling straw on which Ninian was lying. 'For now, sleep, recover your strength, drink water, eat bread and cheese.' He indicated a platter covered with a cloth. 'Tomorrow, we shall seek out the Count of Foix.'

Ninian was deeply asleep when some small sound disturbed him. Shocked awake, his heart thundering in his chest with alarm, he reached out for his knife. The sound came again; a soft fumbling against the sheet of heavy fabric that protected the lean-to from the elements. His hand closed over the handle of his knife, gripping it tight. When this nosy intruder finally came inside, Ninian would be ready . . .

A hand slid under the fabric. It was holding the handle of a heavy earthenware jug. It vanished, to return almost immediately bearing two stubby mugs. Then a bearded face appeared.

'I hoped you'd be awake!' Roger of Pépoulie said. 'I've just broached a barrel of my own rosé, and it's rather good. I wondered if you'd like to share it with me?'

In the morning, Ninian disposed of his headache with a combination of breakfast, several mugs of water and an invigorating wash in the stream that burbled along behind Roger's house. Garnet stood saddled and bridled, and beside him was a small, stocky pony, whose bridle was old and worn and over whose broad back was spread a piece of sacking. Roger of Pépoulie might be related to one of the wealthiest and most powerful families in the Languedoc, but his disguise as a poor grape-farmer was very convincing.

Bearing in mind they were about to go before a count, Ninian brushed down his tunic as best he could, buffed up a shine on his boots, and was in the process of trying to smooth his tangled hair when Roger, observing him, burst out laughing.

'What's so funny?' Ninian demanded.

Roger shook his head, still chuckling. 'Wait and see.'

*   *   *

The Count of Foix's castle was on the knees of the mountains, and the ride up to it took the form of a long climb that varied only in the intensity of the incline. By mid-morning Ninian and Roger had left the wine-growing regions far below. Ninian thought he saw an eagle soaring in wide circles high above. They must, he realized, be roughly on a level with Alazaïs's village.

The castle was well-concealed behind a huge rocky outcrop, and Ninian did not see it until they were almost upon it. It was more of a fortress than a castle, ringed by high walls from which sentinels looked down. Roger must have been recognized as a friend, for as they approached the formidable gates, they were opened from within. Roger, riding ahead, led them into a narrow courtyard bustling with men, women, children, horses, dogs and chickens. Ninian stayed on Garnet's back while Roger dismounted and went to speak to the huge man who was marching across the yard towards him.

Was this the count? Ninian wondered, staring in wonder at the giant's enormous red beard. There was no time to ask, for Roger turned and said, 'Come with us; leave your horse with him.' He indicated a skinny youth who had materialized from the shadows.

They followed the giant in through an arched opening – the big man had to duck – and then up a steep flight of stone steps, emerging on to a platform set high up on the fortress walls. Ninian had a quick glimpse of a huge patchwork of land, spreading out impossibly far below, and then Roger grabbed his arm, spun him round and hissed, 'Bow to the count.'

He had not known what to expect but, perhaps affected by the possibility that all these mountain men were like the giant who had ushered them into the count's presence, Ninian was surprised to see that he was a small, wiry man, on the face of it hardly meriting the reputation for audacity, savagery and ruthlessness that he had won. Then he looked right into the count's small, dark eyes, and he realized his mistake.

'I'm told you have information for me,' he said, the eyes holding Ninian's. His voice was harsh, like the caw of a raven.

Roger dug his elbow into Ninian's ribs, and the spell was broken. 'Yes,' he said. 'I went to de Montfort's winter camp, pretending to be newly arrived from the north and eager to join the crusade. He is planning to attack Lavaur, and he is expecting the imminent arrival of a very large column of German knights to support the siege.'

The small black eyes seemed to bore into him. 'Lavaur,' the count mused. He glanced at the bearded giant, then at Roger, beckoning both men closer. There was a muttered conversation, and the bearded man crouched down – Ninian could almost hear him creak – and drew a diagram in the dust. The count nodded. 'Yes,' he said, 'an ambush *there*—' he pointed at a spot on the diagram with the toe of his boot – 'at Montgey, where we could utilize the contours of the land to conceal us.' He turned to the giant, his face twisted with cruel lust. 'A bloodbath, yes?'

The giant grinned, revealing huge teeth full of gaps. 'Yes,' he agreed.

'The German column will be bleeding into the dust before the besiegers at Lavaur even know they're coming,' the count said with relish. 'By the time they come to help, nobody will be left alive.' Spinning round as fast as a striking snake, he fixed his eyes on Ninian again. 'So, what do you want?' he demanded.

'What do I—?'

'He's asking what you expect to be paid for this information,' Roger hissed.

'What do I say?' Ninian hissed back.

Roger grinned. 'I'd advise against excessive greed, but, other than that, it's up to you.'

Ninian thought swiftly. There was nothing he could think of for himself, but what about his village friends? Some of the young men he had been training were lacking swords; this might be the perfect opportunity to put that right.

He said, 'In the village where I've been living we are short of weapons. If you could spare any swords, or even knives, that would help them greatly.'

The count laughed, a sound like metal scraping on stone. 'Weapons we have,' he replied. 'Take what you can carry.'

Then, without even a wave of his hand in dismissal, the count turned his back and, bending close to the giant, a fist punching the air for emphasis, began to issue an intent and inaudible stream of orders. Roger jerked his head towards the steps, and they backed unobtrusively away.

Roger offered to ride with Ninian as he set off for Utta's village; in the euphoria of meeting the Count of Foix, and glowing with the success of his mission, Ninian had almost forgotten that he had offered to seek her out and suggest she remove herself to the relative safety of the village high in the mountains. Roger was carrying his share of the count's reward; the sound of clanking metal accompanied them as they rode along.

For some time it was the only sound, other than the soft thud of the horses' hooves on the turf. Roger, it seemed, had something on his mind. Ninian waited, and presently it emerged.

'You have proved a good friend to the bonshommes,' he observed. 'You train their young men in the art of fighting, and now you have provided very valuable information that will help their cause.'

Ninian, taken aback, agreed. 'They, also, have been good friends to me,' he replied, 'and have housed and fed me ever since my arrival.'

'Bearing a treasure they have been longing for, if I hear right,' Roger murmured.

Ninian was not sure whether or not to confirm it; was the presence of the precious manuscript meant to be a secret? 'I had need of a place to hide,' he said instead, 'and I—'

'Yes, I'm aware of your story,' Roger said calmly. He turned to look at Ninian, studying him intently. 'I think, my young friend, you must ask yourself if, having given so freely of yourself to these people whose battle is not yours, you intend to stay with them for ever.'

'I can't go home!' Ninian protested. 'I'm wanted for murder!'

'Do you not have loyal family and friends who will have fought to clear your name?' Roger demanded.

Ninian thought piercingly of Josse, and his heart gave a painful lurch.

'Yes, I thought so,' Roger went on softly. 'Will they not now be desperate to hear news of you, praying that you might be preparing to return?'

'I'm not sure I dare take the risk,' Ninian admitted. 'If I *am* still wanted, my chances of escaping with my life will be slim.'

'Are they any better if you stay here?' Roger countered. 'You heard the count back there.' He jerked his head in the direction of the castle, far behind them now. 'You are in the middle of a war here, my friend, and both sides will fight to the death. The Cathars—' and, amid everything else, Ninian was surprised to hear him use that term – 'will lose.'

'But—'

'It isn't your fight, Ninian,' Roger said. He sighed. 'I'm not sure it's mine, either.'

'I thought you were on their side!' Ninian protested.

Roger looked at him. 'Putting aside ancillary issues such as the pope's resentment over an upstart faith that threatens his precious Church's dominance, and the king of France's hunger for territory in the south, what we have here is basically a difference of opinion over the nature of a supreme being. In which,' he added with a smile, 'I do not believe.'

Ninian felt as stunned as if Roger had hit him. He'd heard it whispered – very quietly – that there were such people who denied the existence of God, but he had never before encountered one. And then, penetrating through the shock, he heard again what Roger had just said about his friends.

Roger's was not the first voice that had uttered those defeatist, depressing sentiments. Now, with an impact as forceful as a fist in the face, Ninian recalled that strange episode in the little chapel where he had stood before the Black Madonna. He heard again those words: *this battle will not be won. Church and king together can draw on endless resources and are ultimately invincible.* And, regarding his friends in the village, that chilling condemnation: *they made use of you.*

Now memory was returning fast, words and images flooding his mind with such force that he put up a defending hand to his head, as if to beat them away. But the gesture was useless; he sat on Garnet's back and endured as again he saw the familiar sights and the beloved faces that culminated in the one single word: *home.* Even as he felt the tears of homesickness and longing form in his eyes, the final image was forming, and he saw once more the towering edifice reaching up as if to scrape the heavens, the cone of brilliant, dazzling light surrounding it, spinning round like a huge vortex of power.

If the message urging him to leave the south was so forceful, perhaps he ought to start listening to it . . .

Utta was delighted to see him and, inviting him and Roger inside her tiny house, instantly began to bustle about preparing food and drink for them. She talked so quickly, and her accent was so thick, that Ninian caught about one word in four, hardly enough to make adequate sense of her outpourings. As she went about her work, she frequently paused to stare at him, sometimes taking his face between her hands and twice kissing him with great affection.

Roger, watching, sent Ninian an amused glance. 'She appears to be quite fond of you,' he remarked.

Ninian, embarrassed, muttered, 'She once came to England, and she met my mother.'

Utta picked up the word *mother*, which engendered further demonstrations of emotion. 'Mother saved my life,' she said to Roger. 'Mother risk herself, her baby, to keep Utta safe from man who would kill her.' She nodded emphatically, as if to underline her words.

'Her baby?' Roger asked. 'Was that you?'

'My sister,' he said shortly. 'My half-sister, in fact. Same mother, different fathers.' Again, he thought of Josse, in truth the only father he had ever known. His true father had been a far more elevated yet vastly inferior man, whose identity he certainly wasn't about to reveal to Roger.

Utta, still chattering, seemed to be asking about Joanna. 'My mother is dead, Utta,' Ninian said gently. 'I told you when you came to see me up in the village, didn't I?'

Utta stared at him, her blue eyes intent. Then her round face broke into a smile. 'Dead?' she echoed. Then, shaking her head, 'No, oh, no. She is here—' she clasped both hands over the clean white apron that covered her full chest – 'and here.' Now one hand was in the air over her head, waving in a slow circle. 'Not *dead*,' she repeated insistently, 'for I hear her voice, I see her lovely smile in her face that is now lined, and I see her hair, still beautiful even though now it is streaked with grey.'

Stunned, Ninian tried to rationalize the extraordinary remark. Utta must have an active imagination, he told himself. She remembered his mother – of course she did – and her mind had added the details of the lined face and greying hair because she guessed that was how it would be if Joanna were still alive.

That had to be the explanation; it was, after all, the only one.

It was strange, then, that the image of Joanna that Utta had just described exactly matched Ninian's vision of her in the tiny chapel where Roger had found him . . .

Utta leaned closer to him, one hand clutching his arm. 'You have seen her too?' she whispered.

Slowly, he nodded. 'It's – she's just a vision,' he said, his voice breaking on the words.

Utta smiled, a very sweet expression. 'She watches over those she loves,' she said. Then, her voice barely audible, she added something else. Ninian thought it was: *go and find her.*

But I can't, because she's dead, he wanted to protest. Yet he found he could not say it.

As he and Roger left Utta's little town and headed up into the mountains, such was Ninian's state of mind that he found himself wondering if the visit to see Utta had been manufactured by some sort of power from beyond the earth purely so that he could hear her speak those words about Joanna. Because it had otherwise proved pretty pointless, since Utta would not even consider leaving her cosy little house for the sanctuary of the village in the mountains. 'Here I am happy, have many friends, have good, plain work to keep hands busy, I have my life,' she had said. As if she had heard Ninian's unspoken protest – that, when de Montfort's army came crashing through the narrow streets, she would lose all those things, including her life – she had given him her sweet smile and said, 'I am old woman now. Have had good life, am ready for death when it chooses to take me, for then will come paradise.'

It had been useless to try to shake her serene certainty.

Now, plodding along behind Roger, Ninian wondered if he should have done more, or whether it was Utta's destiny to quit her earthly existence in that friendly, cheerful little house. He could have—

'This is where we go our separate ways.' Roger's voice had broken into his thoughts and, looking up, he saw that they had stopped at the foot of the narrow and barely discernible track that led up to the village. 'My road leads on down there,' Roger went on, pointing ahead, 'and I don't want to tire my horse by making him go all the way up to the village.'

They both dismounted. Roger untied the bundles of weapons he had been carrying and handed them to Ninian, who added them to the load already on Garnet's back. The path was steep; he realized his horse would have enough to bear without carrying his weight too, and decided to walk up.

He and Roger stood facing each other. 'Thank you for all you've done for me,' Ninian said.

Roger waved a hand. 'I've done nothing,' he replied. Then, giving Ninian a suddenly astute look, he added, 'Unless, that is, I've succeeded in putting some doubt in your mind.'

Not waiting to explain, he mounted his horse, put heels to its sides and rode away.

Of the men who had ridden out on the mission, Ninian was the last to return. His friends greeted him with relief and, when he admitted his failure to persuade Utta to come, said that many of the others had experienced similar disappointment. The weapons were greeted with delight and many questions concerning their provenance, which Ninian politely declined to answer; his account, he felt, should be given first to the village elders.

He stashed the bundles under his bed and was just trying to smarten himself up in preparation for seeking out Alazaïs, when a young woman came to summon him to her presence. Word of the weapons must have spread already, he thought as he hurried across the tiny square to her house.

When he was ushered inside, he found her sitting alone, in exactly the same pose as when he had first met her nearly half a year ago. 'Sit down, Ninian,' she said. He sank on to a wooden stool. She sat in silence, regarding him.

'I couldn't persuade Utta to come to the village,' he said, as the silence became awkward. 'She—'

'It is not important,' Alazaïs said dismissively.

'I've brought swords and knives,' Ninian hurried on, 'which I was given by—'

Once more she interrupted. 'When you did not return with the others,' she said, 'I hoped it meant that you had decided to go home.'

He was angry that she would think that. 'I would not go without telling you,' he said stiffly. Straightening his shoulders, he added, 'I was brought up not to desert my friends.'

'You came here for two reasons,' she intoned. 'One, because you were running from a false accusation of murder, and two, because my son told you there was a refuge here where nobody would find you. In addition, he made sure that you brought to us our treasured manuscript, although you did it unknowingly. Neither action provides any reason for you to take on the mantle of our friend, Ninian.'

He could not understand why she was being so harsh. 'But – I've lived here with you all, and I've been useful, training the young men. Haven't I?' He was distressed to hear the note of pleading in his voice.

She was watching him dispassionately. 'The result will be the same,' she said softly.

He wondered if she was being deliberately cruel to drive him away. 'You don't need to—' he began.

'Ninian, there is something I would ask of you,' she said. She smiled thinly. 'You may think, with justification, that I have a fine cheek, to ask a favour of you when I have just implied that you are an outsider and not welcome here. However, let me explain.' She was quiet for some moments, apparently thinking. Then: 'While you were away, we had some visitors.' She mentioned several names, all of which Ninian recognized and some of which were those of the most important leaders of the bonshommes. She must have seen his expression, for she said, 'Esclarmonde of Foix and I are old friends, and we took the consolamentum together. Peter Roger of Cabaret I have known for years.'

She was of the St Gilles family, Ninian recalled. It was one of the leading clans of the region, and it was probably no surprise that such revered elders had made the arduous journey up to the village to visit her.

'They had only one reason for coming here,' she murmured, 'and it concerns you, and the favour I would ask of you. That *we* would ask,' she corrected herself, 'for, in truth, it concerns us all.' She paused, studying him intently out of narrowed green eyes. They were, Ninian thought absently, very like her son's.

'You came here bearing a treasure you did not know you carried,' she said, her voice now powerful, as if, having decided on how to phrase her request, her strength and determination had flooded back. 'Would you, Ninian de Courtenay, be prepared to return to the north, leaving behind this tortured land, and take something equally precious to safety?'

His mind filled with questions and objections. Ignoring them, he took a deep breath and said, 'You'd better tell me what this something is.'

She gave a faint smile. Reaching inside a fold of her robe that lay over her heart, she drew out a small rectangular object, wrapped in black silk. Unfolding the silk, she put on the little table in front of her a set of the images that he'd noticed the bonshommes carried, and which they used to help others understand the complexities of their faith. Most sets were simple, crudely drawn on thin paper. The ones that Alazaïs now spread out before him were painted on to heavy card and were stunningly beautiful.

'Behold,' she said, 'the secret heart of our faith. Encoded in these twenty-one images, Ninian, hidden in symbols that no outsider could penetrate, is the journey of the soul as it passes its years down here in its earthly existence.' He was staring down at the images, his eyes dazzled by the glorious colours and the high degree of the artistry. He was also experiencing the disconcerting illusion that cool fingers were walking their way down his spine: the images seemed to generate a strong, mysterious power. 'Would you like to take the journey with me?'

He found his voice. 'Yes.'

She had laid the images out in a particular sequence – three rows of seven – and now she straightened the edges so that they were perfectly in line. Pointing to the card on the left of the top row, she said, 'Here we begin, for this is the Lost Soul; the angelic spirit trapped in an earthly body and torn out of its true home in the spirit realm. Here—' she went on to the second image – 'is the Free Spirit, and a door opens just a crack to admit a tiny light, representing the faint hope that the Lost Soul may find his way home again if he can overcome all the challenges and dangers that await on the journey. Here—' she indicated a strange, robed figure which, although clearly an authority figure, was female – 'we have the female face of religion, or perhaps you would say Mother Church, and she is our enemy; after her comes her male counterpart, the human head of that church.' She paused, and he thought he detected a tremor in her hand.

She went on, pointing to the next two images and identifying them as the Queen and the King, representing temporal power on earth, and the one that came next, symbolizing the temptations of the carnal – love and procreation – both of which tried to pull the Lost Soul from his true path. 'Finally in the first row comes the Wagon,' Alazaïs said, 'and here, see, is the picture of a rich man's worldly goods loaded high on a runaway wagon that is out of control and about to crash, to the ruin of everything on it. This is the temptation of materialism, and the image illustrates its ultimate futility.'

The low, steady voice compelled him to listen as her finger went on to the next row, describing each image as she came to it, setting out for him the journey and the qualities needed to endure it. Fortitude. The strength to withdraw and seek extraordinary courage. A warning not to seek justice within the confines of the world. The wheel of fate, and the assessment of the soul at the completion of each turn.

With a sudden light in her eyes, she said, 'Now we come to the soul commencing transition. Great suffering must be endured as the end of physical existence approaches, but the agony is assuaged by the promise of the glory ahead. Here is Death, the end of life incarnate, and here Alchemy, as the consolamentum purifies and releases the soul, allowing it to quit the body.'

Her hands now spread over the last line of seven images. 'Here is the ruler of the material world in all his evil, waving in fury as he tries to call the soul back. But, see, he is impotent in his rage, for the soul is already free, flying up towards the Angelic Realm. Now the great material edifices of the world collapse, shattering and breaking; many choose to see these building as symbols of the Church, ultimately failing. Here is the Star—' she indicated a beautiful image of a fragile, ethereal star bathed in silvery light – 'which is the first level of spirit; and here is the Moon, which is the second. Here is the Sun, whose fire and heat burn off all the impurities that the Lost Soul has gathered during its time on earth, leaving it pure and clean as it was before its long imprisonment. Now, at last, it is ready for Transcendence—' she pointed to the penultimate card – 'where the soul completes its long and arduous journey and is once more simple free spirit.' She paused, catching a quick breath. 'Here the soul may at last hear the first snatches of the heavenly music, speeding him on his way. And finally, here is the Angelic Realm.'

She fell silent. Ninian, looking up, saw tears rolling down her face. Hastily, he returned his attention to the final image.

It was the most glorious of all. The Angelic Realm was depicted in colours that seemed to glow, radiating heat that he thought his tentative, questing fingers could actually detect. The landscape was beautiful in its clean, pure simplicity, and the softly-rolling green hills and sparkling streams were tinged with gold, appearing transparent. There were figures in the picture, although they were vague and indistinct. They seemed to float over the shining ground as if they were too light to touch it.

Ninian's heart filled with a joy so intense that he could barely contain it. He tried to speak, but no sound came. He felt Alazaïs's hand gently touch his own.

'You see?' she asked softly. 'You understand?'

He shook his head. 'No, oh, no. This – this journey, this story that symbolizes the basis of your faith, it's too complex for me.' He raised his head and met her eyes. 'But I do under-stand now why you asked for my help.'

She was nodding. 'Yes, I see that you do.' She paused, weighing her words. 'These images represent our deepest secrets,' she said, her voice grave. 'I have explained the journey very briefly, for I would have you know what it is you carry, yet our wisest elders spend years – lifetimes – studying the symbols, and there is always more to learn.' She sighed. 'When we are gone, we would be happy to know that our precious images still exist somewhere in the world we leave behind. While just one set remains, there is the hope that what we were and what we believed will not be entirely lost.'

He wanted to make the obvious objection: that, if the images were so complex and the symbolism so obscure, then, without anybody to translate them, the hope was a pretty faint one. But he didn't.

What he did say, as many different strands finally came together in his mind and he looked up into her eyes, was, 'Yes. I'll do it.'

TWELVE

It seemed to Josse that he had been searching for the Brown Man for days, although in truth it had only been the afternoon and evening of one day and the early part of the next. Yesterday he had scoured the forest closest to Hawkenlye Abbey, going back in his memories and seeking out all the places where he had ever known somebody to hide. He had wondered briefly about going to check in the area immediately around Joanna's hut, probably the best hiding place of all, since even he, who was well aware of its existence and would have said he knew how to get there, quite often had a problem locating it. In the end, he didn't bother. According to Helewise, Meggie had gone to the hut to fetch supplies, and he very much doubted it was the first time. If there had been any sign that someone had been there, she would have noticed and told him.

He had found nothing and, as darkness fell and made further searching impossible, he had turned for home. This morning, with an eager Geoffroi by his side, he had been concentrating on the area further east, closer to the House in the Woods. Heartbreakingly, they had checked the camp where Ninian had briefly stayed last autumn, before he fled. Full of memories and images of Ninian, the place had clearly lain undisturbed since its former occupant had left.

Now, Josse made up his mind to go back to Hawkenlye, and, if there was no news there, on to Tonbridge. He was deeply uneasy, although he did not know why. Mentally, he went through all the people he loved, reminding himself where they were and what they were doing. Apart from Ninian – and his absence was an ongoing pain that Josse could never make himself get used to – everyone was accounted for.

He realized that his distress was on behalf of the Brown Man; he had failed to find him, and perhaps that meant that he'd been wrong about the man choosing to hide in the forest. Supposing he had stayed close to Tonbridge? Supposing Lord Benedict's gang of thugs and bullies were even now surrounding him, closing in on him while he lay in an exhausted sleep, preparing to jump on him, beat him, bind him and take him captive to some foul prison from which he would only emerge for his hanging?

Having decided, Josse took Geoffroi back to the House in the Woods and left him in Gus's care, with strict instructions to keep a close watch on the lad. 'I am going to seek for news, at Hawkenlye first and then down in Tonbridge. Geoffroi is wild to come with me,' Josse said quietly to Gus, 'but there is danger there, and I would not put him at risk.' Briefly, he explained.

'I know of Lord Benedict,' Gus said, a look of disgust twisting his pleasant face. 'If one of his gangs finds this Brown Man of yours, I pity him.'

'Let's hope they don't,' Josse replied.

'Amen to that,' Gus muttered. He helped Josse back into Alfred's saddle. 'Good luck,' he said.

'I'll need it,' Josse replied.

Since he had to ride almost right past the clearing by St Edmund's Chapel to get to the abbey, he decided to make the brief detour and speak to the three women there. He would not be long, he told himself, and if there was news at the abbey, it could wait for that short while.

It was almost noon. A fire had been lit in a newly-built hearth behind the chapel, and the smell of whatever broth or stew was simmering over it filled the clearing. Josse's rumbling stomach reminded him he had not eaten since the sparse breakfast he had snatched at dawn. Slipping off Alfred's back, he tethered the big horse at the edge of the tree line and headed over to the group gathered around the fire.

There were perhaps a dozen people there, ranging in age from an elderly, toothless grand-dame wrapped in an old sack to a baby bound snugly in a shawl against its mother's chest. With the exception of the baby, every man, woman and child was rapidly shovelling in food, as if the crude wooden bowls were about to be snatched away. Studying these people, many of whom looked as if they hadn't seen food for days, Josse was ashamed of himself. He, who'd already eaten that morning, had been about to demand a share of the broth.

His eyes sought out Helewise, who was standing beside the hearth with a big white apron tied round her waist and a ladle in her hand. She was watching the hungry people, smiling in satisfaction as they ate. She had not noticed him.

I have to do something to help, she had said to him when she told him she was planning to come back here. Well, she was succeeding. In just a few days, she and the others had got this little sanctuary up and running, with food available, advice on injuries and sickness from Meggie, and, in Helewise herself, the firm support of a woman whom most of the local people knew and trusted.

He had to admit she had been right.

He glanced around, looking for the others. There was Little Helewise, talking to the woman with the baby. The girl was pale, he thought, and she looked anxious. As if she felt his eyes on her, she turned. He could hear her gasp even from several paces away.

What was the matter with her? Helewise had told him only yesterday that the girl's spirits were much improved, yet there she was, looking at him as if he was the last person she wanted to see.

Suddenly, cold fear clutched at his heart. *Where was Meggie?*

Not stopping to think, he ran into the chapel, flinging back the door so violently that it banged hard against the stone wall. Not there. He turned and raced across the clearing, past the lay brothers' shelter and into the little cell. His eyes scanned it – three tidily-made cots, the hearth swept and kindling laid ready, the women's belongings neatly stowed on and under their beds.

No, that was wrong. Two sets of belongings were stored by the owners' beds; the third cot was bare.

Meggie was no longer there.

He spun round and was about to burst out of the cell when Helewise rushed in, her granddaughter on her heels.

'*Where is she?*' he demanded, his voice a roar of pain. 'And don't tell me she's at the hut,' he shouted, before Helewise could speak, 'because it'd be a lie and I won't believe you – she's taken *everything!*'

Helewise took his arm in a firm grip and steered him to the largest of the three beds. 'Sit down, Josse,' she said, and her voice was once more that of a former abbess of Hawkenlye. He sank on to the bed, and she stood over him, Little Helewise lurking uncomfortably behind her.

'Tell me the truth,' he said hoarsely.

'I would not lie to you,' she replied. 'We have been waiting for you, for we must pass on to you all that we know.' She shot a quick glance at Little Helewise. 'We guessed you would return to the abbey, but we resolved that if you had not done so by noon – now – we would seek you out at the House in the Woods.'

His heart was thumping painfully. 'To say what?'

She sat down beside him, taking his hand in hers. 'Dear Josse, Meggie has gone to search for Ninian.'

He tried to leap to his feet, but she held him back; he had forgotten how strong she was. 'I've got to go after her!' he cried. Rounding on her, he shouted, '*Why didn't you tell me as soon as you found out?*'

Helewise glanced at her granddaughter, and he thought he read reproof in the look. Pointing at her, he yelled, 'It's *your* fault, is it? You're to blame, for keeping my daughter's disappearance to yourself!'

Little Helewise went white, and one hand clutched at her stomach. Josse barely saw the gesture; he wanted to leap at her and shake the truth out of her.

'Don't shout at her, Josse, she's—' Helewise began, quickly getting to her feet and going to stand protectively in front of her granddaughter. But then, to Josse's surprise and, to judge by her expression, Helewise's too, the girl gently moved Helewise out of the way.

With a lift of her chin and her eyes full of determination, she said, 'Josse, it is true that I knew she had gone, and, indeed, my fault that you were not notified immediately, but I think you should hear the whole story.'

'Go on,' he said coldly.

'She was at her hut yesterday,' Little Helewise began, 'fetching—'

'Fetching supplies. Aye, I know.'

'Yes,' Little Helewise agreed. 'She came back here, and we all ate supper together. Grandmother told Meggie that you'd been to see us and explained how you'd told us about the Brown Man being hunted by Lord Benedict's men, and how you thought he was innocent and was probably hiding out in the forest, where you were going to look for him and tell him he should flee.' She paused for breath. 'Well, not long after that, we all settled down for the night. We fall asleep quickly, because it's warm and cosy in the cell and we're usually very tired. Anyway, something woke me up – I've no idea how much of the night had passed – and I opened my eyes to see Meggie. She was kneeling on the floor beside her bed, fully dressed and with her heavy cloak on, and she was packing her leather bag. She was putting everything in it, and, even though I was still half asleep, I realized she wasn't just taking a few things to go off to the hut for a day or two.'

She hesitated. Josse, desperate to know, was about to demand that she continue, when she drew a shaky breath and spoke again. 'Meggie said she thought she'd found a way to bring Ninian home. She told me she was setting off to do everything in her power to achieve that aim.' She paused, clearly thinking. 'She must have already been out to the hut,' she added, 'and accidentally woken me up when she came back here to the cell to fetch her belongings.'

Josse sank back against the stone wall of the cell. Going after Ninian. Meggie was setting off into the huge, dangerous outside world to find Ninian. *I tried and failed*, he thought bitterly. *Why should she do any better?* Oh, dear God – anguish flooded through him – his adopted son gone, and now his own precious daughter too.

Little Helewise had sunk down and was kneeling before him. 'Look at me, Josse,' she said, and, amid the storm of emotion whirling through his head, he was surprised at the note of authority in her voice. She was not the child of the Warins for nothing . . .

He did as ,she bade him. Her eyes, cool and grey like her grandmother's, held his. 'She hasn't gone alone,' she said.

'*What?* Who has she gone with, then?' He tried to think who it could be and failed. For one strange moment, he thought this mysterious companion might even be Joanna . . .

'She didn't tell me who it was,' Little Helewise said gently. 'But I think we might guess,' she added, shooting a look at Helewise.

Josse, his mind full of his daughter and desperate for reassurance, hardly heard. 'Did she—' He cleared his throat and tried again. 'Did she say anything else?'

'She sent you her love and said not to worry. She trusts the person she's travelling with.'

'But who is it? Why didn't she say? She—'

Helewise sat down beside him again and put her hand on his shoulder. 'Meggie knows, better than anyone else of my acquaintance, who she can and cannot trust,' she murmured. 'Have faith in your daughter, dear Josse, for she richly deserves it.'

'She really believes she can find Ninian,' Little Helewise added, her eyes shining. 'I so wanted to go with her, and I pleaded with her to take me with her.' Her voice broke, and for a moment she seemed to slump into misery, but quickly she recovered. 'But she wouldn't.' She turned to Helewise, and Josse saw her fine eyebrows raised in enquiry.

'It's up to you,' Helewise said softly to the girl. She smiled. 'Tell him, if you wish.'

Little Helewise nodded. Then, once more facing Josse, she said, 'The reason Meggie wouldn't take me with her was because I'm pregnant.'

Josse felt his mouth open in a silent exclamation. 'Pregnant,' he repeated. Images flashed through his mind. Little Helewise, grieving when Ninian went away, in despair because neither she nor anyone else knew when – if – he would be back. Ninian, a man now, tall, strong, and, wherever he was, with no idea that his beloved girl was carrying his child. Little Helewise again, pining through the long winter months and then, unexpectedly, turning up at the House in the Woods . . . where, *of course*, she knew Meggie lived. Meggie, the obvious person to turn to for a young, unmarried woman who had discovered she was pregnant and needed advice.

'She didn't tell me,' he murmured.

'No, but she said I ought to,' Little Helewise replied. 'She said you of all people would not see it as anything to get upset about if a baby was born to an unwed woman, since both your own children were. *Oh!*' Belatedly, she clapped a hand in front of her mouth. 'I am so sorry, Josse. That was very tactless.'

He found he was smiling. Despite everything, a big grin was spreading over his face, and he did not seem to be able to stop it. 'Tactless but true,' he remarked. Then, opening his arms, he took her in an enfolding hug. Kissing her soft cheek, he said, 'I am very happy for you.'

She kissed him back, then, pulling away so that she could look into his face, she said earnestly, 'Meggie said my duty was to stay here where it's safe because whatever happened to me would happen to her too.' Her eyes widened. '*Her,*' she repeated, frowning slightly. Then, excitement and joy flooding her face, she whispered, 'When she said *her*, she meant the baby, didn't she?' She put both hands over her stomach and, before either Josse or Helewise could speak, she cried, 'Oh, do you think she could tell? Did she know? I would *so love* a girl,' she whispered.

Josse glanced at Helewise, whose mouth was quirked in a smile. He was well aware – and he was quite sure she was too – that, if ever Meggie could be persuaded to predict the sex of an unborn child, she was never wrong. He said softly, 'Maybe you'll get your wish.'

For a moment, nobody spoke; it was, Josse reflected, as if all three were picturing Little Helewise with a small baby girl in her arms. Then, indicating her granddaughter with a tilt of her head, Helewise said, 'Er, Josse, I think she may have guessed right.'

His mind still on babies, he did not at first realize what she meant. 'Guessed right?'

'Just now, Little Helewise said she thought we could guess who Meggie's gone off with. It must surely be the Brown Man. Don't you think?' she prompted when he did not immediately reply.

He considered it. The Brown Man had killed the three

brigands back in January, and the other two attacks had been
in the last few days, so he must obviously have found a safe
place in the vicinity in which to hide out. Since Meggie hadn't
been near the hut until recently – ironically, because Josse had
feared the sort of violent man who, it seemed, had in fact
been using the hut – the Brown Man could very easily
have been living there since he arrived in the area.

Perhaps his daughter's good judgement was affecting him,
but he found he was not as alarmed as he would have expected
by this news that she had gone off with a probable murderer.
But there was murder and there was execution; what had
Sister Estella said? *Something bad done for a good cause.*
Yes. If the man camping out in Meggie's hut had in fact been
the Brown Man, and he was responsible for the revenge
killings and assaults, then he was surely on the side of good,
not evil.

Or so Josse tried to convince himself.

The two women were waiting for his response, with evident
impatience. 'Aye,' he said eventually. 'It all appears to fit with
what we already know, although I suppose we should try to
keep open minds, for we may be quite wrong.'

'We're not,' Little Helewise said decisively. 'And, anyway,
even if he wasn't who we think he is, one thing's for certain.
She—' Abruptly, she stopped, as if suddenly doubting she
should go on.

'What?' Josse and Helewise said together.

Little Helewise shrugged, as if to say, *very well, then.*
'Whoever he is, Meggie really liked him,' she said. She looked
at her grandmother, then at Josse. 'I've never seen her like that
before,' she added softly. 'It was as if – as if a candle had
been lit within her, making her glow.'

'Could it have been excitement at setting off to look for
Ninian?' Helewise suggested. 'You said she appeared very
certain of success, and she is very close to her brother.'

'I don't think it was that.' Little Helewise shook her head.
She smiled. '*I* think Meggie's fallen for him.'

Josse was almost certain there was little point in going out to
the hut to see if he could find any trace of Meggie and her
mysterious companion, but that did not stop him trying.

Accordingly, leaving Helewise and her granddaughter to tend to the afternoon's visitors, he set off through the forest.

On this occasion, he had no problem in finding the hut, making his way straight to it. Looking around the clearing, he saw the signs that a horse had been tethered beside the stream, and, thinking he might find hoof prints leading away from the hut to indicate which way they had gone, his hopes rose. Only to be dashed again, when he discovered that the ground all around looked exactly the same: the Brown Man must have walked backwards away from the clearing, scuffing up the prints with a length of branch. It was a device Josse had used more than once himself. This man, he reflected, was no fool.

The worry he had been trying to suppress rose up again. What would happen if Lord Benedict's men caught up with the Brown Man when he had Meggie with him? Would they assume she was his accomplice and arrest her too, throwing her into a neighbouring but no less dreadful prison? Against his will, the terrible pictures formed.

And then, quite clearly, he thought he heard a voice: *do not let your anxiety blind you to what you have just observed.*

The man is no fool, he repeated to himself. Then, very faintly, he smiled.

Putting out of his mind the identity of that wise and very familiar voice, he crossed the glade and opened the door of the hut, fastened with Meggie's usual intricate knot. Inside, all was as neat and tidy as she usually left it. There were a few gaps on her shelves where she stored her herbs, and he guessed she had taken some essential remedies with her. This departure had been done thoughtfully and carefully.

He went up the ladder and studied the sleeping platform. Meggie had been born up there; he and Joanna had made love there several times.

'Look after her,' he said aloud to Joanna. 'As, I hope, you've been looking after Ninian. She's going to find him.'

It was probably only his imagination, or the wind softly blowing through the bare branches outside, but he could have sworn that same voice said, *I know.*

*   *   *

He fetched Alfred and rode on home. He needed to speak to his household and inform them where, and for what purpose, Meggie had gone. As he rode, he felt again the stab of fear concerning Lord Benedict's men and was very tempted to hurry on and try to catch up with Meggie and her companion. But very soon he realized there was little point. He might strike lucky and make his way to the port from which they were indeed planning to embark, although it would be a miracle if he did. If he failed, how long was he planning to go on, riding from town to town, asking about a young woman and a man dressed in brown with chestnut-coloured skin? No; it was useless.

Reluctantly, he turned Alfred's head for home.

Nearing the House in the Woods, it occurred to him to wonder how Meggie was all at once so sure she knew how to find Ninian, and what it had to do with whatever the Brown Man had said. Knowing Meggie, it was quite possible she had been trying some sort of spiritual link with Ninian, and that, through some mysterious mind-meeting process that Josse couldn't even begin to imagine, she believed she had an idea of his present whereabouts. Oh, dear God, did that mean she too was about to hare off for the Languedoc and plunge right into a war? But no; he arrested the thought. Like the whole family, she had known full well where Ninian was ever since Gervase had told Josse, and had showed no inclination until now to go and look for him.

Logic suggested to Josse that somehow – and probably via the mysterious stranger – Meggie had learned something else; she had heard, or surmised, or intuited, that there was a way to get to Ninian and bring him back.

And, he realized in a flash, how much more urgently he was needed here, now it was known that his beloved Little Helewise was carrying Ninian's child. Meggie, of course, knew; Josse could think of nothing more certain than that to persuade her that *any* risk was worth taking if it brought Ninian back.

He was almost home. Suddenly, he remembered the day that Gervase had visited, when, unknown to Josse, he had already received word from his mother far away in the south, concerning the precious Cathar manuscript. That message had reached Gervase, although Josse had no idea how. It had somehow been passed from person to person, whispered from mouth to mouth, all the long miles from the Mediterranean coast to the Kentish Weald.

If a message could travel from south to north, could word similarly be sent the other way?

Wondering why he had not already thought to ask, Josse kicked Alfred to a canter for the last half mile. Tomorrow, he resolved firmly, he would ride down to Tonbridge and put the question to the sheriff.

THIRTEEN

The sturdy horse called Auban had an extremely comfortable gait, something between an amble and a trot. To Meggie, sitting securely behind Jehan as they covered the miles down to the coast, it was as if she'd been perched there half her life.

She felt as if she was in a dream. So much had happened in such a short space of time, and her own actions still amazed her. Had anyone asked her if she'd be willing to give up everything she knew and leave the country of her birth in the company of a total stranger, she'd have given them short shrift. *I cannot possibly leave my work and my responsibilities*, she'd have said; or, *my father loves me deeply, and he is already bearing the loss of one child*. Or even, *my mother is gone, and I need to stay close to the places she frequented in order to keep her spirit with me*.

Yet when she had come across Jehan Leferronier sitting so calmly in her hut, and he had told her he was about to leave and where he was bound, she knew as if it had been planned out for her that she would go with him. She was still not ready to think about that; about why it was she did not even pause to question whether he was a threat to her or whether he would keep her safe.

She already knew.

The one thought hammering through her mind as she'd raced back to the cell beside St Edmund's Chapel to stuff her few belongings into her bag and gather up her heavy cloak

had been: *oh, please, please, make him wait for me! Let him
still be there when I get back!*

He had, and he was. The reddish-chestnut horse stood ready,
bridled and with a simple saddle on his broad back, attached
to which were two worn leather saddlebags. Jehan, it appeared,
travelled light. The man himself was busy with the knot that
fastened the door. Not turning round – he had known without
looking the very moment she stepped into the glade – he'd
said, 'I believe I now can do it precisely as you do.'

Approaching, she had checked. He could.

They had set out straight away, and by the time dawn had
begun to light the sky in the east, they were already out on
the south side of the great forest and in the valleys and small,
wooded ridges between the Weald and the South Downs. Now
it was mid-morning, and, as the big horse trod carefully along
a narrow little track that wound and twisted along the high
ground behind a small village, Meggie wondered what was
happening back at home.

It had been quite easy to persuade Little Helewise not to
come with her, desperate as the girl was for news of Ninian.
With the pregnant woman's instinct to protect her child, she
had readily accepted that the journey Meggie was about to
undertake was too risky for her and her baby girl. That, Meggie
reflected, was her one regret: she had let it slip that Little
Helewise was carrying a girl.

My one regret? she thought now. *What about making my
father suffer agonies of anxiety and pain because I've ridden
off without saying goodbye?*

She wasn't going to turn back; she couldn't. She could only
appeal to the kindly spirits, imploring them to soothe Josse's
sore heart and tell him she would be all right.

As the sun reached the zenith, Jehan turned his head and said
over his shoulder, 'Are you hungry?'

'Yes,' she said instantly. She was surprised he hadn't heard
her empty stomach grumbling. Perhaps he had.

'We are sufficiently distant from any house or road to make
a small camp,' he said, looking around, 'provided we keep
well hidden.' He pointed to a steep bank to the right of the
path, behind which was a patch of woodland, the mixed

deciduous and evergreen trees growing close together. He slipped off Auban's back. 'Wait while I look?'

It was a question, not an order, and she nodded her agreement. Auban shifted his large, feathered feet as Jehan dismounted, and, moving forward into the saddle, Meggie took up the reins and spoke some quiet words. The horse flicked his ears, and she sensed his interest. She patted his neck, urging him forward a few paces and then back again. He responded readily, and she felt she was making a friend.

Jehan's head and shoulders appeared above the bank. 'It is a good place,' he pronounced. 'Will you bring Auban? The bank is lower along there—' he indicated – 'and I think you will be able to enter the woods.'

He was testing her, she thought. Seeing if she was ready to ride the big horse and guide him in what was quite a difficult manoeuvre. 'Yes,' she said.

Auban moved easily beneath her, negotiating the gap in the bank and then picking his way back to where Jehan waited. The dark man smiled. 'I thought you might get off and lead him,' he said. 'But you rode.'

Slipping down now, she put her face close to Auban's and breathed gently against his nose. 'I like him,' she said.

'He, I think, likes you too. Now—' he was already reaching for one of the saddlebags – 'food for Auban, and food for us.'

She was collecting hearth stones, kindling and firewood. 'And I will prepare a hot infusion to refresh us.'

Sometime later, with welcome food in their bellies, they sat finishing Meggie's brew. She had included some herbs to stimulate, for there were still many hours of daylight and they would no doubt ride on as long as they could. She wondered which port they were making for.

He was watching her, his dark eyes thoughtful. Meeting them, she said, 'We'll have to break out of cover at some point, won't we?'

He frowned slightly. 'Cover?'

'I've noticed that so far you've been very careful to keep to the most remote places and the little-used tracks.' He began to speak, but she stopped him. 'Not that I'm complaining – with Lord Benedict and his men after you, it makes very good sense not to leave a trail, nor to allow us to be seen by people in hamlets and villages who might remember and report having noticed us when asked.'

'Very good sense,' he echoed. '*Oui.*'

'But, although I don't know the land around here very well,' she went on, 'I *do* know that there are open stretches where it'll be hard to hide. The great forest ends to the north of us, and, from what I've seen, it looks as if the patches of woodland are starting to thin out.'

He did not answer for a while. She guessed he was thinking about what she had said. 'When I came to England,' he said eventually, 'the ship on which I sailed arrived at a port to the south-west of here, on the eastern side of the great inlet that cuts into the south coast.' He smiled ruefully. 'It was a small ship, and the winter winds blew hard, so we were very glad to reach dry land. The port was big and bustling, with many ships sailing in and out, and many people to see who passed through.'

'Yes, but I don't think we need worry about Lord Benedict's men finding us so far away,' she began, 'because they won't know—'

'We should look for a much smaller place from which to set sail,' he went on, as if he hadn't heard. 'I propose that we carry on along this ridge – which bends southwards as it goes west – and, when we emerge into open country, make for the coast with all speed.'

It made sense, she supposed. Having been so careful up to now, it probably was better to seek an out-of-the-way place to look for a ship. 'Very well,' she said. 'It is wise, after all, not to assume that danger is behind us.'

He looked at her gravely. 'Danger is all around,' he said. 'We must be watchful.'

They packed up, and Meggie cut turves to cover the mark of their little fire, tossing the stones back into the undergrowth. Jehan led Auban down on to the track, and soon Meggie was once more mounted behind him.

They rode on for some miles, with an ever-thinning line of woodland on their right and open downland to the left. Something was niggling at Meggie; something he had said. She worried at it, and presently it came to her. 'Jehan?'

'*Oui?*'

'You said you crossed to England in the winter?'

'*Oui.*'

'Not – not *this* winter, just passed?' He couldn't have meant that, could he?

A shiver went through her.

He had done those dark deeds out of revenge, because all his victims had been cruel, violent bullies who had preyed on the weak. If he had only been in England a matter of weeks – at most, a couple of months, she reasoned, if he'd arrived as early as December – then how had he known? How had he identified so quickly the men he had killed and punished?

From Jehan, there came no answer. After a moment, he reached an arm behind him and his warm hand clasped her knee. 'Meggie,' he said, 'I am not the man you believe me to be.'

Whatever he had been about to tell her – and she barely dared think what it could be – he did not utter the words. Because just then there was a sound from within the line of trees that ran along perhaps a hundred paces away to their right; it sounded like a large animal, suddenly moving where it had been still. There was a muttered curse, and then a cry, and four horsemen burst out of the trees.

Jehan yelled, '*Hold on!*' and then they were flying, Auban's big feet pounding on the turf, racing over the ground with a speed she could never have imagined. She risked a quick look behind.

The horsemen were on the track behind them.

They seemed to be gaining on them.

In a small house standing alone on the lip of a valley beneath the great forest, Tiphaine was hard at work. In the house were two women. Neither of them, for very different reasons, was capable of doing much for herself. The older woman was lost in a world of her own; a world which, to judge by her perpetual tears and frequent outbursts of bewildered grief, was not a happy one. The younger woman had lost a lot of blood and was barely strong enough to sit up.

On arrival, Tiphaine had briefly surveyed the interior of the house, frowned, then rolled up her sleeves and set to work. She had lit a fire, built it up to a good, cheering blaze, and put pot after pot of water on to boil. Most of the room needed to be cleaned, but, before that, what was most urgently required was a heartening infusion. Tiphaine mixed valerian, chamomile and linden flowers, and, as the sweet smell of the dried linden blossoms permeated the room, she sensed a very slight lifting of the prevailing mood. When both mother and daughter had finished their drinks, Tiphaine made a further medicine for Melania, now including herbs to slow the blood flow.

Soon there was no sound from either woman except for steady, soft breathing; both slept. Tiphaine nodded in silent satisfaction. She had made the sedative deliberately powerful, knowing that what her patients needed more than anything else was sleep.

Presently, she realized that she was going to run out of fuel for the fire. The trauma that had hit this household in January had thrown the inhabitants far out of the usual pattern of their lives, and such tasks as collecting firewood and swabbing the floor had been largely ignored. Casting a quick eye on her patients – both were still fast asleep – Tiphaine went outside and strode off into the forest.

When she returned a little later, she was carrying enough fuel to last until dusk. Nevertheless, she was smiling, for her mission had not been solely to collect wood. The other, more important part of it had been accomplished, and Tiphaine was satisfied. All she could do now was wait.

Tiphaine had found some vegetables, some grain and a hard rind of bacon, and, with the addition of some fragrant culinary herbs, she had made a big pot of stew. There was much more than was necessary for the appetites of three women, two of them invalids. Tiphaine, however, fully expected that more than the three of them would eat that evening.

Melania was first to wake. Tiphaine examined her, gave her the good news that she was now barely bleeding and reassured her that, with enough to eat and drink, plenty of rest and the relief of knowing she could now put her dreadful experience behind her, she should soon recover her health.

Melania nodded briefly. 'Thank you,' she said quietly. Then, her face creasing in distress, 'I don't think I could have borne it if—' She did not finish.

'I know, lass,' Tiphaine replied. 'A child of that foul trio would have reminded you for the rest of your life. Best to have sent it on its way.'

'It's a sin,' Melania said. 'A priest would tell me I had taken life.'

'A priest wouldn't have had to deal with the consequence of a brutal rape every day,' Tiphaine said shortly. 'Easy enough for a man to stand up there on his high horse and talk about sinning.'

Melania smiled; it was a thin smile, soon gone, but the first Tiphaine had seen since the catastrophe that had ruined her life. 'To think,' Melania said, 'you used to be a nun.'

Tiphaine snorted. There really was no answer to that. She stood up and went to look at the older woman, still sleeping. Returning to Melania, she sat down again and said, 'While Marta's asleep, we must talk about her and what you're going to do.'

Melania sighed. 'What *can* I do? She's lost her mind, but she's my mother, so I'll look after her.'

Tiphaine studied her. Melania was strong – or she had been before the rape – and, to the best of Tiphaine's knowledge, had always been a good and dutiful daughter. But now she was facing an unknowable length of time in which she would have to care for a mother turned into a feeble, querulous and totally dependent child.

Tiphaine did not think that Marta would live very long, although she would not say so to Melania. The old woman's steep decline was yet another crime to lay at the feet of the men now buried at Hawkenlye; whoever had killed them, Tiphaine reflected, had rid the world of three people it would not miss. Nevertheless, help was needed, no matter how long or short a time remained to Marta. Tiphaine looked towards the door. If her plan was going to work, help might even now be on its way.

They came after dark, their arrival announced by a soft tap on the door of the lonely house. Marta lay on her bed with her eyes open, gazing out at visions none but she could see. From time to time, she gave a shudder that shook her thin body like an ague. Melania was sitting cross-legged by the fire, arms folded tight against her belly, staring into the flames.

Tiphaine, who had been expecting the visitors, got to her feet and went to the door, removing the chest that she and Melania had propped against it to hold it closed.

Nobody had repaired it after Wat had broken it down.

Tiphaine studied the newcomers. There were two of them: one was a boy in early adolescence, the childish plumpness of his face just beginning to harden into its adult shape; he carried a large bag that clanked as he moved. The other was an older man: short, lean, clad in soft brown and green shades, and with watchful hazel eyes. Tiphaine nodded her satisfaction. Of all men, she would have selected him had she had a choice.

He was called Luis, named for the rowan tree. Tiphaine bowed to him, for it was said he knew high magic. She was glad to see him for less elevated reasons, for he was also a healer, especially of those whose minds were disturbed. He had trained with the elders of the people, over in Brittany, and he was both respected and loved.

'Come in,' Tiphaine said, stepping back so that the man and the boy could enter. They did so, standing just inside the entrance while Tiphaine pushed the door shut and replaced the chest. Luis, watching, spoke some quiet words to the boy, who nodded eagerly and murmured a question. Luis turned to Tiphaine. 'He says, is there any good, seasoned wood? If so, he will repair the door.'

Tiphaine told him where to find what he needed and the boy pushed aside the chest and slipped outside again. 'There are tools in the outhouse,' she said.

Luis smiled. 'He has brought tools.' Then, advancing into the room, he crouched down beside Marta. Tiphaine watched, ready to offer an explanation, but Luis did not appear to need one. He put his hands either side of Marta's head, softly stroking the wild grey hair, and it seemed to Tiphaine that the agitation in her eyes was stilled. Luis spoke some quiet words, and a smile spread over Marta's lined, haggard face. Presently, her eyelids drooped and then closed. She turned on her side, and Luis covered her with a soft blanket.

'She will have no further need of your herbal sedatives tonight, Tiphaine,' he said. Then, moving to the hearth, he sat down beside Melania, who, ever since he had come into the

house, had been watching him with wary eyes. He looked at
her, not speaking.

After a long pause, she said tentatively, 'I don't know you,
do I?'

'No, Melania. But I know of you. I know that you and your
parents have always been friends of the forest people, offering
an open door and a hot meal when times have been hard for
us. Living out here on the edge of the forest as you do, you
have always been aware of us, knowing when we are in the
area and leaving out small gifts for us.' He twisted round so
that he could look into her face, for she sat with bent head.
'Is that not so?' he prompted.

'Yes,' she whispered.

Tiphaine watched, fascinated, as Luis's hand edged towards
Melania's, slowly, so slowly, until it was finally close enough
for him to touch his little finger against hers. She flinched,
but did not pull away.

'We knew you and your parents were vulnerable out here,'
he went on, still in the same soft, hypnotic voice, 'and we
should have watched over you. We had heard that bandits were
abroad in the wild places, and we tried to protect those whom
we knew to be at risk. But we are few,' he said with a sigh,
'and, on the night when they came here, we were far away.'
He waited, and Tiphaine wondered if he was giving Melania
the chance to speak of her ordeal.

She will not tell you, she said silently to Luis. It had taken
Tiphaine days to persuade Melania to say anything about that
terrible night, and, even now, she had only revealed the broadest
outline.

But then, to Tiphaine's surprise, Melania began to speak.
'They broke down the door,' she whispered. 'Father took up
his knife, but they just laughed at him. Poor Father, he tried
so hard, and then when those two men were – were raping
me, and Father was dying, I begged and begged them to allow
me to get up off the floor and fetch him his medicine, but they
wouldn't.' Luis's hand now encircled hers. She cried, 'I heard
him dying, and I couldn't save him!'

She wrenched her hand away and covered her face, her
hands muffling the sobbing.

Gently, Luis took hold of her wrists. 'Weep, Melania,' he

said. 'Grieve for your father, for he was a good man and deserves your tears. Weep for your poor mother, and between us we shall try to ease her broken mind.'

Melania stared at him, and Tiphaine felt she was torn between wanting to pull away – for he was a man, was he not, and her recent memories of men were frightful – and wanting to lean against him and accept the comfort and the strength he was offering.

The room stayed perfectly still on the point of balance for some moments. Then, with a wracking sob, Melania collapsed against Luis's broad chest.

Later, when Melania was deep in as peaceful sleep as her mother, Luis and Tiphaine sat together beside the hearth. The repaired door was back on its hinges, and two stout planks sat in brackets set into the wall on either side, barring it securely. Tiphaine had served up her stew – most of it was still in the pot, since neither of her patients had been persuaded to eat more than a few mouthfuls – and the two visitors had gulped it down as fast as she had been able to ladle it into their bowls. Now the boy was curled up like a puppy in the far corner of the room, sleeping.

'You are rightly revered as a healer of minds, Luis,' Tiphaine remarked.

He sighed. 'Neither woman is healed,' he replied, 'for tonight has been just the first step in a long journey.' He glanced at Marta. 'For the old woman, I fear it will not be many weeks before the deep peace of death claims her, although I hope to restore her to herself before she dies.' He turned to where Melania lay, and Tiphaine thought his expression softened. 'The young woman has been very badly damaged, and her soul is tormented by her memories. She shuts them away, and they grow and grow until they threaten to annihilate her.'

'But you can help her?' Tiphaine prompted.

He smiled at her. 'Yes, Tiphaine.'

Still she was not satisfied. 'I can stay here and help them. I must return to Hawkenlye for more supplies, but I can come straight back. I could watch over them, and—'

He put his hand on hers. She felt the power in him, radiating out of his flesh and into hers like the welcome heat of flames on a cold night. 'You have been a true friend,' he said, 'and without your herbs, Melania would now be forced to face carrying and bearing her rapist's child. You—'

'I did not provide the herbs; Meggie did.'

'Meggie,' Luis said softly. 'Yes. Her mother would have done the same, as would her grandmother. We still remember Mag Hobson, and it is good to know that her blood still runs in one who dwells in the forest.' He was silent for some time, and then, coming out of his reverie, he murmured, 'Please thank her when you see her.' Then, recalling the earlier conversation, he said, 'You offered to stay here, but there is no need.' He jerked his head towards the sleeping boy. 'He and I will look after them now, although you will always be welcome here. Come as often as you can, and bring others, for it will do the women good to feel part of the wider world again.' He paused, his face intent. 'We *will* make them better, Tiphaine.'

Studying him, she knew he spoke the truth.

There was something else she wanted to ask him. It was a matter that had been on her mind for some time; a worry that she had not been able to assuage.

She guessed he shared her anxiety. She said very quietly, 'Is there any news?'

He sighed. 'No.'

FOURTEEN

Early the next morning, Josse left the warmth of his hall and went outside to the stables to fetch his horse. He had asked Will to prepare Alfred, announcing to the household his intention of riding down to Tonbridge to seek out Gervase de Gifford. His optimism of the previous day seemed, however, to have deserted him, and now he was pretty sure that going to ask the sheriff about some weird and highly unlikely means of passing a message from England to the Midi was going to be a complete waste of time.

He was, however, stuck for any other ideas.

As he entered the stables he heard voices and thought at first it was Will passing the time of day with Alfred and the other horses. One of the voices was indeed Will's, but the other was a woman's. Rounding the partition between two stalls, he saw Helewise.

'What are *you* doing here?' he demanded, realizing straight away that, as a greeting, it was neither polite nor cordial.

'Looking for you,' she replied calmly. 'I thought I'd ride with you, if you do not object.' She inclined her head, and he saw that Daisy, her grey mare, was also saddled and bridled.

'Why?' he asked.

She took the mare's reins from Will with a murmured *thank you*, leading her outside to mount up. Josse followed, swinging up on to Alfred's back. Together they rode out of the yard and off down the track.

'Why?' she repeated. 'Because I thought it was high time Daisy had some exercise.'

'Aye,' he said impatiently, 'and what's the real reason?'

She turned to look at him. 'Dear Josse, isn't it obvious?'

'Not to me.'

'To the best of our knowledge, Ninian is still far away, and there has been no word from him. Now Meggie, too, has left, racing off on this mission of hers with a man we know nothing about.'

His heart gave a twist. 'I *know*,' he managed. 'There is no need to remind me.' Bracing himself, he added, 'I still don't know what you're doing here.'

Her expression very tender, she said, 'I've no idea where you're off to and what you plan to do, but it doesn't really matter.' She hesitated, then went on in a less certain tone: 'Little Helewise can manage perfectly well on her own at the chapel for one day. I – I just thought you might be glad of some company.'

Amid the pain and the worry, briefly he felt very happy. She had been thinking about him and, perceiving his need, had come to offer the help he would have asked for had he known it was available. Not sure if he could speak without the emotion showing, he merely nodded.

Her smile suggested that she understood.

*   *   *

'Where *are* we going?' she asked presently. He told her; to
his relief, the moment of weakness was past and he sounded
just as he usually did. Her eyebrows went up in surprise. 'Do
you really think we might get a message to Ninian in this
way? Oh, Josse, I do hope you are right, although—' She did
not finish.

'Aye, it seems unlikely to me, too,' he admitted. 'But I have
to do something. I can't just sit in the house waiting for—'
He, too, found he could not complete the sentence. Just then,
he didn't want to contemplate receiving news of his daughter
or adopted son, because, in his present low state, he could
only think it would be bad.

'We shall try, anyway,' she said stoutly. 'And then, if Gervase
either cannot or will not help, you and I will put our heads
together, as so often we have done before, and think of
something else.'

The thick fog of Josse's gloom shifted, just a little, and it
seemed to him that the thinnest ray of sunshine glowed down
on him.

They were nearing the place where the road turned down to
the right, towards Tonbridge, when there came the sound of
clattering, hurrying hooves and shouting from behind them.
Josse and Helewise drew rein, moving to the side of the road
to allow the group past.

There were perhaps eight or ten of them: burly, rough-
looking men, some mounted on inelegant but serviceable
horses, some on foot. All were armed, with knives, clubs, stout
sticks and, in one case, a crossbow. With a sinking heart, Josse
thought he recognized who they were.

'Get off the road and let us pass!' yelled the man riding in
front, waving an arm holding a club. He was clad in a worn
leather tunic and, despite the cold, his brawny arms were bare.
'Move!'

Josse thought that, since he and Helewise had already
positioned their horses one behind the other beneath the low
bank on the left of the road, the man was being unreasonable.
'We can hardly get further out of your way, unless you're
suggesting we climb the bank,' he protested.

The man in the leather tunic reacted as if Josse had just

insulted him, letting out a stream of insults and kicking his horse so that it raced towards Josse, foaming at the bit, its eyes wild.

Josse held his ground. 'Watch your foul tongue,' he said coolly. 'There is a lady here.'

The man glared at Helewise. He opened his mouth as if to add another crudity, then thought better of it. 'You're obstructing an officer of the law in the fulfilment of his duty,' he said grandly.

Josse wondered where he'd picked up the phrase. Although he thought he already knew, he said, 'What officer are you, and what duty are you carrying out?'

The man's chest swelled under the dirty leather tunic. 'Tomas is my name,' he pronounced, 'and Lord Benedict gives me my orders.' It was as Josse feared. 'As to my duty, if it's any of your business, we're taking this here violent criminal to that there abbey, which is the nearest place as is likely to have a secure prison. We're going to put him safely under lock and key till Lord Benedict can come to collect him.' He grinned, revealing a few stained teeth in otherwise bare jaws.

He raised his arm, the hand in a fist, and made a gesture to his men, who were gathered behind him. With a mocking bow, he turned to the figure now revealed in their midst.

He was dressed in the colours of the earth, predominantly brown, and the coarse cloth of his garment was stained as if from living rough. He was tall and slim, standing proudly with his shoulders held stiffly. There was a dignity about him, Josse thought, despite the sacking hood that had been thrown over his head, tied around his throat with a length of rope and completely concealing his face. His hands were bound behind his back.

'Why is he hooded?' Josse demanded.

Tomas shot him a sly look, his eyes full of malice. 'My men don't like the way he stares at them.'

Horrified, Josse was trying to think. Oh, dear God, if this was who he thought it was, then where was Meggie? Had she managed to escape when Tomas and his men had encircled and taken this Brown Man? Had she abandoned him to his captors – surely not! – or was she even now close by, awaiting the chance to try to help him?

She must not do that, Josse thought desperately, terrified for his beloved daughter. There was nothing she could do against so many, even with Josse and Helewise there to help, and if she showed herself now, it was highly likely they would take and imprison her too . . .

He must *do* something.

'Why have you taken him prisoner?' he demanded. 'What evidence is there against him, that you should treat him like this?'

Tomas glared at him. 'Evidence enough for us,' he growled. 'A witness saw him fleeing like the cesspit rat he is after he drowned our poor Rufus, and she described him to us. Good friend she's been to us, and she'll have her reward.' He gave a twisted grin. 'It's him, all right, and she'll swear to it.'

'Whatever you believe this man to have done,' Josse said, speaking loudly so that Meggie might hear, 'he is entitled to a fair trial, and I will not stand by to see him roughly treated.' There was a snigger from one of the men; another grabbed the bound man's arm, turning him so that his back was towards Josse. The brown robe was torn, and there were the raw, bleeding marks of a whip across his shoulders.

'Oh, you won't?' taunted Tomas. 'Well, whoever you are up there on your fine horse, this bastard's responsible for at least four deaths, including that Rufus from down Tonbridge way, and he flogged our poor old Matthew.' He put on an expression of mock regret. 'I'm not at all sure as how I can stop my men taking a bit of revenge, them being a tad cross on old Matthew's behalf, not to mention Rufus's, only he's not here any more to appreciate it.' There were mutterings from behind him and sounds of feet scuffling in the dust.

Josse urged Alfred forward. 'I shall accompany you to the abbey,' he stated firmly, 'and I shall make quite sure that no further harm comes to your prisoner.' It was not the moment for further discussion, so he waved for Tomas to lead his party on ahead, falling in behind.

'I do not care for this,' Helewise muttered, riding close beside him. 'Should we not fetch Gervase?'

'He claims he cannot stand against Lord Benedict,' Josse replied tersely.

'But Gervase is sheriff here!'

He glanced at her. 'Lord Benedict is a close friend of the king.'

There was nothing more to add.

He could sense Helewise's unease, and suddenly realized that, as well as feeling distress at the prisoner's capture, she must also be anxious not to go inside the abbey. Catching her eye, he said, 'Go up to the cell. I'll find you there.' She nodded. Her eyes held his and he tried to get across the unspoken message: *find Meggie! Don't let her do anything foolish!*

Helewise nodded again, then kicked her horse and turned away towards the forest and the short cut that led across to the clearing.

Someone at the abbey must have seen the horsemen approaching, for Abbess Caliste was there at the gates as they rode in. Tomas leapt down from his horse, tossing the reins to one of the abbess's escorting group of nuns, and he stood facing her, a swagger apparent in his stance.

'I require use of a secure cellar, Sister,' he began, 'where I can lock up my prisoner till Lord Benedict of Vitré gets here. He—'

Josse, also off his horse, pushed past Tomas and his men and went to stand before the abbess. 'Good morning, my lady abbess,' he said, making a courteous bow.

Abbess Caliste turned to him, frowning. 'Sir Josse? Are you involved in this business?' She looked very doubtful.

'Only by chance, my lady. I encountered this man and his companions on the road, where they overtook me on their way here.' He paused, thinking hard. 'They *claim* to have caught the man responsible for the recent assault and deaths hereabouts.' He laid careful emphasis on *claim*.

Abbess Caliste's eyes were on him, and she said softly, 'What would you have me do, Sir Josse?'

He took her arm and, turning away from Tomas and moving off a few paces, out of Tomas's earshot, he muttered, 'We have to do as he asks, my lady, for I understand that Lord Benedict has jurisdiction in this matter. Have you a place where he can be locked up?'

'There is the punishment cell,' she said uncertainly.

Josse knew of it. It was a small, windowless chamber built into the stones of the undercroft below the nuns' dormitory. It was always cold, the walls often running with water, and, once the door had been locked, totally dark. It was so small that only someone of less than average height could stand or lie down stretched out.

It was a terrible place.

'Is there nowhere else?' he muttered.

'Nowhere that is truly secure,' she whispered back. 'We do not usually expect to lock people up.' He went to speak but she forestalled him. 'Sir Josse, if I suggest some less harsh alternative, they will surely reject it and hunt around until they find what they are looking for.'

Aye, he thought, *she's right.*

Abbess Caliste stepped past Josse. Fixing Tomas with cool, assessing eyes, she said, 'Follow me.'

Josse, walking behind the men roughly dragging the hooded man along, felt the abbess's distress as acutely as he did his own. This penning up of a man within such a foul place was wrong, surely, whatever he had done.

With a lay brother now leading the way, the party went in through the low archway into the undercroft. Someone pushed the prisoner's head down to prevent him bumping it on the lintel. They half-pushed, half-dragged him along the passage to the tiny door at the end. Someone flung it open, and the prisoner was hurled inside. They heard a thump as he fell, hard, on to the stone floor.

Abbess Caliste's voice rang out, firm and authoritative: 'Remove the hood and unbind his hands. You will not leave him lying there unable to help himself.'

There was an instant's silence, and Josse was sure Tomas would argue. The man stood facing the abbess, eyes fixed to hers, mouth open for some crudely-worded refusal. But Hawkenlye Abbey appointed its abbesses wisely; in this her own place, Abbess Caliste was not to be gainsaid. After a short, tense moment, Tomas turned away, nodding curtly at one of the men who had shoved the prisoner inside the cell. The man went down the low steps, and there was the sound of a knife sawing through rope. Then he emerged once more, slamming the door behind him, and Tomas rammed the bolts home. Then he turned the big iron key in the lock, removing it and swinging it on its ring.

He turned a triumphant face to Josse. 'Let's see him try to get out of *that*,' he said.

Shocked and horrified, Josse stood looking at the door. There was so little space in the tiny room.

And the prisoner was tall.

Tomas was rubbing his hands, his delight palpable. 'I'm leaving my best men here to watch over him,' he announced, 'while two of the others come with me to fetch Lord Benedict.' He leered at the abbess. 'Don't you or your ladies go getting any ideas about handing in some little treats, Sister, because my men won't approve of that.' Then, chest thrust out, he strutted away.

Josse and Abbess Caliste were ushered back along the passage.

As the sound of their receding footsteps rang out, for the first time there was a reaction from the man in the punishment cell: a thin animal howl of anguish, swiftly cut off.

Josse went with the abbess to her room, both of them deeply shaken by what had just happened.

'I am not at all easy in my mind that the prisoner's fate is to be decided by Lord Benedict,' the abbess said as she sank into her chair. 'Sir Josse, we must inform Gervase de Gifford, who surely will not stand by and allow a man to be condemned without trial?'

'I do not know, my lady,' Josse replied. 'In these times, it is not easy to stand up to a man who has the favour of the – er, of those in very high places.'

She understood; he could tell by her suddenly wary expression. 'I see,' she said neutrally. Then, passionately, she cried, 'But, Sir Josse, even if the man in the undercroft is indeed he who carried out the revenge killings, he should be allowed to explain himself and give his reasons! Many people, I believe, would applaud his actions, not punish him for them. Yet I fear that, as soon as Lord Benedict arrives, our poor prisoner will be dragged out and hanged from the nearest suitable tree.'

Josse had the same fear. His mind was working frantically, trying to think of a way either to get the prisoner out of the cell or find some argument that would make Lord Benedict see the sense and justice of a proper trial, but so far he could think of nothing. He had briefly wondered if it would be worth speaking to the witness, but, from what Tomas had said, it was clear she had been promised a hefty bribe. Times were so tough, for the vast majority of the population, that, although it was deeply upsetting to think that this woman would see a possibly innocent man hang for something he might not have done, it was hardly surprising.

Absently, he let his eyes roam around the room, going back in his mind to the many times he had sat here with Helewise. As if Abbess Caliste could read his thoughts – perhaps she could, for she was an extraordinary woman – she said softly, 'Go and find her, Sir Josse.'

In the little cell by the chapel, Josse found Helewise and her granddaughter, huddled in quiet conversation with Tiphaine. Helewise got up to greet him as he went in.

'There's no sign of Meggie, Josse,' she said, her worried eyes holding his. 'Little Helewise and I have searched through the forest in a wide arc all around the clearing, and, unless she's deliberately hiding from us, too, she's not here.'

'She'll have gone to the hut!' he cried. 'We must—'

'I've just come from there,' Tiphaine said. 'I've come to fetch herbs from the abbey, but there's one or two things Meggie keeps that they don't have, so I called in at the hut before I came here. Sorry, Josse, but she's not there either.'

His legs felt suddenly weak. He sank down on to the nearest bed and dropped his head in his hands.

He heard the rustling of fabric and felt Helewise's hands take hold of his, removing them from his face. 'Dear Josse, if *we* can't find her, then there is little chance anyone else can,' she said gently. 'If she was with him when he was taken—'

'No *if* about it,' he protested.

'If she was,' Helewise repeated, 'then she had the good sense to realize that she could help him far more if she remained free than by hurling herself impotently at a company of men and demanding they release him.'

It made sense, as far as it went, but he could see one big

objection. 'Then why isn't she here, setting about helping him?' he asked.

Nobody seemed to be able to answer him.

After a pause, Tiphaine spoke. 'Seems to me someone ought to tend to the man,' she remarked. 'Helewise said he's been whipped, and that punishment cell's a dirty place.'

Josse looked up at her. 'Tomas's men are guarding the door,' he said. It sounded feeble, even to his own ears.

Tiphaine grinned. 'There's a pretty young nun I'm training in the use of herbs,' she said. 'Reckon if the two of us go along and she bats her long eyelashes at the guards, they'll see their way to allowing us to tend their captive.' She crossed to the door. 'Worth a try, anyway.'

Josse watched her stride away down the long slope towards the abbey. His mind seemed to overflow with anxieties: uppermost was the need to protect his daughter.

But he did not know how.

Helewise was still crouched beside him, and he was tempted simply to lean against her, close his eyes and rest. She, however, had other ideas. 'Josse?' she said, giving his shoulder a nudge. 'Josse, we were on our way to see Gervase, weren't we?'

'Aye,' he sighed, recalling. The problem of finding Ninian seemed very far away just then.

'No matter what you say about Lord Benedict taking control in this matter, I still think Gervase should know what is going on,' she went on.

'He probably does already,' he replied.

'In that case, he should be here,' she said with spirit. 'He is sheriff of Tonbridge, and he cannot just absolve his responsibility like this.'

'He's not doing that, he . . .' But Josse found he had no heart for the defence of Gervase that he'd been about to present. In essence, she was right. Maybe it was time someone pointed it out to Gervase.

He got up, straightening his tunic. 'Come on, then.'

The surprise in her face suggested she had expected to have to work harder to make him agree. Quickly recovering, she wrapped herself in her cloak and followed him out.

FIFTEEN

Ninian knelt in front of the strange black figure, his mind wandering. In the near-darkness of the tiny chapel, the goddess and her child were illuminated only by a solitary votive candle, which Ninian himself had lit. It was late; everyone else appeared to have gone to bed.

He was in a small town called Rocamadour, which was built into the side of a limestone cliff, so its streets and lanes were formed largely of steep tracks and flights of innumerable steps. Pilgrims to the shrine of the Madonna, Ninian had learned, often ascended from the valley floor up to her little chapel on their knees.

It was a long climb.

He was not entirely sure why he had come. He'd had to travel long past the usual time he stopped for the evening to get there, answering a silent but imperative voice that often spoke inside his head.

He had learned to trust that voice, for he believed it was his mother's. And, indeed, black goddess statues, like the one he was now looking at, were featuring quite strongly in his journey . . .

He had come, he estimated, roughly a third of the way. For the first week on the road, he had been forced to travel via tracks so small and difficult to find that, had it not been for the succession of guides who had helped him, he would never have found his way. The bonshommes and credentes who rode with him on those lonely, secret trails did not know what he carried; they had only been told that they must help him, for his mission was of great importance. As he shared with his guides the hardships of travelling through the mountains when the snows were only just melting, he grew close to each one. But he was leaving them, leaving them all, just as he had left his friends back in the village. He knew – or perhaps had been persuaded – that it was the right thing to do, for them and for himself, but, nevertheless, all his training had led him to believe that you did not run out on a friend when that friend was in danger and needed you. He had done something to help – the information he had taken to the Count of Foix would surely result in the massacre of one big group of freshly-arriving crusaders – but it would do little to arrest the steady progress of Simon de Montfort. And, sooner or later, the front line of the battle would reach the village he had left behind.

It was particularly painful to recall his parting from Alazaïs. She had been his first real friend in the village; she had provided the warm hearth and the kindly, welcoming affection that had helped him when the ache of homesickness became too much to bear. And she was old; even if other, fitter women and men survived the onslaught, it was not likely that she would. Ninian had wondered if he should suggest she came back north with him; there would surely be a home waiting for her with her son Gervase and his family. But he knew, without even having asked, that she would shake her head and, with a gentle smile, refuse.

She had held him in her arms as they had said goodbye. 'I will keep you in my heart,' she had whispered. 'I shall pray for you, every day, and picture you as you journey north.' He had told her the route he was planning to take. 'You will see the Great Mother's shrine at Chartres in the spring,' she added. 'Her time of most profound mystery.' Then she had kissed him and let him go.

They had all turned out to see him off, and he'd left with their promises of prayer and undying friendship echoing in his ears.

And then, as now, his heart had ached to leave them. No friends could have been in graver danger, now that winter was over and the brutal crusade against them was starting again.

He gazed up at the statue high above him. Not including the figure that he had taken back to Hawkenlye from Chartres, she was now the fourth he had encountered. The first had been in the deserted village where he had met Roger of Pépoulie, and it was she, he supposed, who had set his feet on the homeward path. He'd come across the second in the hands of a fellow traveller, staying, like Ninian, in a rough inn at the foothills of the mountains. The man, seeing Ninian's eyes on her, had kindly handed his treasure to him for a moment. She was about the size of the man's outstretched hand, and, as he informed Ninian, she kept him safe. The third, he'd found in a church beside the mighty Garonne River, at a spot where travellers waiting to cross went to pray for a safe arrival on the north bank. He had been told that there were many more of them, all over the Languedoc, as if the images touched on some fundamental part of the people's faith.

And now this one, this Black Madonna of Rocamadour, was looking down on him, silently communing to him some blessing that he felt like a soft stole around his shoulders.

He had once asked Alazaïs why the dark figures were so important. Her answer had been enigmatic: 'She is the Mother Goddess, and her history is ancient. In Egypt she was Isis; she was also Virgo, Kore, Demeter and Persephone, for her nature is the heart of the feminine and she is both mother and daughter.'

The names meant little to Ninian. He waited to see if she would say more. Presently, she did. 'She is depicted with her son, usually at her breast or on her knee, but very occasionally still in her womb.' Vividly, Ninian imagined the Hawkenlye figure. 'Isis and Horus; and, as depicted by later artists, the Holy Mother and the Holy Child,' Alazaïs said dreamily. Then, eyes suddenly intent on Ninian's: 'As to whether the child is Christ himself or the child of Christ, that is for each person's own heart to decide.'

The child of Christ?

At first, Ninian had been shocked by the blasphemy. It was only later that a chance, overheard remark had allowed him to understand the truth that had been staring him in the face: the bonshommes believed the Black Goddess to be Mary Magdalene. The baby she bore was the child of Christ. And, far from being the wild, outlandish fantasy of one mad old woman, it was the belief of most of the bonshommes and many of the dominant aristocratic families.

But he understood there was something yet beyond that extraordinary idea; something to do with the female side of god, which seemed to symbolize the whole essence of the feminine. It appeared to be embodied in the shape of the Black Goddess figures, and they were deeply revered.

Ninian did not fully understand what had happened to his
mother in Chartres Cathedral. He and Josse had spoken about
it briefly, and Ninian realized Josse was as confounded as
he was. It must therefore, he reflected, be in his soul, or
somewhere – a place, anyway, that was not his conscious,
thinking mind – that he perceived a very important thing: the
Black Madonna was connected with some sort of eternal,
female, divine figure, and that, in turn, was connected to the
mystery that surrounded his mother's disappearance.

No wonder the Black Goddess seemed so intent on leading
him towards Chartres.

'What's he supposed to have done?' Tiphaine's young
apprentice asked as the two of them made their way to the
undercroft where the prisoner was shut up. The young nun
carried an empty bowl and a flask of hot water. Tiphaine
had packets of lavender and comfrey in her worn old satchel,
as well as a small pot of healing cream made to a recipe
invented by Joanna. Its ability to prevent scarring was
legendary.

'They say he's killed,' Tiphaine said shortly, hoping to
indicate by her brevity that she did not wish to gossip.

The young nun's eyes widened. 'Will we be safe?' she
whispered.

Tiphaine took pity on her. 'Perfectly safe. It's not nuns he's
accused of murdering, and anyway we're here to help him.'

The four guards left by Tomas were lounging around the
entrance to the undercroft. One of them, seeing the two figures
approach, got up from his leaning pose against the wall and
went to block the door, a cudgel in one hand. 'No entry here,'
he said. 'Dangerous prisoner inside.'

Tiphaine regarded him steadily. 'His wounds need to be
cleansed,' she said. 'The punishment cell is filthy and probably
rat-infested. If those cuts become inflamed and the fever starts
up in his body, your prisoner will die before you have the
chance to take him out and hang him.'

It was apparent from the men's expressions that they didn't
like the sound of that. They put their heads together and
muttered for a while, then the man who had blocked the door
turned round and opened it.

'Go on, then,' he said grudgingly. He handed her the key. As the young nun slipped past him, he shot out a hand and pinched her bottom. 'We'll have to search you when you come out again, so don't go trying to smuggle him out under your skirts, Sister!' They heard the sound of the door being firmly closed and locked behind them.

'That *hurt*!' the nun said, rubbing her buttock as they hurried along the dank passage.

'I'm sure it did,' Tiphaine replied. It had been courageous of the girl not to cry out.

They reached the door, and Tiphaine inserted the key and turned the lock. She struggled with the bolts, finally managing to push them back. She looked at them thoughtfully for a moment, then, reaching in her satchel, took out a small pot of grease. Taking the bowl and the water from the young nun's hands, she gave her the pot. 'Put some of this on those bolts,' she instructed the nun.

'Why?' the girl asked, taking the pot. 'You've got them open now, and—'

Good Lord in heaven, Tiphaine thought, *what were young nuns coming to, asking questions like that?* 'Just do it,' she said tersely. Then she stepped down into the tiny cell.

She waited for her eyes to adjust. The passage was dim enough, with just two little windows set high up in the walls admitting light. The only illumination within the cell was through the open door.

He was lying on his side, his long legs curled up, his face to the wall. His instinct to prevent his cut flesh hurting even more by contact with the ground had probably saved his life, Tiphaine reflected, since he had kept the deep wounds out of the filth on the beaten-earth floor. Crouching down, she placed the bowl on the ground and poured in the hot water, adding the fragrant herbs. The clean, sweet smell of lavender quickly permeated the enclosed space, and Tiphaine felt the usual uplift of the heart.

The prisoner stirred. 'Keep still,' Tiphaine said. 'I have brought water and herbs, and I will clean the wounds on your back.'

He nodded. She sensed him tense, preparing for the pain that her ministrations would cause, and her hands were as gentle as a mother's with a newborn baby. She bathed, wrung out the soft cloth, bathed again, and he made no sound. Finally, when the wounds were as clean as she could make them, she smeared on generous amounts of the healing ointment.

'What is that?' came his muffled voice; he had, she realized, buried his face in his sleeve to silence any cry that fought to escape him.

'A tried and trusted remedy which seals the flesh and minimizes scarring,' she replied.

'And it really works?' Despite everything, there was a touch of sardonic amusement in his tone.

'It does.' She rubbed in a little more, then, sitting back on her heels, sealed the pot. It was hard to see in the darkness, but she thought she had put a good coating of the cream on each cut. She was about to replace the pot in her satchel when his hand shot out and grasped her wrist.

'Will you leave it with me?' he asked softly.

'I will, yes.' She put it into his hand, and his fingers closed round it. 'You'll have to feel for where to rub it on, but I dare say that won't be difficult.'

'The pain is already much lessened,' he said, 'but that's not why I want it.' He hesitated. 'It smells of the outdoors,' he went on, a catch in his voice.

The brief comment all but broke her heart. She heard a gasp and felt a hand on her shoulder, and only then realized that her young apprentice had followed her down into the cell. Tiphaine glanced up at the girl, whose face was wrung with compassion. The wide, blue eyes were filled with tears. 'We can't leave him here,' the girl hissed in Tiphaine's ear. 'We *can't*! We've got to—'

'*Hush*,' Tiphaine commanded. Such horrified anguish would not help the poor prisoner.

Too late; he had heard. He turned round, looking first at the young nun and then at Tiphaine.

It was Tiphaine's turn to gasp. Remembering, grabbing hold of the girl, she said urgently, 'Is this him?'

The nun shook her head, bewildered. 'Is it who?'

Trying to hold on to her temper and speak calmly, Tiphaine tried again. 'You said that, six weeks back, you'd met a man in the vale who was seeking a priest because he was about to do a bad deed. You described him as a brown man. *Is this him?'*

Her eyes gazing down at the tall figure before her, Sister Estella, apprentice herbalist, said, 'No, it's not.'

For Tiphaine, the reply was both relief and anguish. Relief because the prisoner was not the man who had been looking for forgiveness for a sin he was going to commit; not the legendary Brown Man who was wanted for murder. The anguish because, all the same, he was lying helpless in the punishment cell, accused of killing three men and flogging another.

His presence there was affecting Tiphaine deeply, for she knew who he was.

Moreover, the thought of leaving him there was making her feel physically sick, for he was a man of the outdoors who had never lived within walls. And now he was penned inside this tiny space, cut off from the light, the sky, and the air, only to emerge again to walk to his hanging.

Not if I can help it, Tiphaine thought grimly.

She reached down and tightened the man's grip on the pot of ointment. 'Remember the smell of the forest,' she said softly. 'Do not despair.'

Then she got up, slung her satchel over her shoulder and, grabbing Sister Estella's hand, hurried out of the cell.

Tiphaine dismissed her apprentice, sending her off to make some more white horehound and lungwort cough mixture, a remedy she had recently learned. In fact there was plenty of the mixture on the shelves in the herbalist's hut; Tiphaine needed to be alone because she had a great deal to think about.

For the young man in the punishment cell to be hanged was out of the question. For one thing, he was not the Brown Man whom Josse and the others believed had committed the revenge crimes. Whether or not the prisoner had murdered anybody was not, as far as Tiphaine was concerned, relevant. Knowing who he was – more important, knowing *what* he was – she knew he could well have killed, although she also knew he would not have done so without a very good reason.

He could not die because he was a good man. He was loyal

and true, protecting those who could not protect themselves, looking out for people on the point of starvation or despair and doing what he could to help them. He was the respected, valued, beloved leader of a group of others like him, and if Lord Benedict were to bring about his death, the world would be a poorer place.

Tiphaine strode away from the abbey, heading for the deep forest. The beginnings of a plan were forming. She sent a silent prayer of gratitude to whichever divine being had put it into her head. It was a wild plan, depending on several things outside Tiphaine's control. The chances of it working without a hitch were slim.

It was, however, the best she could do.

She hitched up her robe, lengthened her stride and sent out a long, silent, continuous call to the person she urgently needed to find.

SIXTEEN

Jehan had insisted that they stay in their hiding place for the remainder of that day and all the following one. Or, rather, he insisted *she* stay hidden, while he repeatedly slipped out to see what was happening. When she complained, with increasing vociferousness, about her enforced captivity, finally losing her temper and yelling at him that she was leaving right that moment, and would get across the narrow seas and find her way to Chartres by herself, he had put his hands on her shoulders, stared intently into her eyes and said, 'Please, do no such thing. If they are who I fear them to be, the men outside want to kill me. They saw you with me, and so I am afraid that means you are in danger too.'

She was not sure why, but she had believed him.

Meggie had hoped that, at some moment during all that time, he might have found the opportunity to explain the comment he had made just before the attack came, or, indeed, to tell her why the men were so intent on harming him. She had hoped in vain; all she managed to extract from him was a solemn promise to reveal all she wanted to know once they were safely out of England.

She found she believed that, too.

Around dawn of the morning of the second day after their flight from the band of men, Jehan was at last prepared to continue on their way. The hiding place had been comfortable enough, but, all the same, it was a huge relief to leave it.

Meggie was still not quite sure how they had managed to escape. Auban's surprising turn of speed had been crucial, for he had succeeded in outdistancing their pursuers sufficiently to get out of sight of the four men. Then Jehan had taken what Meggie thought was a big risk: slowing the horse to a casual lope, he had ridden right into the heart of a small town that crouched in a narrow valley among the downs. The place was busy, with a row of stalls selling the tired-looking remnants of winter-stored vegetables. 'We'll be seen, and someone will tell the four men which way we've gone!' she cried.

'No they won't,' he had replied, as calmly as if they were out for a springtime stroll. Then, with a swift movement that almost unseated her, he turned Auban's head into a narrow alley between two buildings, following it to the far end, where there was a dilapidated barn. Quite sure that they must have been followed, that, any minute, a loud, challenging voice would demand to know what they thought they were doing, she turned to look back up the alley.

Nobody was following. People were milling about in the road beyond the end of the alley, all of them apparently too intent on the day's business to bother about much else. Jehan slipped off Auban's back and, shouldering aside the barn door, led the horse inside. There was a narrow stall, concealed behind a partition, and Jehan put Auban into it, tending the horse carefully and whispering words in a language Meggie didn't understand. At one point he turned to her, nodded to a bucket lying in a corner and asked if she would go and find water. She took it, went back up the alley again and, in a courtyard opening off the far end, found a well.

Once Auban was settled, Jehan set about preparing their own quarters, up in the hay loft above the stall. And there, safe, warm, adequately fed from Jehan's supplies – reasonably comfortable, in fact, other than the constant pique of her burning curiosity – Meggie had spent the next day and a half.

Now, it was so good to be moving again that she was prepared to be reasonable and wait a little longer for explanations. In any case, there was enough to think about without giving her attention to whatever story Jehan was going to tell her; for they still had to get out of the little town and down to the coast, where there might or might not be a boat that would take them across the water.

The town appeared to be still asleep, and they did not encounter a soul until, passing an outlying farm, they met a young woman leading a small herd of cows in for the early milking. Other than an uninterested nod in their direction, the milkmaid ignored them.

There was a stretch of woodland to the south of the little town, and they used its cover for many miles. When they emerged, halfway down a long, gentle shoulder of land, the sea lay sparkling below them. Narrowing her eyes against the bright sunlight, Meggie could make out a tiny harbour, surrounded by a few simple dwellings. Several small but sturdy fishing boats were tied up along a wooden jetty, as well as a couple of craft being loaded with cargo. Jehan smiled in satisfaction. 'That,' he said, 'is just the sort of place I was hoping to discover. Come; we will find out if one of those mariners will carry us over the sea.'

Still cautious, he made Meggie wait with Auban, hidden in a stand of pine trees, while he went on alone. He was not gone long, and when he returned he looked pleased. 'The boat at the far end of the quay can carry us and our horse,' he said. 'We sail with the tide.'

Not entirely sure what that meant, she nodded. He looked at her enquiringly. 'Come on, then!'

'We're going now?'

'*Oui*. On the tide, as I just said.'

Another lesson learned, she thought, studying the heaving sea that filled the little harbour and slapped up against the foot of the low cliffs.

The boat was sturdy but basic, with a space let into the deck for the storage of cargo – and, on this trip, a horse. It was fortunate, Meggie reflected, that it was a fine day, for there was not even a rudimentary cabin and no shelter up on deck. She and Jehan sat down aft, opposite the helmsman, and wrapped themselves in their cloaks and one of Jehan's blankets. They ate a little of their remaining food, and one of the sailors offered them a sip of some fiery spirit from his flask. It brought tears to the eyes, but, as Meggie discovered, it set a heat in the blood as if you were beside your own hearth.

In silence, Meggie and Jehan watched England receding behind them. No quartet of horsemen stood on the shore yelling and waving weapons at them. There was no place for any pursuer to hide on the small boat, and the sailors busy going about their duties were plainly exactly what they appeared to be. For the time being, Meggie and Jehan were safe.

'Now,' Meggie said, leaning closer to Jehan so that he would hear her quiet voice, 'I believe you owe me an explanation.'

He turned to smile down at her. '*Oui*,' he agreed. 'You have been very patient, Meggie, and you shall indeed have your reward.' He paused, eyes still on the shore – rapidly disappearing now as the wind picked up and the boat put on sail – and then he began to speak.

'I told you, I believe, that I am a Breton,' he began.

She nodded.

'I do not know if you in England know the story, but, seven years ago, our beloved Prince Arthur of Brittany disappeared. He was captured by his sworn enemy: his uncle John, king of England.'

Meggie, still recovering from the surprising starting point of Jehan's tale, thought she had heard something to that effect. 'King John believed Arthur would be the Lionheart's heir, didn't he?' she asked.

'So did everyone, including King John and Prince Arthur. Arthur would continue to be a threat to his uncle, even once the crown was on John's head, and so he killed him.'

Meggie stifled a gasp. Was it safe, to say such things out loud? Not that there was anyone to hear . . . 'The king himself killed his nephew?' she whispered.

'*Oui*. With his own bare hands. Then he had the corpse weighted with a heavy stone and thrown into the Seine, so that we who loved him could not even have a body to bury, or a grave to visit where we could pray for him and remember all that he had meant to us.'

She was surprised at the emotion that shook his voice. The Bretons must have really loved this prince of theirs, she reflected. She was not sure she understood – she could think of no one who displayed a similar devotion to King John, or had done so for his late brother – but then, perhaps Prince Arthur had been a particularly good leader of men. 'I am sorry that you lost him,' she murmured.

He bowed his head. 'Thank you.' Then, as if eager to change the subject, he went on: 'I began with this matter because I wish you to understand the hatred that exists in the heart of the Bretons for King John, for he is a man who committed a terrible crime and yet was not called to account for it. He will answer one day before the power that judges us all, but for many of us that is not soon enough, especially as we see King John continuing to flourish. We have – spies, I think is the right word, in Britain; men, and women, who watch, who wait, and who, when opportunity presents itself, come back over the water to inform us. These spies, these brave people, they know where to find groups such as mine, who, while keeping up the illusion that we are nothing but hard-working men who travel to wherever there are tasks suited to our skills, yet constantly wait for the word that we hope and pray will one day come. Back in the late autumn, one such spy came to us in Chartres and reported that the king was planning a spring advance into Wales.'

Meggie remembered Josse having referred to the same thing. Not that she had taken a lot of notice; the doings of the king were very far removed from the daily, small details of their own lives. Save, of course, that campaigns cost money, and each new one meant more tax demands. 'I heard tell of it,' she said.

'You did?' He sounded amazed. 'From whom?'

'My father.' Josse's beloved face swam before her eyes, and her heart gave a painful lurch. 'He keeps himself informed about such things.'

Jehan nodded thoughtfully. 'I see. So, to return to my tale, we now had information that the king would move against the Welsh prince Llewelyn, pulling together many of Llewelyn's enemies and making them his allies. For we who would see revenge taken against King John for the murder of Arthur, it was too good a chance to pass up. Accordingly, word was sent in secret to many clandestine organizations for men of like mind, and a company set sail for England's southern coast. From there, the plan was to separate into small groups and make our way to Wales, where we would offer our swords to Llewelyn, standing shoulder to shoulder with him as he prepared to take on the king.'

A plan which, Meggie reflected, must have somehow gone wrong. 'What happened to this company?'

He sighed. 'The majority of its members will, I hope and pray, even now be in Wales, preparing to defend that land against the king's advance.'

'Yet you are here, with me, sailing back to where you came from,' she pointed out.

He sighed again, then gave a soft, ironic laugh. 'I will tell you what happened to me,' he said. 'I sailed with one of the last groups to embark. We were few in number – no more than ten – but our hearts were high and we looked forward eagerly to catching up with our compatriots and setting off on the long march into Wales. But a storm sprang up, and a strong south-westerly wind blew us far off course. Our companions had sailed due north from Brittany, aiming to make landfall at Plymouth, and, since they would have reached England before the storm, I trust they arrived without mishap. We, conversely, were almost shipwrecked, and when finally we made port it was to find ourselves far to the east, on the further side of the great inlet behind the island that guards it.'

She was not sure what place he meant, but she caught the general drift of his tale. 'Go on,' she prompted.

'King John, it would appear,' he said, 'keeps a watch on the ports along his southern coast. Those who guarded, moreover, were on high alert; perhaps because reports had reached the king concerning the arrival of many groups of Breton fighting men making their way to Wales. Whatever the details – and I can only guess – there were men waiting for us when we arrived. Our group was attacked, and we broke up and fled for our lives.' He hesitated, his face grave. 'Two of my companions were killed. As for the others—' he shrugged – 'I do not know. I tried to find them, but without success.'

She tried to imagine what it had felt like, alone in a strange land with men out to kill him. 'Could you not have made your way to Wales and found the rest of your company?' she asked.

'I could,' he acknowledged, 'and, indeed, that is what I planned to do, once I had recovered.'

'Recovered?'

'I was injured during the storm. A piece of broken mast fell on my head, and I was—' He searched for the word. 'As if asleep? Unaware?'

'Unconscious,' she supplied.

'Unconscious, *oui*, thank you. I was unconscious for two days.'

He'd had concussion for two days, she thought. No wonder he'd needed to recover. And, in that state, newly back on his feet after such an injury, he had landed in England and instantly had to fight for his life. She leaned closer to him, feeling the strong thud of his steady heartbeat.

'I found a place to rest,' he was saying, 'in a miserable, dirty lodging house that stood close to a junction of two major routes, one traversing the land from west to east, one running north up from the coast. It was, in truth, the first place I found that offered accommodation, such as it was. There I paid a small fortune for a bed in a dirty room, where I took off my boots, wrapped my sword in my cloak and hid it under the thin mattress on my narrow bed, and slept for a day and a night.'

As he spoke, she noticed, his hand had gone down to the sword at his side, absently stroking it. The professional healer in her was thinking that, to sleep for so long, he must surely still have been suffering the after-effects of the concussion. That or he had simply been exhausted . . .

'When finally I woke,' he went on, 'it was dark, and by the silence I guessed it was the middle of the night. I lay trying to remember where I was and what I was doing there, and then, as memory came back, I realized something: my sword had gone. I leapt up, making myself so dizzy that I began to retch and would have vomited had there been anything in my belly. I went over every inch of that filthy, squalid room, and, although I found my cloak, flung in a corner, my sword had indeed disappeared.

'When I could stand without falling over, I left the room and searched the rest of the house. It was run by an old woman and her daughter, and, as I ran through the other rooms and the silence continued, I began to be very afraid for them. With good reason: the house had been wrecked, the few objects of the least value stolen and the remainder smashed to pieces. The old woman lay on the floor of her kitchen, and somebody had beaten her very severely. Her daughter crouched in a corner, mute with shock, for she had been raped.'

'What did you do?' Meggie whispered.

He raised his head and looked up into the blue sky, as if praying. Then he said, 'I tended them as much as they would allow, fetching blankets to cover them and setting a fire in the hearth, to warm them – for they were shivering with cold and shock – and also to heat water, for both had wounds that needed treating. However, in the state they were in they did not welcome the ministrations of a stranger, and a man at that, and so I did as the daughter asked and fetched a neighbour, who shoved me out of the way and told me she would take over.' He smiled faintly. 'As for me, I set off after the bastard who had stolen my sword.'

She had been listening, fascinated, to his tale, in thrall to his quiet voice speaking so close beside her. It was a moment before the obvious question occurred to her: 'How did you know which way the thief had gone?'

'The old woman must have been made of granite, for, despite the beating she had received, she had kept her wits about her and listened to the three thieves' talk. She said they came from the West Country – many travellers lodge with her, and she is familiar with regional accents – and one of them made reference to moving on eastwards. I told you, I think, that the lodging house was on a crossroads between roads going north–south and east–west?'

She nodded.

'It did not take much of a guess to decide they had gone east, and that's the way I went.'

'And you followed them all the way to Hawkenlye.'

'I did, yes, eventually. It became easy to pick up their trail, once I understood their habits, for they preyed on the weak. They picked lonely houses, isolated hamlets, dwellings inhabited only by women or old men, the sort of people less likely to fight back when three brigands broke down the door.'

He frowned. 'I grew to despise those men; to realize that they did not deserve life.'

'So you went to the little chapel in Hawkenlye Vale seeking a priest, because you knew you were about to commit a sin and you wanted absolution.'

He turned to her, surprised. 'You know about that?'

Again, she nodded.

'Then you will know, too, that no priest was to be found. I had forgotten that England lies under an interdict.'

They had reached a familiar point, she thought. It was her turn to pick up the narrative. 'Then – then you sought out the three men and, quickly and mercifully, you killed them with a stab straight into the heart. You carved a bind rune into the chest of the biggest man, telling anyone who cared to look that his death was in revenge for the terrible crimes he had done. You buried them out on the edge of the great forest, and there, a few weeks later, they were found and taken to Hawkenlye Abbey.'

He drew breath as if to speak, and she waited. He must have changed his mind.

'You remained in the area, living in my hut,' she went on, 'and, when eventually you and I met, you told me you were returning to Chartres, and I said I wanted to come with you because I have to find my brother.'

She thought back over the last three days, remembering how they had run from the four men who had suddenly appeared and chased them. Remembering how frightened she had been.

She thought she understood now why Jehan had insisted they took such care not to be found by the horsemen. 'You didn't think those four men were Lord Benedict's men, hunting for you, did you?' She did not give him time to reply. 'You thought they were the ones who attacked your group as you landed. They were, weren't they?'

He smiled grimly. 'Not the same men, no, I do not think so, for our landing was many miles further to the west. It is possible that they were looking out for men such as me, which I take as an encouraging sign, for it means, perhaps, that my countrymen are still finding their way across the water to unite with the king's enemies in Wales.' He glanced at her, a faint smile on his face. 'I believe now, though, Meggie, that possibly

I exaggerated the danger, and that the four men who chased us were no more than opportunist thieves.'

She nodded. It hardly seemed to matter now, anyway. She and Jehan were safe on the water, making good speed. Soon – early tomorrow, perhaps, if the wind did not change – they would arrive in some small port, and the last stage of the journey would begin.

She leaned against Jehan, glad of his warmth beside her under the cloaks and blanket. Tonight would be cold. She was just congratulating herself on how calmly she had revealed to him that she knew about the men he had killed when she was struck by a frightening thought.

He'd slain the three men whom he had known to be evil. He had followed the trail of their cruel, brutal crimes for many miles across southern England, and he was right not to show them any mercy.

But what of his other victims? What about the man he'd flogged, and the man who was found in the river, drowned? All right, they had only received what they had dished out, but how had Jehan known, he who was a stranger in the area? Had he deliberately gone out looking for violent men on whom to administer retributive justice?

Or did he just like beating and killing people?

Some tiny, involuntary movement must have given her away. Perhaps, as the sudden doubt was quickly replaced by fear, she had shrunk from him.

Then she remembered what he had said: *I am not the man you believe me to be.*

And, afraid to her very depths, she wondered what she was going to do.

SEVENTEEN

'They say he is the man responsible for the three men's deaths, and for Matthew's flogging and Rufus's killing,' Josse said. He and Helewise were sitting together in the cell by St Edmund's Chapel, and, for the time being, they were alone. Little Helewise was once more helping the nursing nuns in the Hawkenlye infirmary, and there had been no sign of Tiphaine for a couple of days.

Meggie had not returned.

Josse had told himself many times each day that his daughter could take care of herself; that seeing her companion arrested and taken away must have been very frightening, driving her to hurry away and hide somewhere that nobody could find her. Meggie knew the forest better than anyone other than its own people; she would have found somewhere safe by now.

Somewhere safe. Following the usual natural progression, his thoughts moved on to Ninian. Was *he* safe? Where was he?

Josse thought back to the brief and unsatisfactory meeting that he and Helewise had had with Gervase de Gifford. The sheriff had told them bluntly that the matter of the prisoner in the Hawkenlye punishment cell was out of his hands, Lord Benedict de Vitré having issued Gervase with a direct command not to interfere. It had hurt the sheriff's pride, Josse and Helewise had agreed afterwards, to make that admission.

Josse had found a moment to ask Gervase about the possibility of getting a secret message out to the Cathar community in the Languedoc; with an ironic lift of an eyebrow, Gervase replied that, while communications did occasionally reach him from the south – although none had done since winter – he had not the least idea how to initiate the passing of a message in the opposite direction. He added, sounding more than a little offended, that, had such a means of communication been available, didn't Josse think he'd have suggested it long ago, the moment Ninian's name had been cleared?

But it wasn't available. Josse and his missing family were on their own.

As he had also done many times each day, Josse forced himself now to think about something else.

Word had spread that Lord Benedict de Vitré had been informed of the prisoner in the punishment cell. It was rumoured that he was in no hurry to come and collect him. Lord Benedict, Josse thought, must have a cruel streak and was relishing the thought of a man being confined in a cell so small that he could not stretch out; so dark and airless that sometimes he must gasp for breath.

As if her thoughts echoed his own, Helewise said, 'I hate to think of him in that dreadful place. His guards have orders to make sure he stays alive, but I do not imagine they are providing anything but the most basic food and water.'

Josse doubted they were doing even that. Water, aye, probably they'd give him water, but it took several weeks for a man to die of hunger.

He looked at her. She was pale, thin, and had dark circles beneath her eyes. He guessed she had sacrificed rest and sleep in order to pray for the prisoner. Sensing him watching her, she raised her head and met his eyes. 'Do *you* think he is guilty?'

'They claim to have a witness who saw him running from the site of the Tonbridge man Rufus's death.'

Her scornful expression told him what she thought of that. 'We should ask ourselves what motive he has for the killings,' she persisted. 'Who is he? Why has he taken it upon himself to deal out vengeance on the victims of crime? That's supposed to be the sheriff's job,' she muttered, 'and, ultimately, God's.'

God, Josse reflected, didn't seem too bothered just then about taking revenge on the cruel and the heartless, the robbers, rapists and murderers. But he did not think he ought to say so. 'I don't believe anyone knows who he is,' he said. 'He's just the Brown Man, as Sister Estella would say.'

Helewise was looking thoughtful. As he studied her, her expression changed, and now she looked slightly abashed. 'I suppose—' she began, then stopped.

'What is it?' he asked.

She smiled ruefully. 'Oh, I'm probably just being silly, but I was just wondering . . . Josse, it *is* the Brown Man who's in the cell, isn't it? He was *dressed* in brown, after all – you and I saw his garments, even if not his head and his face – and we have all assumed he's the man who met Sister Estella in the vale when he was looking for a priest.'

'And we've all assumed also that the Brown Man is responsible for the beating and the deaths, because he was here in the area at the right times and was seeking forgiveness for a grave sin.' Josse was on his feet, grabbing Helewise by the hand. 'Come on.'

She knew without his having to explain what he intended to do. She pulled her hand away, shaking her head. 'You go,' she urged.

And he remembered that she still would not go within the abbey. Giving her an encouraging smile, he hurried out of the little cell and ran off down the slope to the abbey.

He knew he ought to have sought out Abbess Caliste first, but he could not wait. He did not know where the sister he must find usually worked, and so wasted time searching down in the vale and in the infirmary, where a harassed nun carrying a reeking bowl of bloody bandages told him curtly to go and look in the herbalist's hut.

Where, very shortly afterwards, he found her, calmly pouring a glutinous liquid into a small bottle.

'I'm sure it's not meant to be as thick as this,' she greeted him. 'I really need Tiphaine's help, but she seems to have disappeared.'

'Sister Estella,' he said, leaning against the worn wooden workbench and trying to get his breath back, 'I've come to ask you a favour, and I'm afraid it's something quite unpleasant, although I hope that won't prevent you agreeing.'

She put the bottle down carefully on the bench, then wiped her hands on her apron and turned to him, the big blue eyes serious. 'I will help if I can, Sir Josse,' she said. 'What is it you want me to do?'

'There's a man in the punishment cell,' he began, 'and he's been accused of—'

A look of relief spread across her round face. 'Sir Josse, if you're going to ask if I'll take some remedies and bathe his wounds, you can set your mind at rest because it's already been done.' She looked down. 'I must confess that it was not I who tended him, for I only went to help Tiphaine, and she did the work.' Meeting his eyes again, she added, 'We left him a special little pot of stuff that's very good at preventing scarring, so probably he'll mend well.' The beaming smile she gave him suggested he would be as delighted as she was at this good news.

She really was a very sweet girl, Josse thought.

He reached out and took hold of her hand. Trying to think

how best to phrase the question, he said, 'Did you catch sight of his face, Sister? He was hooded when I saw him, but I recall that the guards took the hood off, once he was in the punishment cell.'

She was nodding. 'Yes, they did. He was lying facing the wall when I went in to join Tiphaine, but then he turned and looked at us, and it was then I realized.'

She believes I already know, Josse thought.

Still careful not to betray his desperate impatience, he said, 'Realized what, Estella?'

'That he wasn't the man who I spoke to down in the vale. The one I told you and Abbess Caliste about, when you wanted to know if there had been any strangers about back in January,' she added helpfully.

He kept hold of her hand. 'Are you quite sure?' he asked urgently. 'It's dark in the punishment cell.'

But she was smiling, confidence radiating from her. 'I am absolutely certain,' she said. 'I told you, didn't I, about the Brown Man? How his skin was a beautiful colour, like glossy leather, and he had a beard and an earring and very dark eyes?'

'Aye,' he agreed, 'you did.'

'Well, the only *brown* thing about the prisoner in the cell is his robe, which, as you probably noticed, is an earthy sort of colour, and quite dirty, as if he's been sleeping outdoors. Oh, his hair's brown, too, but, as I told you, I never saw the Brown Man's hair because he wore a cloth wrapped round his head, but his beard was black, not brown. The man in the punishment cell's got very *pale* skin, nothing like the Brown Man's, and his eyes are blue.' There was a short silence. 'Actually, he's very handsome too,' Sister Estella said thoughtfully.

'I don't suppose,' Josse said, with more optimism than expectation, 'you know who he is?'

Her face fell. Josse guessed that, having thought she was being so helpful, it was disappointing not to be able to provide the answer to his question.

'I'm afraid not,' she said. 'Sorry, Sir Josse.'

Ninian was nearing the end of his journey. He was south-west of Paris, and now the roads were in better condition. The weather stayed fine, so he managed to keep up a consistent number of miles covered per day. Garnet was in good health – Ninian said a daily prayer of thanks each morning for that small miracle – and so was Ninian himself. To save the horse that had carried him faithfully over so many miles, often Ninian would dismount and walk for the last part of the day.

As he had travelled steadily north, he had been dismayed to find so many people going in the opposite direction. There were great companies of mounted knights, calling to one another in loud, braying voices about the exploits they were about to undertake, the fine lands in the south they were going to win. The heretic blood they were going to shed. There were also long lines of foot soldiers, slogging along with their heads down, determined expressions on their faces. They, too, were seeking the shedding of blood, and all in the Lord's name. Even the lowliest of them expected to receive the reward of the promised remission of sins and the hope of fewer days in purgatory that the priests said awaited all the faithful who answered the call and went on crusade.

Ninian feared for the friends he had left behind. On many occasions, he had felt the urge to turn round and go back. Each time a firm voice in his head had said *no*. As he neared Chartres, the forbidding voice had become more authoritative, and he was quite sure it was his mother's. Sometimes he even fancied a man's voice joined hers, and the fancy took him that it might be that of his illustrious father . . .

Not that it was in the least likely, since, as far as he knew, his parents had not so much as set eyes on each other after the Christmas that he had been conceived. Josse was Ninian's father; if not in the flesh and in the blood, then in the heart and the strong love between them. Nevertheless, Ninian could not prevent himself from wondering, just occasionally, about the man who had sired him. Would he have turned round and gone to help the bonshommes in their desperate fight?

No, came the voice in his head, *because that fight is unwinnable. Only a fool takes up arms in a struggle in which he has no hope of victory.*

Perhaps it *was* his father, after all.

*   *   *

Tiphaine had done all she could. Now there was nothing to do but wait; and, from the rumours flying around, she knew the wait would not be long.

She had slipped, unnoticed, back inside the abbey, and she was quietly working away in the little hut that had been her domain when she was Sister Tiphaine, the Hawkenlye herbalist. Abbess Caliste, bless her understanding heart, made no objection to Tiphaine's presence, and the other nuns all took their cue from the abbess. Tiphaine still worked as hard as she had ever done, and she knew that the many ointments and remedies she constantly turned out were much appreciated. As was her wealth of wisdom, acquired over a long lifetime, much of which she was now intent on passing on to young Estella. Now *she* was a promising healer if ever there was one.

The rumours were spreading right there within the abbey walls, and it was precisely to pick them up that Tiphaine had returned. She smiled grimly to herself as she worked, thinking about the guards that Lord Benedict's man, Tomas, had left to watch the prisoner. They obviously knew practically nothing about life within an abbey, and they had neither the intelligence nor the common sense to work out what it might be like. They appeared to think that women and men vowed to the service of God would be above gossiping like old wives round the well, and, in consequence, they didn't bother to lower their voices when they spoke of confidential matters. Such as what the rider who had raced through the abbey gates that afternoon, both he and his horse in a lather of sweat, had come to tell them. And the effect his news had had on arrangements for the prisoner.

Two lay brothers tending the blowing horse, and a nursing nun heading for the infirmary had overheard the muttered conversation. It was not long before virtually the whole abbey knew what the messenger had come to say. Lord Benedict de Vitré had apparently had enough of making his prisoner suffer inside the punishment cell and was coming in person to fetch him next morning. The messenger had added a directive from Tomas to his men: Lord Benedict had commanded that the prisoner be kept fed and watered, so the guards had better make sure he got something to eat and drink, and they'd better clean him up a bit before morning.

Now Tiphaine was praying as she worked, her lips moving soundlessly as she repeated the same incantation, over and over again. *It has to be tonight. Let it be tonight.*

The plans had been laid, and everything was ready. They had not appreciated the urgency when the finishing touches had been put in place, but Tiphaine did not think it made any difference. Once they saw that the idea had a good chance of working, nobody was going to delay it by even a day.

It *would* be tonight. Tiphaine was quite sure of it.

As the day drew to a close, Josse wondered if he ought to set off for the House in the Woods. He did not in the least want to, for he was as tired as he ever recalled being. He was lying stretched out on Meggie's bed in the cell by the chapel, boots off, soft pillow under his head, warmed by the glowing fire in the hearth. He and Helewise had been out all day, searching near and far through the forest once more, looking for any sign of Meggie, but they had found nothing. They had been forced to conclude that, wherever she was, she was far beyond their reach.

They had no answer for the question that had been burning through Josse since he had spoken to Sister Estella: if the unknown man in the punishment cell was the killer of the three brigands and Rufus, then with whom had Meggie had ridden away? If the prisoner wasn't the Brown Man, then perhaps that dark stranger really was Meggie's companion; but, if so, then why had he come to Hawkenlye, what was the sin he was preparing to commit when he had spoken to Sister Estella, and why – presumably having done whatever he was planning to do – had he hung around in the immediate vicinity for a further six weeks?

And, if the man in the punishment cell wasn't the Brown Man, who was he?

It was too much for one head to contain, Josse thought with a deep sigh. Helewise, hearing him, looked up from her sewing. She was sitting on her own cot, her face glowing from the warmth of the hearth, and the scene would have been one of cosy domesticity had it not been for the anxiety that ripped the air like summer lightning.

'Do you want to talk about it again?' Helewise asked.

He smiled at her. 'Not really,' he admitted. 'I can't think of anything new to add, and you and I have been over it all so many times that my head's spinning.'

'Mine too,' she said feelingly. She looked down at the neat darn she was making in the hem of one of Little Helewise's robes. 'At least I can keep my hands busy. It helps, believe me.'

'Perhaps I should take up sewing,' he said.

She had folded the garment and set it aside, and now she got up and went over to the corner where they stored their food. 'I'm going to start on the meal,' she announced, 'such as it is.'

He, too, got up. 'I'll do it,' he said. 'You get on with the darning.'

She smiled at him. 'Are you sure?'

'I hope you're not doubting my ability,' he said.

'Not in the least.' There was a twinkle in her eyes that suggested the contrary.

He set water on to boil, and then peeled a few very tired-looking carrots to add, with some handfuls of oats, once it was ready. There was a little of the stock saved from yesterday's pot, which would add some much-needed flavour, and half a mangy cabbage to shred into the mix. Little Helewise had promised to bring a loaf of bread back from the abbey when she returned. It was the most basic food, Josse reflected as he chopped and shredded, but probably better than most people would eat that night.

The pot was bubbling nicely when Little Helewise came in, her face flushed from the chill in the outside air. She flung the bread down beside Josse and, before he even had time to acknowledge it, said, 'Josse, I've remembered something!'

Helewise, picking up her agitation, had swiftly got up and was now standing beside her, an arm round her waist. The girl leaned against her, and Josse noticed in that instant that both faces wore the same expression and were suddenly very alike.

'Sit down,' Helewise commanded, gently but firmly pushing Little Helewise on to her bed. 'Get your breath back.'

Little Helewise was indeed out of breath, panting hard.

'It's the growing bump in the belly,' Helewise said over her shoulder to Josse. 'You can't seem to breathe as deeply as you want to.'

'Oh, I see,' Josse said.

Little Helewise, recovering, gave her grandmother a smile. Then, eyes on Josse, she said, 'I told you how I was awake when Meggie came to fetch her pack?'

He nodded, tense with anticipation.

'Well, she said she'd found a way to bring Ninian home. That's the bit that stuck in my mind, because suddenly I began to hope he might actually be with me again before – well, before the baby.' Her hands went to the bump under her gown. 'But just this evening I was talking to a woman in the infirmary, and she very much wanted to give thanks to God because she's recovered from a fever, and since she's got four children, all under six years old, it's really important that she's healthy, and she— Sorry, I'm digressing. Anyway, she was saying it was a shame nobody was allowed to go into the abbey church any more, and even the shrine in the vale was locked, and so I said she ought to slip away and come up to St Edmund's Chapel, because nobody seems to watch it and it's stayed open. I didn't tell her about the secret down in the crypt, but I did say there's a power in the chapel that particularly watches over mothers and children, and she said it was nice to think of a church being more about women and babies than men and their need for power, and *then* I remembered what else Meggie said!'

Her triumphant expression suggested she thought Josse and Helewise would understand without her telling them. With a frustrated frown at Josse, Helewise crouched by her granddaughter's side and said, 'You'll have to tell us, since we weren't there.'

'No, sorry, of course you weren't.' Little Helewise took a steadying breath. 'I'm pretty sure she – Meggie – thought I was more asleep that I was, because she was muttering quite a lot, and it didn't really make much sense. She said something about the goddess's resting place, and a summoning voice, and links in a chain, and she mentioned Ninian and her mother.' She glanced at Josse, a quick look with an unspoken apology in her eyes. 'She seemed to be driven, as if she'd heard a voice calling and suddenly everything made sense. As if—' she paused, searching for the right words – 'as if something that had greatly puzzled and worried her did so no longer, for the way was now clear.' She stopped, eyes going from Josse to Helewise and back again. 'Does it mean anything to you?' she asked, her gaze resting on Josse. When he didn't speak, she went on, 'Oh, I'm sorry if I've raised your hopes for nothing, but I—'

He reached out and took hold of her hand, clasping it firmly. 'Not for nothing, dear girl,' he said, a grin spreading over his face. 'And as for meaning anything, oh, aye, it does that, all right.'

He looked up at Helewise, whose expression suggested she understood the implications as well as he did. 'What do you think?' he asked her softly. 'Shall you and I ride off again, with a little more purpose this time?'

She didn't speak. She didn't need to, for he could see her answer in her shining eyes.

EIGHTEEN

Hawkenlye Abbey lay serene and quiet under a clear night sky. The springtime constellations stretched out above, stars shining brightly in the inky blackness. Here and there, soft lights burned still; in the infirmary, a nun sat beside a restless patient, and a candle still burned in Abbess Caliste's little room. There was so much work to do, and she was in the habit of staying up late to complete a few outstanding tasks at a time when there were no interruptions.

The four guards that Tomas had left to watch over the man in the punishment cell were bored. The days had seemed very long, for the prisoner was so secure in his tiny cell that there was no chance he might escape, and little point in trying. Occasionally, they had heard him banging on the door, and once or twice that unearthly howl had split the air.

All four of the guards loathed that howl. It made their flesh creep, and they feared it just as they had feared the prisoner's clear, deep-blue eyes. Tomas had told them to put that hood over his head; good old Tomas, always one to look after his men. The prisoner wasn't wearing his hood now, but they

could usually contrive not to look into his face on the few
occasions when they had to open the cell door to chuck food
or water inside. Not that they'd done much of that.

The guards were unsettled by the prisoner. There was
something about him . . . To a man, they would be heartily
relieved when this bugger of a duty was over and done with,
and the prisoner had been handed over to Lord Benedict. He
wouldn't live long, once that had happened. He'd soon be
dangling from the end of a rope, feet dancing in the jig of
death.

It was an image to cheer a man on a cold night of guard
duty.

One of the men stood up and went to urinate around the
corner of the high stone wall of the dormitory building. As he
stood there, his water steaming in the cold air, he looked up
at the place where the nuns lay sleeping. Some of the younger
ones were quite pretty. He grinned, imagining a plump young
novice suddenly turning up and offering to warm him with
her soft flesh . . . Reluctantly, he tucked himself away and
went back to join the others.

He settled down with them again, all four of them huddled
inside the partly-open door of the undercroft, and they were
beginning on the nightly ritual of arguing over who would do
the first watch when they heard soft footsteps.

The door was pushed further open, to reveal the abbess
standing on the step. She had an earthenware jug in one hand
and four stacked wooden cups in the other. Giving them a
faint smile, she stepped inside and closed the door.

They sat where they were, looking up at her in the light
from a lantern placed on the floor beside them. Not one of
them was aware that it was courteous for a man to stand up
in the presence of a woman, especially when that woman was
the abbess of a large foundation and, as such, worthy of
respect.

She held up the jug. 'It is a chilly night for being on guard,'
she said, keeping her voice low, 'and I have brought you a
warming draught.'

The nearest man scrambled to his feet and took the flask,
pulling out the stopper and sniffing at the contents. 'Smells
good,' he commented, giving the abbess a toothy grin.

'Drink it while it's hot,' advised the abbess. 'Here.' She handed him the cups, which he laid on the ground, filling each to the brim with the hot drink.

The four men slurped greedily at their cups. 'Mmm,' said another man appreciatively. 'What's in it?'

'Wine, honey to sweeten and herbs for flavour,' Abbess Caliste replied. 'It is a sovereign remedy prescribed by my nuns to keep out the cold and bring heart to those who are weary.'

The guards smacked their lips, grinning to each other. The drink was better than anything they'd tasted since they had been put to this tiresome duty, and they all took a refill. The abbess watched them, a faint smile on her lips.

The guards were coarse, ignorant men, chosen by Tomas not for their sophistication but for their strength and their brutish willingness to do anything he told them to, the crueller, the better. As a consequence, none had more than the sketchiest idea of how an abbey operated. They didn't care, for they took their cue from the men of power who ruled their lives, and they, in turn, took theirs from the king. King John had no respect for the religious foundations, viewing them simply as a rich vein of wealth to be tapped whenever he saw fit. The four men who now sat chuckling with each other, finding the same old lewd jokes suddenly amusing again, were merely a despicable by-product of the world which John had brought into being. Had they ever had the least curiosity as to what life in an abbey was like, and had they made the smallest attempt to satisfy that curiosity, they might well have found it odd that the abbess herself had brought out refreshments.

They steadily drank their way through the spiced wine until the jug was empty. So sweet, so spicy, it was hard to resist. Sweet, spicy . . . and drugged, with one of Tiphaine's more potent sleeping draughts.

The abbess watched as the four men fell asleep. It was quite amazing, she thought; although she had known what to expect, still the swiftness with which one man after another abruptly slumped down on to the floor took her by surprise. Hitching up her skirts, the abbess leaned down and grasped the shoulders of the first man, dragging him down a couple of shallow steps and inside a small room set into the wall beside the door. The second man was lighter, and she was able to move him more easily. Panting, she went back for the third – a heavy, thickset man – and had to resort to rolling him over and over in order to move him. His head bumped once or twice on the hard floor. The fourth man was almost more than she could manage, and it took her a long time to get him into the little room with his companions. When at last all four were laid out in a row, she checked to see that they were still breathing, removing the key on its iron ring from the belt of one of the men as she did so. She then hurried out, closing the door.

She picked up the lantern and, clutching the heavy key, went on down the passage to the punishment cell and turned the lock, then slid back the bolts, which moved more easily than she had expected. Then she hurried inside, almost falling down the steps in her haste. She put the lantern on the floor and stared down at him.

He was lying with his back to her, and she saw immediately that the wounds on his shoulders were already healing. She sent up a prayer of gratitude for Joanna and her ointment; and for Tiphaine, who'd had the good sense to bring it to where it was needed. She took hold of his upper arm, shaking him.

He turned towards her, a frown creasing his brow. Then he saw her face. His eyes widened in surprise, and he opened his mouth to speak.

'Hush,' she whispered, 'no time now for explanations. Can you walk?'

'I will walk,' he muttered.

She helped him to sit, then to stand. It broke her heart to see that he was unable to straighten up. For a tall, long-legged man like him, the punishment cell must have been a torment.

She stood, supporting his weight as he tried to get his balance. She could tell he was very weak; she cursed under her breath, calling down every horror she could think of on those who had treated him in this way. After a while, she felt the heavy pressure of his arm across her shoulders lessen; he was standing unsupported.

'Come on,' she murmured. She helped him up the steps and out of the cell, locking and bolting the door once more.

Then she led him back along the passage, pausing to put the key back beside the man who had been entrusted with it. Now they were at the door to the undercroft, the abbess and the man from the punishment cell, and they spared a moment to embrace, for the love between them was deep and enduring.

They hurried towards the gates, and she helped him shin up the wall. Propping herself on the top of it, she watched as he dropped down on the other side. He looked up at her. 'Aren't you coming? We should hurry.'

'Soon,' she replied. 'There is one more thing I must do.'

He nodded, understanding. 'Very well. But be careful.'

'I will.'

'I'll wait for you. You know where.'

'Yes. Keep out of sight!'

He grinned, teeth white in the soft moonlight. 'I usually do.' Then he turned away and began to run, and in a few moments had merged into the night landscape.

The abbess let herself fall back inside the abbey wall, brushing the dust off her habit. Then, hurrying light-footed over the hard ground, she went back to the little room at the end of the cloister and quietly let herself in.

Early the next morning, Josse and Helewise arrived at the House in the Woods. Josse had not slept much, and he doubted if she had, either. They had slipped out of the little cell by the chapel soon after dawn, leaving Little Helewise asleep. She knew where they were going, and why; apart from saying how much she wished she could be setting out with them, she was more than happy with their plans. The lay brothers still slept in their shelter by the cell; Little Helewise would be quite safe. One of the nuns from the abbey stables helped Josse and Helewise prepare their horses and wished them God's speed as she saw them off.

As predicted, Geoffroi was very angry at being left behind. 'It's not *fair!*' he cried, the eternal protest of the child, and Josse took some time to explain all the reasons why he couldn't go. To no avail, since the boy was still cross and upset when Helewise quietly came to stand beside Josse and announce that their provisions were packed and they were ready to go.

'Keep an eye on him,' Josse muttered to Gus. 'He'll probably try to follow us.'

'Don't worry, sir, Tilly, Will, Ella and me'll keep him out of mischief,' Gus replied. He reached out his hand and, in an unexpected gesture, clasped Josse's. 'Good luck, sir,' he added. 'We'll be praying for you.' He paused. '*All* of you.'

Josse opened his arms and embraced him. 'We'll be back as soon as we can manage it,' he said gruffly. Then – for this was proving more painful than he had expected – he grabbed Helewise's hand and hurried her out of the house, across the yard to where Will was waiting with the horses. They mounted, then put heels to the horses' sides and hastened away.

For a few moments, the House in the Woods rang to the echoes of goodbyes and the clatter of hooves on stone. Then the deep silence fell again.

Helewise was very relieved to see that Josse looked his old self. She had been worrying about him for weeks – months, really – and had been at a loss to know what to do to restore his usual optimistic good spirits. He'd been missing Ninian, of course, ever since the young man went away, and their failure to catch up with him and bring him back last autumn had hit Josse very hard. As had her own role in the matter; she hoped he might at long last have forgiven her. It was going to be a rough trip, she mused with a wry, private smile, if he hadn't.

Then, to add to poor Josse's woes, Meggie too had gone, and perhaps only Helewise understood in full how much pain her departure had caused him. *That's why he's himself again*, she thought now, riding hard to keep up with the pace he was setting as, away from the forest, the countryside opened up before them. *Because the waiting is over at last and he's actually able to* do *something*.

She was glad – more than glad; glad didn't begin to describe it – that he had asked her to go with him.

She had used the time of Josse's distraction to do a great deal of thinking. Several things had happened – one, in particular – and she did not view the world, and her place in it, in quite the same way any more.

She hoped very much that there was going to be a chance to tell him so.

The forest was a great bulge to the west and, eventually, the north of the road. They were going at a steady, sustainable pace, for there were many miles to go. Presently, there came the sound of fast-moving horses from behind.

Josse turned and met Helewise's eyes, realizing that she, too, was remembering the last time this had happened.

The horsemen came galloping round the bend and into view; not a big gang of roughs but just two men, Gervase de Gifford and one of his deputies. The deputy drew rein and Gervase came on alone, trotting up until his horse was close beside Alfred.

Leaning towards Josse, Gervase said, 'They told me at the house that you hadn't long left. I had to catch you, Josse. There's something I must tell you.'

Instantly, Josse feared that something had happened to the prisoner; that Lord Benedict had arrived in a surprise dawn visit, dragged the man out and hanged him.

But Gervase was shaking his head, smiling. 'It's not news from Hawkenlye that I bring,' he said softly, 'for, indeed, I did not stop to call in on my way up from Tonbridge.' He paused, his light-green eyes intent on Josse's. 'The news is from much further afield.'

And then Josse knew. 'He's safe? He's all right?' He felt his heart thumping in his chest like the feet of a galloping horse.

'He left the south several weeks back,' Gervase said, still in the same low voice, as if this were too secret a matter to be overheard even by Helewise or his own trusted deputy. 'I'm told he's making for Chartres.'

Josse could have sung. A huge bubble of joy seemed to swell up inside him, making it hard to breathe for a moment. Then, reaching out to grasp Gervase's hand, he said, the grin spreading right across his face, 'So are we.'

At Hawkenlye Abbey, the cry went up as the nuns were leaving the abbey church after tierce, which was the third office of the day. It was only then that the four guards, stumbling around after their long and exceptionally heavy sleep, had thought to go and check on the prisoner. Puzzled at finding themselves waking up in the small room by the undercroft door, they had wasted quite a lot of time wondering how they had got there and blaming each other for being too heavy-handed with the wine, of which they had a dim memory.

The guard who looked after the key had been fooled by its presence, on the floor beside his hand, into believing nothing was amiss. How could there be, he had thought vaguely, when he still had the key?

It might be incomprehensible, but the fact remained: the prisoner had gone. The four guards were all yelling at one another, their anger swiftly turning to fear as they realized the unpleasant truth: Tomas would be bringing Lord Benedict to the abbey later that morning, to collect a man who was no longer there.

A man whom they had been ordered to guard.

'It's that bloody abbess's fault,' one of the men cried, loud enough for several Hawkenlye nuns and monks to overhear and making them frown their disapproval. 'She shouldn't have brought us that spiced wine!'

Another of the men rounded on him – the leader, if anyone was. 'And that's going to be our excuse, I suppose? The abbess brought us something tasty to drink, out of the kindness of her heart, and we forgot all about being on guard and drank it down till we were all so pissed we fell asleep?'

'She probably put something in it to make us sleep,' muttered the first man. 'They know about potions and that, these nuns.'

The leader swore in frustration, grabbing his companion by the collar. There was a ripping sound. 'And Tomas is going to believe that, is he? He's going to take your word – the word of a man facing the very serious charge of falling asleep on duty and letting his prisoner escape – over an abbess swearing blind she only brought us some warmed wine because it was a cold night?'

'How *did* he get out?' a third guard said.

One of the others shuddered, making the sign against the evil eye. He muttered something.

'What's that?' the leader demanded.

'I said, he's got magic powers,' the man repeated, only slightly more loudly. 'It's them eyes, and that weird howling. Reckon he summoned the spirits, and *they* fetched him out.'

The leader gave a furious, disgusted snort. 'Try telling that to Lord Benedict!'

'I still reckon we was drugged,' said the man in the torn jerkin.

The leader rounded on him, clutching his wrist so hard that he winced. 'And *I* say I don't want to hear another word about that!' he hissed. 'We're in deep enough shit as it is without you going hurling accusations at the abbess. Who d'you think's going to believe you?'

'I'm only saying,' the man mumbled.

'Well, *don't* say.' He released him, and he stumbled and fell. The grumbling went on as the four men went back inside the undercroft.

Tiphaine had been approaching the undercroft entrance as the exchange began, and had stopped, out of sight of the guards, to listen. Now she continued on her unobtrusive way over to the abbess's room, smiling to herself.

So far, so good.

Abbess Caliste felt as if she were in a dream. The night just passed had been extraordinary. Her head buzzed with questions, although in her heart she understood, and already she was beginning to accept. Now she needed to decide how best to act and speak over the next crucial few hours.

She stood up and strode around her room. She felt strange, even now; as if she were still half asleep.

There was a quiet tap on the door. Caliste's heartbeat quickened; were they here already? Oh, and she had had no time to work out what she would say . . .

'Come in!' she said loudly, with a confidence she was far from feeling.

The door opened, and Tiphaine entered, shutting it quickly behind her. *I might have known*, Caliste thought with a wry smile. It was unlikely that Lord Benedict and his men would even bother to knock, and if they did, it would not be quietly and considerately.

Caliste sank into her chair. Opposite her, Tiphaine stood quite still, watching her. Caliste waited. After a long pause, Tiphaine began to speak. She went on for some time, and Caliste did not interrupt.

'How long had you known about him?' she asked when finally Tiphaine fell silent.

'I'd suspected what was going on for some time,' she replied. 'There's a group of them, but it was his idea and he's always been the leader. They look up to him. He's special, see.'

Caliste could readily understand what she meant.

'They've been trying to protect the households on the forest fringes from these bands of brigands that have been preying on the defenceless. Someone's got to,' she added vehemently. 'The forces of law and order don't seem prepared to do their job properly and look after the vulnerable, and, in addition, the lads from the forest take it as a personal insult when violence occurs on the fringes of their domain.'

'I know,' Caliste said softly. She wasn't sure that Tiphaine heard.

'They hoped that, by demonstrating what would happen to those who attack the weak and helpless and abuse their positions of power, it would discourage others from acting in the same way,' Tiphaine went on. 'He's been the inspiration, and he's a fine leader, partly because he has quite a lot of the old magic about him.' Her eyes darted quickly to Caliste's, as if she wanted to check that this mention of magic was acceptable to the abbess of Hawkenlye. 'He's fierce, and strong, and full of supernatural abilities – they say he can make himself invisible. Some folk even claim he's the Green Man come amongst us again.' Tiphaine gave a rather unconvincing laugh, as if to imply she had no time for such fanciful ideas.

Caliste smiled to herself.

'It's on account of that they all follow him, I reckon,' Tiphaine added. Again, she shot that swift glance at Caliste.

'Yes,' Caliste breathed. She understood.

'Will you be all right?' Tiphaine asked.

Caliste shrugged. 'I don't know.' It was the honest answer. 'They're blaming the wine.'

'How long will it be until he is safe?'

'He is safe now,' Tiphaine replied quickly. 'Already he'll be far away, deep in the forest. He's on his own territory now, and no man will find him unless he allows himself to be found.'

'Will he continue in these acts of revenge?'

There was a long silence. Eventually, Tiphaine said, 'What do *you* think?'

When Tiphaine had gone, Caliste sat gathering herself for what lay ahead. She got up, propped her door open and sat down again. She did not have long to wait, for presently she heard the sound of horses' hooves – a large group of mounted men, to judge by the volume – and, presently, loud, angry voices. Then there came heavy footsteps along the cloister outside, and a large, stout, red-faced man erupted into her room, followed by a second man close behind him; several others were pushing and shoving in the doorway.

The stout man came and leaned his hands on the table in front of Caliste, towering over her. 'I am Lord Benedict de Vitré,' he announced.

'I thought perhaps you were,' Caliste murmured.

A further suffusion of blood flooded the red face. Clearly, he had detected the faint irony. 'What the hell have you done with my prisoner?' he demanded, spittle from his loose, wet mouth spraying over the table.

Caliste drew back. 'I have done nothing with him, save permit my nuns to tend his wounds,' she replied coldly. 'And I will inform you right now, Lord Benedict, to save you the trouble of asking to use it again: the punishment cell is to be destroyed this afternoon.' She had only just made the decision, but this purple-faced bully wasn't to know. 'It will never again house anybody, be they clergy or layman. Is that clear?'

Her firm voice had an effect on Lord Benedict, for he stood up and took a pace away from the table. *It is true, then*, Caliste thought. *Stand up to a bully, and they step down.*

But Lord Benedict was not deterred for long. 'Do what you like with your damned cell,' he growled. 'Where's my prisoner? I've a rope waiting for him and a gaggle of peasants lined up to watch him hang. Those ignorant, insolent bastards need to find out what happens to men who take the law into their own hands.'

'I have no idea where your prisoner is,' Caliste said calmly and with almost perfect truth.

Lord Benedict was eyeing her with deep suspicion. 'You took wine out to the guards last night,' he said, an accusing finger pointing at her heart like a dagger. 'Funny thing for an abbess to do, wasn't it?'

She glared at him. Not prepared to dignify his second comment with a reply, she said, 'I was working late into the night and my cellarer had provided spiced wine for me. I did not want it, so I took it out to the men on my way to the dormitory. We do not approve of waste, here.' She let her eyes rest on his fat stomach. 'Nor of overindulgence; it is your men's own fault, Lord Benedict, if they act like gluttons.'

The man standing behind Lord Benedict stepped forward – Caliste recognized Tomas – and muttered something in his ear. Lord Benedict's anger blasted out of him and, turning to Tomas, he shouted, 'And what bloody good will that do? You can whip 'em all you like, Tomas, and I dare say they deserve it, but it won't bring my fucking prisoner back!'

Caliste stood up. She was secretly enjoying the scene, quite unfazed by the bad language, but it seemed better not to let on. 'Restrain yourself, my lord,' she said reprovingly. 'Such words are not permitted within these walls.'

He rounded on her, about to yell at her too, but she held his eyes with her own and, somewhat to her surprise, he subsided.

'That f— That prisoner got out of a locked, bolted cell,' he said with icy control. 'Any ideas how he did it, my lady abbess?' He laid heavy, sarcastic emphasis on her title.

'Absolutely none,' she replied. 'According to my nuns, your guards think he used his magical eyes and his uncanny animal howl to summon supernatural assistance, so maybe that was it.'

Lord Benedict appeared to comprehend that she was making fun of him, and he clearly did not like it at all. One hand clenched automatically into a fist, and for a worrying moment Caliste seriously thought he was about to hit her. Fortunately, he reconsidered.

She nodded, slowly, thoughtfully, as if something had silently been agreed between the two of them. Perhaps it had . . . Then she said softly, 'Hadn't you better get on with organizing your search parties and looking for him? He probably has quite a start on you already, my lord, and your chances of finding him must surely lessen with every moment you waste here.'

She thought she had gone too far. His face was maroon, his

forehead bulging with veins like small, blue worms. He was covered in sweat, and a nerve pulsed beneath his right eye. Perhaps his heart will give out, she thought. She was quite surprised at how little the possibility worried her.

It was the moment to seize the initiative; before he did. She said pleasantly, 'Now, Lord Benedict, I am, as I'm sure you can appreciate, a busy woman. If there is nothing else I can do for you . . .' She left the sentence unfinished.

There was a moment of stillness. Then the balance shifted as, turning abruptly on his heel, Lord Benedict stalked away.

She made herself wait until evening. It was perhaps the longest day of her life. Then, wrapping a dark cloak over the distinguishing black and white habit, she left her room, went quickly and quietly along in the shadows and slipped out through the abbey gates.

She went up the slope to the forest. She skirted round the glade beside the chapel, for she did not want to be seen. Once under cover of the trees, she began to breathe more easily and the tension of the day began to ease.

She knew where she had to go. It was many, many years since she had gone there, but she remembered.

She hoped there would be someone waiting for her in the distant glade. There was. She ran forward, and the slim figure dressed in grey took her in her arms.

The embrace lasted some time, for it was many years since last the two had met. Then Caliste broke away and, looking into her grandmother's face, said, 'I believe I know how it was done.'

And the Domina replied, 'Yes. I imagine you do.'

'It *was* her, wasn't it?'

The Domina smiled her strange, distant smile. 'You know it wasn't you, Caliste, and so that is the only explanation.'

Caliste allowed the Domina to lead her across the glade to a fallen tree, and they sat down side by side. 'Why did she do it? I understand that what he and his companions were doing is important, in many ways, but to take such risks!'

The Domina turned to her, her eyes intent as if she were searching inside Caliste's very soul. 'No, it is true, you do not know,' she murmured. 'In that case, I will tell you.'

There was a pause, and, when the Domina spoke again, her voice had taken on the timbre of the storyteller. 'Twenty years ago, a child was conceived who was destined to become a great man, born as he was from the very essence of his people. He was special, right from babyhood, for it became apparent that he had many unique gifts. As he grew through boyhood and became a man, his belief that he was in some way the protector of the forest, and of her people and those who live on her fringes, intensified. As conditions in the forest and the outside world became increasingly hard, and men in their desperation took to theft, to rape and to murder, he developed the idea of taking vengeance on the cruel and the brutal.'

'The avenger of those who cannot defend themselves,' Caliste said softly. She felt a fierce joy flood up through her entire body, that this brave man had risked his life – had very nearly lost it – to right a wrong that nobody else was going to.

'He killed the men who raped Melania and were responsible for her father's death and her mother's descent into madness,' the Domina continued. 'He left a bind rune on the dead flesh of the most brutish of the three.'

'Vengeance. Yes,' Caliste said. 'Meggie translated it.'

The Domina nodded. 'There were other acts of revenge: the flogger flogged; the man responsible for innocent lives lost by drowning left dead in the river. And then he was caught.' She paused, her face working.

'He could not be left in that terrible cell until they took him out to die,' the Domina went on. 'Tiphaine had recognized him, and it was her idea. She made the sleeping draught; it was very effective, apparently.' She turned to Caliste, an affectionate smile on her face. 'Were there any after-effects?'

'No.' Caliste was trying to work it out. She thought she had it all now. 'She must have waited until it was dark to come inside the abbey,' she said slowly, 'hoping I'd still be at work in my room.'

'She knew you were,' the Domina said. 'Tiphaine told her.'

Tiphaine again. Of course. 'She must also have known that it is my cellarer's habit to bring me spiced wine when I work late; of inferior quality recently, I'll admit, but welcome just the same.'

The Domina nodded.

'I remember falling asleep,' Caliste went on, 'or I *think* I do – I had very vivid dreams, and it's hard to distinguish what was real and what was a dream.'

'I imagine so,' remarked the Domina.

'Then, when I woke up, I was amazed to find myself still sitting in my chair,' Caliste went on. She shook her head wonderingly. 'She did it so well! I would never have guessed anything had happened, except I *know* it did, for how else did he escape?'

'She looks just like you,' the Domina said gently, 'which is no surprise, considering that you are twins. Once you were asleep, she removed your habit and put it on, leaving you wrapped up in her cloak. She filled up the jug of wine – Tiphaine had brought more – and took it across to the guards. When they too were asleep and hidden in the small room beside the undercroft door, she went along the passage and let the prisoner out. She saw him safely over the wall and away, then went back to dress you in your habit again and make sure you were comfortable.'

'She was right there beside me,' Caliste said wonderingly, 'and yet I did not know.' All at once it seemed so sad, such a lost opportunity, that she felt her eyes fill with tears.

Beside her, she sensed the Domina move; she raised her arm in a beckoning gesture. And Caliste saw her twin sister emerge from the trees and walk towards her.

That embrace was also long, and Caliste was aware of a deep, fierce joy as once again, after so many years, she held her sister in her arms. Then, breaking away, she stared into Selene's face.

'It was such a risk!' she said softly. 'What if one of the guards had woken up and caught you? You'd have hanged, too. Why would you take such a chance with your life?'

Selene smiled at her. 'Can't you guess?'

'*No!*'

'Think, Caliste! Think what happened, in this very place, twenty years ago.'

Caliste thought. Then she turned to the Domina, eyes wide, and back to Selene. '*Really?*' she whispered.

Selene was beaming now, pride and love shining in her eyes. 'His name is Coll, Caliste. He's my son.'

*　　*　　*

Caliste could have stayed all night there in the glade. It was the first time in years that she had been with her own close kin, and the experience was both bitter and sweet. Sweet, for she knew then how much they loved her; bitter, because soon she would have to leave them. Their lives still belonged to the forest. Hers was given elsewhere.

When she had bowed before her grandmother to receive her farewell blessing, she knew she must ask the question burning in her mind.

'Domina, is Coll safe now?' she asked, grasping her sister's hand and pulling her close. 'Tiphaine said he was, but I have to be sure.'

The Domina looked at her for a long moment. 'He is back where he belongs,' she said enigmatically.

'Yes, but is he *safe*, wherever he is?' She turned to her twin. 'And you, Selene – what about you? If the truth ever comes out – and, believe me, I pray it won't – is there any chance at all that Lord Benedict's men will find you or Coll?'

The old woman looked first at one twin, then the other. An expression of satisfaction spread over her lined face, as if what she saw pleased her; as if, in their very different ways, both granddaughters had fulfilled their promise. Then, her eyes returning to Caliste, she answered her impassioned question.

'No, Caliste,' she said with a smile. 'No chance whatsoever.'

NINETEEN

Meggie had withdrawn into herself. She could not overcome her anxieties, yet was unable to bring herself to the point where she could accuse Jehan Leferronier outright. Besides, what would be the accusation? How could she explain to him that, while she understood why he had killed the three brigands – he had seen plenty of evidence of their brutality, after all – she could not see why he had felt driven to deal out retributive justice to the Tonbridge deputy and the man who served Lord Benedict.

Did it really matter, she wondered, if he'd hung around the

Hawkenlye area with the sole aim of finding others to punish? All the victims deserved punishment, after all.

Nevertheless, she could not quieten the small voice in her head which said that justice was for the men of law to impose. Even when, in King John's England, the men of law so often failed.

She had managed to avoid further conversation with Jehan on board the boat by saying she was exhausted and needed to sleep. The exhaustion was real enough, but sleep hadn't come for a very long time. This morning they had made port early, and, after stopping at a stall on the quay to buy food and a very welcome hot drink, they had set off inland.

The cargo boat had docked at a small port near Dieppe. Their road now lay almost due south, and Chartres, according to Jehan, was about a hundred miles away. After Rouen, they would be following the route beside first the Seine and then the Eure. It sounded as if the journey would be a fairly easy one, on well-maintained roads over flat lands, and with plenty of other travellers about.

Meggie was reassured by thinking that she would not be alone with Jehan. She kept reminding herself that, no matter what her misgivings, the important thing to remember was that Jehan was taking her to where she hoped – believed – she would find Ninian. She could not get to Chartres without Jehan because, for one thing, she didn't know the way, and, for another, she didn't have a horse.

They travelled for much of the first day in silence, exchanging remarks only out of necessity, in order to decide when to stop to eat, or when one of them felt like getting down from Auban's comfortable back and stretching their legs. By the end of the second day, however, Meggie felt she couldn't keep quiet any longer. In the privacy of her thoughts, she had made up her mind that Jehan was anything and everything from a knight dressed in pure, gleaming white sent from heaven to right the wrongs of the world, to a heartless killer who sought out men to punish purely because it gave him a perverted pleasure.

The truth, she decided as the two of them set about making their camp for the night beside the loops and curls of the Seine, was probably somewhere in-between.

They were camped on an apron of land that projected into the water, surrounded on three sides by the river. The deep, constant sound of moving water was an ever-present background noise as Jehan cut and trimmed branches to make a shelter, and Meggie found hearthstones and got a small fire going. They had a luxurious supper to look forward to: a couple of small, fresh carp just out of the river, some root vegetables purchased at a market stall in Rouen, onions, garlic and herbs for flavour and, to accompany it, a bottle of white wine.

Meggie was so hungry that she gave her entire concentration to the meal, and only afterwards, when their platters were scraped clean and they were leaning back drinking the last of the wine, did she finally nerve herself to ask the questions that had been burning in her.

'Jehan,' she began.

He raised his head and looked at her. A wry smile twisted his mouth. He had removed the cloth that he habitually wrapped around his head, and his long, black hair hung to his chest. His hair was damp: before they ate, he had surprised her by disappearing to go and wash in the river. All over, from his head to his toes. In the firelight, he looked very exotic, with his dark skin and the gold earring glittering in his ear. He also looked very handsome.

But she wasn't going to let that distract her.

'You said you're not the man I believe you to be,' she plunged in, before she could change her mind. 'I think you should explain just what you meant.'

He made a very foreign-looking grimace: a sort of twisting down of the corners of his mouth, accompanied by a slight lift of the shoulders. 'It is – I am not sure where to begin, Meggie.'

'Just tell me the truth!'

'The truth,' he echoed softly. 'Ah, but therein lies my dilemma, for if I reveal to you my true purpose in following those three evil men to Hawkenlye, I fear that you will think the less of me.'

For a moment, her mind was full of the wonderful revelation that what she thought about him mattered to him. She forced herself to concentrate on what was really important. 'You went to kill them, and you put a mark on one of them to indicate that their deaths were done in revenge for their crimes.' He started to speak, but she went on talking. It was now or never. 'Then you found two other wicked men, both of whom had done violence against the innocent, and you punished them too. You—'

But he would not let her continue. 'Meggie, this is what you said before. You did not mention my other two supposed victims, but you did accuse me of killing the trio of brigands.'

'It's not exactly an accusation,' she protested. 'They deserved to die, and I do not think you committed any crime in executing them.'

Now the rueful smile was very evident. 'That, indeed, is the nub of it,' he said. 'I wished to continue to bathe in your approbation, for I have sensed all along that you would admire a man who would take the law into his own hands and coolly murder three such wicked men. But, Meggie, it is high time I confessed: I did not kill them.'

In that first moment, she did not know whether to be relieved or sorry. What she did know as she sat there in the firelight, staring intently into his black eyes, was that she believed him.

'I have disappointed you, I think,' he said quietly.

'No – I don't know,' she confessed.

'I imagine,' he went on, watching her steadily, 'that you are sorry I did not kill the three against whom I had a genuine grievance, yet glad that I am not the man to hunt down the guilty just for the sake of doing violence to them. *Oui*?'

'Yes,' she agreed.

'*Eh bien*, I am glad that you answered honestly. It is right that we should be honest with each other, right from the start.' His words, implying a future between them, sent a thrill through her. 'I must admit to you, Meggie, that, in more than one way, I have allowed you to think I am someone I am not. For your father is a knight and also, evidently, a fine man, and I believe that, loving him as you obviously do – oh, yes, I have seen your face when you have not known I was watching, and I see how it grieves you to think of him worrying about you, missing you. Loving him as you do, you would wish that I, too, should be a man of high birth and property.' He paused. 'You have ancestors who went on crusade, perhaps?'

'Yes,' she said. 'My father's father, Geoffroi d'Acquin, went on crusade with King Louis of France. Acquin is my father's birthplace,' she added, 'although it is his younger brothers who look after it now, since my father settled in England.'

Jehan was nodding. '*Oui*, I surmised that your father's name was of French origin. Well, Meggie, my grandfather went also on the Second Crusade, and his father before him went to Outremer on the First Crusade. But my forefathers were not knights.' He paused. 'They were blacksmiths.'

'You made my little sword!' she exclaimed, drawing it from its pouch at her belt, turning it so that the tiny garnet caught the light from the fire. 'It is doubly precious,' she whispered.

He started to speak, but some strong emotion made his voice break.

After what seemed a long pause, she said, 'Tell me all about yourself, Jehan Leferronier.'

And, once he had collected himself, he did.

'My family have always been blacksmiths, iron workers, and they lived in Brittany, in a place called Paimpont,' he began. 'Our legends go right back into the time of myths, and it is said that one of my forefathers made the magic cauldron for the great sorcerer who once lived in the heart of the Breton forest.'

Meggie stifled a gasp. She knew about that forest; when she was a small child, she had even been there . . .

'My father's grandfather was called Trudo le Ferronier,' Jehan was saying, 'and his *seigneur* was Raoul de Gaël, lord of a large area of the Brocéliande forest, a man who had gone on campaign to England in 1066 with William the Conqueror. Raoul answered the call when the First Crusade was preached, and he took with him to Outremer his faithful blacksmith, for a man who is going to fight has need of someone skilled in metalwork. Raoul had every reason to be grateful to Trudo le Ferronier, for Trudo had refined his skill as a swordsmith, and it was said that his weapons were as good as the great swords made in Spain.'

'Toledo steel,' Meggie muttered.

'How did you know that?' he asked.

She shrugged. 'Probably from my father.'

'In Outremer, Trudo worked alongside a smith from that very city, Toledo, and he learned much of the Spaniard's technique. The process was a closely-guarded secret, but somehow my forefather learned it. It is a question of forging together hard and soft steel,' Jehan went on eagerly, the light of the true craftsman shining in his eyes, 'at a very high temperature, with very precise timing; for if the steel is kept in the heat for too long it will melt, and if for not long enough, the metal will not even reach melting temperature.' He grinned. 'Most swordsmiths recite a particular psalm or prayer, to the same steady rhythm, in order to get the timing exact.'

'But Trudo returned from Outremer?' she prompted. She sensed that Jehan could talk about sword-making all night.

'He did, for Raoul de Gaël died, in 1109, and, with his lord's death, Trudo had no longer a purpose so far away from his home. He came back to his wife and his three children, and five more children were born to them, the last of whom was named Péran, and he was my grandfather.'

'The man who married a woman of Ethiopia,' she put in.

He smiled, clearly gratified that she had remembered. '*Oui, c'est vrai*. Péran went on the Second Crusade, as I said, following his father's example, and whilst there he met a tall, elegant and very beautiful woman of the south whose name was Taya. He wooed her and wed her, and, in time, brought her home to Paimpont, and always he loved and cherished her, for she had given up her hopes of ever returning to her own birthplace and gone willingly with him to his.' He paused, his gaze on something out beyond the fire. 'They had but the one child, my father, Chrétien Leferronier, and he wed my mother, Onenne de Gué, and they, too, had one son.'

'Who is a blacksmith like his ancestors, and who left his forest home to work in the cathedral at Chartres, making beautiful things, where he was distracted by a call to arms from his fellow Bretons because they had seen a chance to get even with King John for murdering their beloved Prince Arthur,' she said in a rush.

'Shhhhh!' he hissed. 'Not so loud!' Then, grinning, he said, 'There you have my life, Meggie. You know what I am and what I am not, and I have told you the truth.'

'I know,' she said calmly. It was time, she thought, to tell him something about her own strange heritage and mysterious gifts. Tomorrow, she promised herself.

He was frowning. 'There is one more thing,' he said. His hand was on the sword that lay in its scabbard on the ground beside him. As she watched, he drew it out.

Despite its sinister purpose, it was an object of great beauty. It was, she realized as she studied it closely, the model for her own miniature weapon. Its hilt terminated in a garnet set in heavy silver, and the crosspieces bore intricate, swirling designs, the very shapes of which seemed to exude mysterious meaning. The long, savage blade was decorated with more curling patterns, and its keen edge shone almost blue in the firelight.

'Did your great-grandfather make it?' she whispered, awestruck by the sheer power of the object before her.

Jehan shook his head. 'No. Skilled as Trudo was, this is an example from an older age, when men put something of their souls into the objects they made.' He ran his hand up and down the flat of the blade, the movement a caress. 'This weapon was presented to Raoul de Gaël on the field of battle, given to him by an elderly knight of ancient and pure lineage, for Raoul had saved his life. The knight was old and had no son to leave his treasure to, and he wanted a fitting gift for his saviour. Raoul, however, did not live long to enjoy his reward, and when he was dying, he summoned the one man who he knew would appreciate its beauty and its power.'

'Trudo le Ferronier,' Meggie murmured.

'*Oui*. Trudo passed it down to his son Péran; Péran gave it to my father Chrétien; my father handed it down to me. And when that thief stole it from beneath my sleeping body in the rooming house, I had no choice but to follow him until I got it back.'

Meggie was thinking hard, trying to remember what Josse had told her about the three dead bodies at Hawkenlye. 'But the sword was buried with the victims!' she said. 'It must have been, because my father saw it on the body of the biggest man, once he and the others had been unearthed and brought to the abbey. They all realized he'd stolen it,' she added. 'My father said it was far too grand an object for a man like that.'

'It is as I thought,' Jehan said with a grim frown. 'When I

came to Hawkenlye, I searched everywhere for the three men, but they had vanished. I guessed perhaps someone else had done what I'd planned to do, and put paid to them and their wickedness for ever.'

'So you *did* intend to kill them!'

'*Oui*, Meggie, I did. But intention is easy.'

'You couldn't kill them if they were already dead,' she pointed out.

'No, indeed not.' He looked as if he were trying not to smile. 'So, I searched and searched, and then I heard that three dead men had been uncovered in their shallow grave and taken to the abbey on the edge of the forest. I watched and I waited, and I took my chance. Shortly before they were taken out and buried, I climbed over the abbey wall, got the better of a lock and made my careful and furtive way to where they lay on their trestles, and took back what was mine.'

'And nobody noticed the stolen sword was gone,' she said softly.

He had put his sword back in its sheath. It was probably her imagination, but Meggie thought the light wasn't quite so bright any more.

Josse and Helewise had made good time, reaching the coast without incident and quickly arranging their passage over the narrow seas in a large trading ship. The ship sailed in the late afternoon, and the captain said they'd reach the far shore round about dawn. He was right; Josse and Helewise were mounting up on the quayside as the first light of the sun brightened the eastern sky.

The boat had docked at Boulogne, and it was a leisurely day's ride from there to Acquin. Josse's heart rose at the thought of returning to his family home again so soon, and, indeed, his kinsmen and women seemed equally delighted to see him, welcoming Helewise with the courteous affection they had bestowed on her back in the autumn. The womenfolk and the servants produced a splendid meal, considering it was at very short notice, and Josse's brother Yves broached a new barrel of wine.

Josse felt quite guilty when he explained to Yves and his calm-faced wife, Marie, that they were only staying one night and would leave very early in the morning. 'We must get to Chartres as soon as we can,' he added, very much wanting his brother to understand. 'We now have two independent sources who have told us that's where Ninian's going, and where Meggie has gone to look for him, and so we really must—'

Marie put out her hands and took his between them. She smiled at him, hushing the rest of his sentence. 'Of course you must, dear Josse,' she said. She glanced at Yves, in her eyes the look of a wife who has known, loved and understood her husband for years. 'If it was one of ours, Yves would probably have to be tied down to stop him setting out right now.'

'Oh!' Josse exclaimed. 'Maybe we should—'

'*No*,' Marie and Helewise said together, exchanging a smile as they did so.

'One night will make no difference,' Helewise added, 'and we had a *very* early start this morning.'

'Come back to us when you have found them,' Yves said. 'We will prepare a party for you all – the biggest celebration this old house has ever seen!'

'We will try to send word,' Helewise said. She shot a look at Josse. 'It's not easy,' she whispered to him, 'preparing a feast – it's nice to have a little warning!'

Josse said a silent prayer. All this talk of feasts and celebrations was, he thought, tempting fate.

Later, as Marie showed Helewise to her sleeping quarters, Helewise confided in her the reason for their urgent need to take Ninian home. Marie nodded understandingly. 'And your granddaughter will deliver her child when?'

'In July,' Helewise replied. 'Of course, they won't be able to marry, even assuming we find Ninian and he comes home, for the interdict still prevents it. But at least there's now a chance that he will be there for the birth.'

'Yes,' Marie said. *The interdict*, she was thinking. *Yes, the interdict . . .*

At long last, Ninian was approaching Chartres. He was tired, Garnet was even more tired, and both of them were dusty, sweat-stained and stinking. Before he entered the city, Ninian

made up his mind to get both his horse and himself as clean
as he could. It was, he thought as he rode through the open
countryside south of the town looking for somewhere suitable,
rather like the ritual cleansing of a man about to be knighted,
where you stripped, washed, donned clean clothing and spent
the night alone in a prayer vigil.

He found what he sought: a spot where a hurrying stream
ran in a shallow valley between stands of willows. It was a
good distance from the road and, down in the water, he would
be out of sight of anyone passing by. He rode down on to the
narrow stretch of sandy bank, slipped off Garnet's back,
unfastened his baggage and removed the horse's saddle and
bridle. He would clean those first, he decided, while he was
still in his filthy clothes.

Garnet had already taken off for the new spring grass and
was on his back, feet in the air, rolling with such abandon that
Ninian thought he'd never stop.

Some time later, washed, dressed in the cleanest of his
garments and mounted on a well-groomed horse whose tack
gleamed as brightly as his rider's boots, Ninian rode into
Chartres. He knew he must find somewhere to lodge – which,
although not impossible, would not be easy, as he had very
little money – but that was of secondary importance.

He found an inn where decent stabling was on offer, leaving
Garnet in the care of a bright-looking young lad. Then he
headed out up the street, across the square and into the
cathedral.

It was very strange to be back. A decade ago, when he and
Josse had been there, the new building had been in skeletal
form, its walls and arches just beginning their soaring flight
up towards the heavens. Now the structure was complete, and
craftsmen were busy working on decorative stone and
metalwork, and putting in magnificent stained-glass windows.

For some time Ninian just stood and stared. He had never
seen anything as beautiful as the evening sun through the
coloured glass of Chartres.

In time, he went where he knew he would: down into the
crypt. To his surprise – for he knew very well where the Black
Goddess figure intended for this place was now hidden – there
was another Madonna statue in the niche that had been

specially built. He stood staring up at her. She too was carved from black wood, and she too was clearly divine, but there the resemblance ended. The Black Goddess at Hawkenlye was the Mother depicted before she gave birth, her belly swelling in a great curve. This statue represented the archetypal mother and child, the infant cradled in her arms and looking up adoringly into her loving face.

'Beautiful, isn't she?' whispered a voice at his side. Looking down, he saw an ancient, tiny woman, eyes bright in the creased old face.

'She is,' he whispered back.

The old woman looked around to check they were alone. Then, leaning closer and enveloping Ninian in garlicky breath, she added, 'Course, she's not the one we was meant to have.'

His heart gave a lurch. 'Really?' he managed to say.

She shook her head. 'No.' Her eyes went misty. '*That* one, she were a small, black, immemorial image.' She paused, apparently lost in rapture. 'Or so they say,' she added, returning to herself. 'This 'ere one's a substitute,' she hissed, laying a bent old finger to the side of her nose. 'Lovely, all the same.' Then, as if fearing she had said too much, she gave him a nod and scuttled away.

He stood alone in the crypt, the Madonna and child before him. The sounds of the industrious workmen high above him faded away as his mind turned inwards and, in a moment like an epiphany, he thought he understood.

There was a greater purpose to everything that had happened, right back to the time when his mother had vanished from this very spot. Somehow she linked everything together. His mother, Joanna. There was a sudden, painful ache of longing for her in his heart, and he put his hands to his breast as if to soothe it.

She had brought him here; acting in some unfathomable way, she had put in his mind the chain that linked together the Black Goddess figures, all the way from the Languedoc to Chartres. And – his eyes were suddenly wide open as further comprehension dawned – the bonshommes were wound up in it all.

The bonshommes, yes, of course, with their worship of the female principle. One hand moved from his heart to where he carried the set of images, wrapped in their silk cloth. 'I will do as you ask,' he said softly out loud, addressing he knew not who. 'I will undertake the task entrusted to me and somehow make sure that the bedrock of your beliefs, hidden deep in these images, will never be lost.'

Then he fell on his knees, closed his eyes and gave himself up to the power of the spirit he could feel humming and beating all around him.

TWENTY

Josse and Helewise were within a few hours of their destination. If the weather remained fine, and if the steadily increasing amount of traffic on the roads and tracks did not delay them too much, then, Josse had announced, they should reach Chartres by nightfall. Helewise breathed a quiet sigh of relief. Although it was only early in the season, already spring seemed to be well into its stride here, and the sun had been beating down on them for most of the last few days. She was hot, travel-stained and weary, and she longed for the relief of getting down from her horse and not facing the imminent prospect of getting back on again.

The good weather appeared to have brought everyone out of their homes, Helewise reflected as she rode along behind Josse. Well, that was understandable; after a long, hard winter, during which you only left the shelter of your own four walls when you had to, and when the days were so short that you got up and went to bed in profound darkness, it was only natural to want to feel the blessed sun on your face again. Everywhere she looked she saw people busy in the villages and fields, tending their animals and their land, mending walls and roofs damaged by winter rain and snow, making sure gates, fences and hedges would be strong enough to contain cattle and sheep turned out on the fresh, new grass. And it seemed that any man, woman or child with time to spare had saddled up and was making for Chartres.

That, too, was no wonder, Helewise thought. Word of the

magnificent new cathedral nearing completion south-west of
Paris had spread to England, so it was hardly surprising that
the people of northern France all knew about the marvel in
their midst and were anxious to see for themselves. Josse had
told her about the fire that had burned down the previous
structure, back in 1194, and how the people, believing this to
have been a sign from the Holy Mother that she wanted a
more magnificent church to house her precious relic, had set
to in their hundreds and thousands to obey her. Men and
women had dragged carts laden with stone from nearby
quarries, the bishop and the cathedral chapter had given up
part of their income, and the king himself had funded
the construction of the grand North Porch. With such a noble
example to follow, other members of the nobility had rushed
to contribute, as had men of lesser rank; it was said that the
merchants of Chartres were donating magnificent stained-glass
windows for the new cathedral, each representing the craft of
the brotherhood that had donated it.

Helewise thought about the precious relic. The Sancta
Camisia was reputed to be the shift that the Virgin Mary had
worn when she gave birth to her holy son. It had apparently
been presented to the great Charlemagne by no less a person
than the Byzantine Empress Irene, although history was less
clear on how the garment had come to be in her hands.
According to some, the Virgin had worn the shift on
the occasion of the Annunciation, not the birth, although
Helewise did not see that one necessarily excluded the other.
Mary had been poor, hadn't she? The visit from the angel,
and the spark put into her womb that had become the Blessed
Saviour, were only nine months apart, so she could easily have
worn the shift on both momentous occasions. Assuming it was
adequately voluminous, her practical mind added.

She turned the story over in her mind. A part of her felt
that she should believe it unquestioningly, and she had an
uneasy feeling that once she would have done just that. Now,
though, now that she had deliberately removed herself from
a place where you were encouraged to think and do exactly
as you were told without protest or demur, it was different.
And a quiet but insistent voice in Helewise's head was asking
if it was really very likely that a fragile, well-used and probably

cheap piece of cloth could truly have survived a thousand years and a journey of several thousand miles, not to mention being turned over, examined and exclaimed over by all the hundreds of people who had handled it.

It could have survived if God had ordered it, she told herself firmly. In which case, the shift was truly miraculous, and people were right to revere it and credit it with magical healing powers. But she found she no longer automatically believed in such miracles. Human hands healed people: hands worked by minds inspired to use the right herbs and administer the correct sort of touch. Yes, it was undoubtedly God who provided the inspiration – hadn't Helewise, when she was abbess, heard so many of her hard-working nursing nuns say that they were but God's instruments, carrying out his work? – but it surely made sense to put your faith in a healer and not in an old piece of cloth . . .

Moreover, were there not more important things for God to do than to ensure the preservation of one small garment? Would not a loving God of power who cared for his creation be more likely to preserve one small life?

Her mind drifted on. Perhaps the true miracle was not the Sancta Camisia itself, but the impetus it had provided. Without it, the great edifice to the Holy Mother might not have been built and rebuilt over the centuries.

Virgin Mary. Holy Mother. Suddenly, Helewise seemed to see the Hawkenlye Black Madonna floating before her eyes, face serene and inscrutable, belly swelling with the growing child inside her.

Virgin, mother, goddess. Were they one and the same? Were the different manifestations simply mankind's attempt to render in wood or stone some great fundamental truth that he barely understood? A *female* truth. Oh, if that were so, then what of the man-made, man-ruled, man-dominant church that had risen up, flourished and now ruled the world?

Helewise rode on, her thoughts profound and troubling. Josse was now some way ahead, and she was separated from him by a cart and a family group consisting of five on horseback and four walking, one pushing a small barrow. Spared from the need, then, to explain her absorbed silence, she allowed her mind to lead where it would.

She had been nursing a secret. She had learned a lesson about herself; a realization that had come to her in the days that she had been back in the little cell by St Edmund's Chapel. She had told Josse that her motive in returning there had been because she felt she must be useful, and she had truly believed that good deeds could only be done within a religious environment; that the very fact of living and working in a place that was a part of a great abbey somehow imbued her efforts with an extra power.

But then that young woman had come begging for help. She had come to Helewise and, forcing down her shame and her horror at speaking of what had been done to her, had asked Helewise to help her get rid of the rapist's child that had taken seed in her. *And I, oh, I thought only of what I had been taught*, Helewise thought, anguished. *I thought in the black and white manner of the men of the church, and I turned her away.*

Where was compassion then? she wondered. Where was the natural understanding that one woman should have had for another, facing as she did the awful prospect of a lifelong reminder of the terrible night that robbed her of her maidenhood and implanted in her the child of a man who had done her and her family such harm?

I should have thought for myself, she told herself. Not sure even now if she could have made and administered with her own hands the concoction that had aborted the foetus, she realized what she ought to have done. She should have told the poor young woman she could not give the help she most wanted, but then have offered another sort of help: to care for and support her through the pregnancy, make sure she had assistance at the birth, and then quietly take the child to the abbey orphanage. Sooner or later, a home would have been found for it; there were always barren couples wishing to adopt, and probably there always would be.

Because of what I did, Helewise thought gravely, *a human being has been robbed of the chance to live.*

I will not allow such a thing to happen again.

The secret that she was hugging to herself – and that she longed to share with Josse, were he to be a little more approachable – was the hard-won realization that she was not, and no longer wished to be, any part of the church as it now was. Her love for the beloved Saviour was as strong as ever, and she knew, without even thinking about it, that it was a devotion that would last until she took her dying breath. But her time back in the little cell by the chapel had made her understand that good deeds could be done even if you didn't belong to an abbey and wear a habit. Many of those who had sought out her help had no idea she had once been a nun; once been an abbess. By those who came in need, she had been taken as what she now was: an ordinary woman offering a little food, a little precious time to listen to worries and anxieties, a hand to hold, and advice when and if it was asked for.

She had prayed in the chapel, and she had spent wakeful hours at night in contemplation. Something seemed to have happened to her, and at last she knew what it was. Perhaps she had needed to be back in the vicinity of Hawkenlye Abbey to understand at last that she no longer belonged there. The time spent with Meggie and Little Helewise – yes, and with Tiphaine – in the cell by the chapel had shown her that there was another way. She might no longer be a Hawkenlye nun, but there was still a vital, important role for her among those who helped the needy and the desperate. That role could be carried out anywhere, and if she moved back to the House in the Woods it would not be long before word spread and those in need found her there; not only her, for there were others who lived there with far more to offer in the way of practical help.

And, as a free woman who answered no longer to the church but only to God and her own conscience, she could do as she pleased and take her own decisions. One, in particular: she raised her head and searched the crowded road ahead.

Yes. Josse.

Images and memories of him rushed into her mind and heart, almost as if they had been waiting for her to complete her long and complicated meditation and, now that she had, were too impatient to hold back any longer. With them came a fresh understanding of what life must have been like for him since she left the abbey and went to the House in the Woods.

I am sorry, Josse, she said silently to his broad back. *I came to your house too soon, and I made you suffer because, not knowing what I wanted, I forced you to question everything you thought was solid and unchanging.*

She knew she loved him; she always had done. She was almost certain he reciprocated that love. Surely, no man would endure what he had from a woman unless he loved her.

She would have to find out. After what she had put him through, it was only right for her to declare herself first, hoping and trusting that he'd respond in the way she prayed he would.

As, at long last, the cry came up from those far ahead that Chartres was in sight, Helewise felt her insides flutter with nerves.

Have courage, she told herself. Then, straightening her shoulders, she stood up in the stirrups for her first glimpse of the town.

Meggie first sensed danger as she and Jehan reached the outer perimeter of Chartres. She thought at first that the growing sense of unease was because the streets were heaving with people, animals, carts and barrows, and she was not used to such a crush. She and Jehan had been forced to dismount, and Jehan was now leading Auban. Admittedly, the roads had become steadily more congested as they'd approached the town – the sunshine had brought out the crowds, and everyone seemed bent on having a look at how the cathedral was progressing – but Meggie didn't think she'd ever before encountered so many people crammed together in such a small area.

Her dismay grew. She was sure there were eyes watching them, and not with any kindly intent. Jehan had headed into the workmen's section of the town, where artisans in the various crafts associated with cathedral building congregated. The streets were narrow and, because of the houses and hovels rising up on either side, relatively dark, especially in contrast with the sunshine outside. Many of the structures were open-fronted workshops, and glaziers, masons and carpenters could be seen hard at work. In a smithy, a great furnace suddenly blazed up as the blacksmith, stripped to the waist with a leather apron protecting his bare, sweating chest, worked furiously at the bellows.

Passageways led off the main tracks, small windows overlooked the street, and the road itself twisted and turned.

There were, Meggie realized, dozens of places where someone could hide and watch, unobserved, the comings and goings.

The warning was now sounding loud in her head. She hurried to catch up with Jehan and, grabbing hold of his sleeve, spoke urgently to him. 'Someone's watching us,' she said quietly.

'I know,' he whispered. Then, giving her a quick smile, he added, 'Don't worry, we'll soon be safely under cover. If I can remember the right way . . .' He stared around him, frowning. Then, his expression clearing, he pointed. 'Up there. The iron-workers' lodgings are at the end of that street.'

He set off again, and she hurried to follow, wanting to keep close. She had not appreciated that the different crafts had their own areas, but it made good sense. In her own craft, people enjoyed the chance to get together and compare their ideas and experiments, and it was no surprise to discover that other métiers did the same.

Jehan stopped outside a low door leading into a one-roomed dwelling, with a beaten earth floor and mud walls. Pushing it open, he ushered Meggie inside. 'Make yourself at home,' he said with a grin, 'if it merits the name *home*.'

'It's fine,' she protested. There was a low bed in the far corner, a rough table and two stools and, on a smaller table, a big pitcher for water and a shallow bowl. The tiny window was unglazed, but the weather was mild, and, besides, she had been sleeping under the stars for the last few nights. This would be no worse than the hut in the Hawkenlye forest on nights when the fire wouldn't draw. 'If you tell me where to find the well,' she added, 'I'll fetch water.' She indicated the pitcher.

He hesitated, looking to his right and left, and she knew that, like her, he still felt that unseen, unfriendly presence. 'The well's down at the end of this street,' he said. 'It's not far. But be careful, *oui*?'

'Yes.' He had turned away, clicking to Auban to get him moving again; presumably in the direction of whatever stabling was available. Instinctively, she reached out, grabbing his hand. '*You* be careful, too.' She met his eyes, almost black in the dim light. She read his expression. 'You feel it, don't you?' she whispered.

He nodded briefly, then hurriedly led Auban away.

She went inside, picked up the pitcher and set off to the well, filling the pitcher and then turning back the way she had come. There were other iron-workers' dwellings on either side of the street, although nobody was busy in the workrooms, and the lodgings appeared similarly deserted. Perhaps they were all up at the cathedral? Anyway, they weren't to be found. If Jehan had expected to meet up with the workmen he had known here before he'd set off for England, it looked as if he was going to be disappointed.

As she went back into the little room, a thought struck her: on the boat that brought them over the narrow seas, Jehan had told her how the men and women spying on King John's movements had come to Chartres specifically to seek out Jehan and his group of Bretons, knowing that they would be eager to answer the summons and take swift advantage of the opportunity to strike against the king who had murdered their prince. Did that mean, then, that all the workmen who had once lived in these empty buildings had been part of the group now, presumably, on their way to Wales? The fact that there was nobody here suggested that it did.

She put the heavy jug down on the little table, pouring some into the shallow bowl so that she could wash her hands and face. The water was cool and very refreshing, and she bent lower, scooping up a handful and trickling it down the back of her neck.

It was thus, bending down with her back to the door, fully engaged in her wash and enjoying it so much that she momentarily forgot her fear and her apprehension, that they jumped her. The first she knew was a heavy hand on her mouth and a brawny arm wrapped round her chest and upper arms, pinning them to her sides. Panicking at the sensation of being so suddenly helpless, she kicked out hard behind her with her right foot, hearing a grunt of pain as the side of her boot sole raked down a shin bone.

The arm round her chest tightened, and she could not draw breath. 'Stop that, bitch,' said a voice in her ear, 'or I'll crush the life out of you.' The arm tightened some more, and she thought she heard her ribs creak. She forced herself to relax.

'Get her over here, behind the door,' a second voice ordered curtly. 'Jacques, get over there too.'

Trying to turn her head to look – difficult, with the brutal hand over her face – Meggie saw that there were three of them. Three big, tough men, armed with knives and their own huge, scarred fists. And Jehan would not know they were there. Oh, dear God, he wouldn't stand a chance!

She started wriggling, twisting and turning, trying everything she could to escape the grip of her captor. He moved the hand from her mouth but, even as she took a deep breath and prepared to shout out, he bunched it into a fist and hit her very hard on the side of her head.

She saw bright lights, and then blackness.

She could not have been out for long, for she came back to herself to see Jehan on his knees, held by two of the men, one each side, who were forcing his head and shoulders down to the ground. His forehead was actually in the dirt.

His sword was propped up beside the door.

'That's more like it,' the third man said approvingly. 'A bit of humility doesn't go amiss, although I can't promise it'll help you any, my friend, once you stand before King John of England and explain why you and your companions were planning on joining those bastard Welshmen, damn their impudence, in their fight against him.' He paused, a smile spreading over his hard face. 'Didn't think we knew about you, did you? Well, let me tell you, you're not the only men to have organized an efficient spy network. Did you really believe England's borders aren't watched? Or that, having picked up one of your lot and persuaded his tongue to loosen, we wouldn't come back here and root out the rest of you?'

Jehan managed to raise his head sufficiently to look the man in the eyes. 'What did you do to him?' he demanded.

The big man laughed. 'We didn't do anything, except give him a bag of gold. He betrayed you, my friend.' He bent down, his face close to Jehan's. 'A piece of advice: if you can afford to *buy* information rather than torture it out of your captive, you'd be surprised at how much better the results are.' He nodded, as if agreeing with himself, and straightened up. Then he gave a curt nod to the men holding Jehan, and one of them put a heavy foot on the back of his neck, forcing him down again.

Meggie's head was thumping, but she knew she must *think*. These were the king's men, and, once they succeeded in getting

Jehan back over the seas to England to face their master, the outlook for him was terrible. She could not let that happen.

She was lying on her side, facing into the room, and the man who had held her was directly in front of her. Nobody was watching her. She drew up her knees and carefully turned over so that her legs were underneath her body. She rested on her elbows for a moment, steadying herself, then, not wanting to wait and risk someone noticing her movements, gathered her strength and pushed herself off the floor, upward and forward, head down, arms held rigid and crossed over her breasts, so that she drove like a battering ram into the big man's back.

He felt as if he were made of stone, and for a terrible moment she thought her desperate plan had failed. But she had caught him unawares and, off balance, he took a step forward, tripped and fell against one of the men holding Jehan. It was enough for Jehan, who was up and on his feet in the blink of an eye, swooping down to pick up his sword and then grabbing her arm with his free hand and flying for the doorway.

She thought they'd got away. But then she felt someone grab her round the legs, and she fell to the ground, her hand dragged out of Jehan's grip. He twisted round, staring at her out of shocked and horrified eyes. 'Go on!' she yelled. 'It's *you* they want, not me – *run!*'

He didn't run. Instead, he reached down and helped her to her feet, pulling her out of her captor's grasp. But in saving her, he had condemned himself, for now the big man had hold of him.

'It is you who must run,' he said. He pushed her very hard away from him, up the deserted street towards the town.

She ran a couple of paces, then turned round. 'I can't!' she wailed.

He flicked his head round very briefly and, for a heartbeat, his dark eyes held hers. 'You must,' he said as he turned back to face his assailants. He had wrested himself out of the big man's grasp – damaging him somehow in the process, for the man was doubled up with pain – and was holding him and the others at bay with his sword. 'I can't come with you just yet. Either they or I must die, for it must end here,' he added softly.

The big man was kneeling on the ground now, but his two companions were edging forward, their eyes on the point of Jehan's sword. They were muttering, heads close together, and Meggie caught a few chilling words that sounded like *let the woman go and kill him right here and now*.

Jehan shot her another quick look, and there was a message in his expression . . . and she suddenly knew what she must do.

She turned and fled up the street, the sound of her feet echoing off the walls. *Either they or I must die. Kill him here and now*. Oh, *oh*, but there were three of them – the big man would surely soon be up again – and Jehan was alone. By herself she could not help him fight them all, but the cathedral was nearby, and surely there were workmen there, maybe even men who knew Jehan, who would help her. If only she could be quick enough – she redoubled her efforts, flying up the street – then there was a hope, a faint hope, that she could bring help before it was too late.

Forcing herself to keep in mind the image of him swinging his sword – that ancient, magical sword with power in its very metal – she burst out of the narrow street and came face to face with the cathedral.

TWENTY-ONE

Ninian was deep in his reverie. He felt uplifted; as if some power outside himself was entering into him, filling him with its own strange force. It was odd, he thought – as much as he was capable of thought just then, in his trance-like state – for, although he was in no doubt about the strength of the weird power, he was also quite sure that it meant him no harm. Quite the contrary, in fact; he felt as if he were surrounded with the warmth of love.

He had no idea of how long he'd been down in the crypt, eyes closed, kneeling before the Madonna and child. Time seemed to have stopped; either that, or somehow he had entered another realm that lay parallel to the real one, a place that closely resembled it but yet was subtly different. Could two worlds exist side by side? he wondered dreamily. If so, then maybe he had slipped unwittingly through the portal.

He thought he might risk opening his eyes.

He was in the same place, or it felt as if he was, for it was cool, dark, silent, and both walls and floor were made of stone. But before him there was not a statue in a niche; there was a ragged-edged hole in the ground. It was filled with water, the surface of which seemed to broil slowly and steadily, as if a spring welled up in it.

The very air was filled with unearthly power, and Ninian knew without even thinking about it that he was in the presence of the spirits.

It was enough – oh, God, it was more than enough. He forced his eyes to close again, pressing his hands hard against his eyelids.

He did not know if it was no more than a product of his imagination, but, just before he shut off the extraordinary sights that his mind could not accept, he thought he saw his mother.

He must have fallen into some sort of swoon.

He was awakened by the sound of voices; a woman, shouting, screaming for help; footsteps running hard; angry protests. The woman's voice again.

Despite his efforts to shut it away and forget all about it, he was still half in his dream world, and for a moment he thought the shouting voice was Joanna's.

But then he realized it wasn't.

Leaping to his feet, he raced across the crypt and up the stone steps. Panting, dizzy, he emerged out on to the floor of the cathedral.

She was standing in the middle of a group of cross-looking officials, many of them in clerical robes and all of them remonstrating with her, angry, apparently, at her unseemly behaviour within God's house. She was frantic, pleading with them to help her, go with her, and all of them were shaking their heads in incomprehension.

It was extraordinary, he thought in a moment's clarity, but he was not in the least surprised to see her.

He pushed his way through the clerics and approached her. He spoke her name, very softly.

She spun round – he noticed she had a large bruise on the side of her face – and, after one swift, delighted look, fell into his arms. Then, allowing herself no more than an instant, she pulled away, glared up at him and, as if he had been deliberately detaining her, said, 'There's no time for that! He's in terrible danger, and we have to help him!'

He didn't even try to get her to explain. Breaking into a run, he followed her across the vast floor, out of the door and down the steps, then across the square and off along one of the dim, narrow little alleyways that led to the artisans' village.

Outside a low, narrow dwelling, three men were held at bay by a fourth, wielding a great sword. His three opponents had lesser weapons, and their reach was shorter. The man with the sword kept sweeping it in broad strokes before him. Even from where he stood, Ninian could see the blueish edge of the steel; no wonder the attackers were keeping their distance.

The man with the sword had deeply tanned skin, a short beard and a gold ring in his ear, and he wore a length of cloth wound around his head. He was dressed in a long robe of an indeterminate shade that was nearest to brown. His eyes, almost black, were narrowed in concentration. He was holding his opponents – the largest of whom was grunting in pain – against the wall of the dwelling. He turned to give a swift glance at Meggie, flashed her a grin and, with a nod in Ninian's direction, said, 'Was he the best you could find?'

Ninian heard Meggie laugh softly. 'Just wait,' she said.

Ninian drew his own sword, and the sharp metal seemed to whistle and hiss as it emerged from the scabbard. He went to take up his place beside the man in brown. 'I'm called Ninian,' he said to him. It seemed only right to identify himself, since he was about to fight shoulder to shoulder with this man. 'I'm her brother.'

'Jehan Leferronier,' the man replied. He seemed on the point of adding something, but then changed his mind.

'What do you want to do?' Ninian muttered. 'Disarm them and hand them to the constables?'

'They will not lay down their weapons,' Jehan said. 'They work for a ruthless master who does not accept such failure.'

'Very well.' Ninian felt the hot uprush of blood. 'Let's take them.'

For a moment the brown-skinned man met his eyes. A glance of understanding passed between them – *he too is a fighter*, Ninian thought – and then, moving as one, they advanced on the three men.

The fight was ugly. The long swords that Ninian and Jehan wielded were less useful at close quarters, and soon both men dropped them in favour of their shorter, stabbing knives. It was quickly obvious which of the three men was the greatest threat: the biggest of the trio was a tough, wily brawler who, surmounting his evident pain, seemed to anticipate and counter every form of attack. Then Ninian, who had been trying to wrest the big man's knife out of his hand, felt a sudden blow to the back of his head and, spinning round, saw another of the attackers swinging a club high in the air in preparation for a second blow.

Ninian wriggled out of the way just in time, and the man, thrown off balance by the lack of resistance to his mighty swing, stumbled to his knees. Ninian fell on him, landing on his back and forcing him to the ground. He pushed the man's face down into the dust, clinging on as he struggled, holding him down until the struggling stopped.

As the red fury abated, he looked up.

Jehan was engaged with the third of the opponents, pushing him back against the wall of the dwelling, one hard hand closing against the man's throat, so that his fleshy face was gradually swelling and darkening. A fierce joy swept up through Ninian.

Then he heard a cry of fear.

Meggie.

She was halfway up the alley, backing away towards the town. The big man was almost upon her, and he had a knife in his hand.

He cannot kill her, Ninian thought wildly. *It will not happen – it can't.*

The man advanced. Meggie took another pace back.

Ninian struggled to his feet, his head spinning and fizzing from the blow he had received. Swaying from side to side, he hurried off up the alley. He stooped to pick up his sword and all but fainted as he straightened up again.

The big man made a lunge at Meggie: a killing blow, except

that she ducked down to her right at the very last moment and, instead of piercing her heart, the knife went into her shoulder. She fell, blood spreading swiftly over the cloth of her robe as the big man withdrew his knife.

Ninian had no idea what she had done to make the big man want to kill her; he did not care. She was his half-sister, his beloved Meggie. He would have given his life for her. The least he could do was take this bastard's life before he gathered himself for another attempt to take hers.

Keep still, he said to her silently. *Stay right where you are, then he too will not move and I can line up my attack.*

He knew he had to get it right first time, for he could not guarantee there would be a second chance.

But she was up, on her hands and knees, backing away from her assailant. The man gave a quiet chuckle. 'Going to make a game of it, my pretty lass, eh?' He chuckled again. 'So much the better.'

Slowly, deliberately, he wiped his blade on his tunic and advanced after her.

Suddenly she was up, haring off up the alley. The big man, as taken aback as Ninian, recovered very quickly and ran after her, cursing. Ninian tried to follow, but his legs were heavy, and he felt as if he were trying to run through thick mud. One step – *come on!* – two steps. He found a little strength and managed a loping run for several paces. Then he fell.

Twisting round, his eyes searched frantically for Jehan. But he was still fully occupied with his own opponent, and Ninian did not dare distract him by calling out.

Get up, he ordered himself. He forced down the nausea, ignored the agonizing banging in his head and got to his feet. Grasping his sword, he ran after the big man.

And saw, in a flash of understanding, that he was too late.

She was only a few paces from the end of the alleyway; she had almost made it out into the square. But by sheer ill fortune, there was a kink in the track just there, and both she and the man about to kill her were out of sight of anyone but Ninian. The big man held her by her hair, which he had twisted round his left hand. He was holding her very tightly; Ninian could see tears of pain in her wide eyes.

The big man's knife was at her throat. He was about to end

her life, as a farmer might dispatch a weakling lamb that was
not going to survive.

Ninian knew it was hopeless, for he was still too far away
and the deadly slice that would take out his sister's throat was
even now beginning. He saw a bead of blood on the soft white
skin of her neck.

Praying for supernatural strength – for any kind of miracle
– he launched himself forward.

The impetus took what was left of his strength, and quickly
his vision clouded, until all he saw was blackness. Out of it
he thought he heard a voice: a powerful, deep voice. It shouted,
Let her go!

Ninian opened his eyes.

Beyond Meggie was a man on a horse. The horse was
golden-coloured, its luxuriant mane and tail dark. The man
was broad-shouldered, and in his hand he held a sword. He
was bareheaded, his dark hair thick. His eyes, full of anger,
were brown, and in them there seemed to be bright highlights,
like sunshine on water.

The big man shouted a furious oath and, as the man on the
horse swung down his sword, he let go of Meggie. The man
turned, broke instantly into a wild, loping, stumbling run . . .

. . . on to the point of Ninian's sword.

He crumpled and fell, a look of astonishment in his eyes.
Then he gave a low moan, and his mouth filled with blood.
His eyes lost their expression, and Ninian realized he was
dead.

He withdrew his sword.

He looked up. The man on the horse had dismounted and
was cradling Meggie to his deep chest, gently touching her
wounded shoulder, murmuring gentle words. Meggie seemed
incapable of speech, other than the one word, constantly
repeated.

Ninian stumbled up to the man, who put out his free arm
and clutched him close.

Jehan! Ninian struggled free and, turning, ran back down
the alley. He met Jehan coming towards him. 'Is she safe?'
he demanded.

'Wounded but safe,' Ninian replied. He raised his eyebrows
in query.

'Dead,' Jehan said shortly.

'Then that's all three of them,' Ninian muttered.

He caught the swift smile of satisfaction on Jehan's face.

Another wave of nausea took him, and he bent over, hands on his knees. With the danger passed, he was beginning to recognize how hard he had been hit.

Jehan put a concerned hand on his shoulder. 'You are hurt?'

'Not badly,' he replied. 'Hit on the head.'

Jehan nodded gravely. 'You must take care,' he said, 'for—'

But there were far more important issues to discuss. Such as, how best to explain to this surprising stranger – with whom, from the look of both of them, his sister had intricately and possibly intimately involved herself – that Meggie's father was standing at the far end of the alley.

It was late in the evening, and Josse had at last found a moment to slip away and go down into the cathedral crypt. He felt he had very good reason to, and he would have gone before had there not been so much to see to.

Meggie seemed to have found herself a man; the Brown Man, in fact, who, on first impressions, did not seem too bad. Josse was cautiously prepared to give him the benefit of the doubt, at least, while he got to know him better. It was a definite mark in his favour that he was not the man who had assaulted and killed the Hawkenlye victims, even if his true purpose in coming to England had been to join in with those who were preparing to stand against the king as he forced his way into Wales. Sometimes, Josse reflected wryly as he strode across the square towards the cathedral, he felt he could understand all too well why a man might take up arms against the king. That, however, was a thought that would have to remain very firmly shut up inside his own head.

And fancy finding both Meggie and Ninian like that! It was quite extraordinary, for Josse and Helewise had only just arrived in Chartres, and, indeed, Josse had been about to seek out stabling for Alfred and for Helewise's mare when they'd heard the commotion. A young woman, people were saying, had affronted the clerics and the high-up officials within the cathedral by racing in and shouting out that she needed help, urgently, and before they could decide how best to deal with her bad behaviour, a young man had raced off with her and the two of them had disappeared down that alleyway over there.

Josse, fear stabbing at his heart and turning his blood cold, had thrown the mare's reins to Helewise, put spurs to Alfred and followed the pointing fingers. To find his daughter in the grip of a fat thug who held a knife to her throat and seemed to be about to kill her.

Josse still could not bear to think about that moment. She had not died, thank the dear, good, merciful God. The man who had been about to kill her had died, however. He and his two companions now lay in the burial ground attached to the town's gaol, borne there by the forces of law and order who, belatedly arriving on the scene, had been convinced by Josse that no crime had been committed other than that three unsavoury strangers – English strangers, to boot – had managed to put paid to each other in a bad-tempered fight.

The town's law enforcers had better things to do than waste time investigating the deaths of Englishmen. Their leader pocketed the generous donation that Josse gave him, and no more was said. Just in case anybody changed their mind and began asking difficult questions, Josse had ordered Ninian and Jehan to leave the town. He described to them the location of a suitable campsite that he remembered and promised to meet them there the next day.

Meggie's shoulder wound was deep and dirty. Helewise had made the very sensible suggestion that they take her to the convent where Helewise had stayed the previous time she had visited Chartres, and now Meggie was being cared for there. Helewise had stayed with her. Apart from some slight embarrassment over explaining to the mother superior that she was no longer an abbess, or even a nun, all had been accomplished smoothly. The convent's healers had washed and stitched the cut, and already Meggie was sufficiently recovered to ask questions about her treatment and offer her own suggestions.

Amid all that had been going on, Josse had kept a part of himself back; a part that, recognizing this busy, crowded town as the last place where Joanna had been in her earthly existence, was already communing with her spirit.

So it was that, now, he was quietly letting himself into the soaring, silent cathedral and making for the steps down to the crypt.

He had a very strong sense that he would never come here again. Before he left for ever, he wanted to take the opportunity of trying to say a last goodbye.

Goodbye and thank you, he reflected as he made his way down the stone steps. Ninian had told him – tried to tell him, although indeed the lad's explanation had been all but incomprehensible – that he'd detected Joanna's hand in everything that had happened concerning his return from the Languedoc, from first promptings right up to the moment in the crypt, when for an instant he had thought himself in another realm. The realm, perhaps, that Joanna now inhabited.

Ninian. Josse thought with love of the young man. They hadn't yet told him exactly why it had been so imperative to summon him home. Ninian had asked about Little Helewise, of course he had, as soon as there had been a moment and they weren't trying to save each other's lives, and Josse had overheard Meggie say, 'She's very well. She sends her best love.' Josse was content to leave it to Meggie to tell him, when the time was right. Women seemed to understand about such things better than men. Better than Josse, anyway.

He was in the crypt. Slowly he walked forward, across the central area where everyone went, and on into the shadows further in its cavernous depths. There had been a sacred spring here years ago, thousands of years, perhaps, long before the building of the great edifices to Christianity had begun. Joanna had always said it was a very special spot . . .

He knew he was no longer in the crypt beneath the new cathedral. He was in the same place, yet it was different. He heard chanting and smelt incense. It was a pungent smell, and it made him slightly dizzy. He seemed to see shapes, lights, floating before his eyes.

He did not know if she was there. But she might be, so he said softly, 'Thank you, Joanna. You brought him back to us, and I reckon you had a hand in today's events too.'

Silence.

'You're going to be a grandmother,' he went on, smiling. 'How do you feel about that?'

He wondered how she would look now. Would the years have changed her, as they did ordinary mortals? Would the long, dark hair now be grey; the dark, shining eyes dimmed? Or did people in whatever spirit world she now inhabited remain as they were when they left their earthly existence? She might be—

She was beside him.

He sensed her; he thought he saw her, although it was hard to distinguish between his vivid memories and what was actually before his eyes.

He certainly heard her. 'Hello, Josse,' she said quietly. 'How do *you* feel, Grandad?'

He grinned. 'Not quite yet. The baby isn't due until—' But he had forgotten.

'July,' she supplied. 'It's a girl, and she's going to be as bonny as her mother. Don't tell them I told you,' she added.

'I won't,' he said.

There was a silence; quite awkward, on his part, for there was so much that he wanted to ask her and he did not know how. But, as she had so often done in life, she picked up his thoughts.

'I am fine, dear Josse,' she said. 'I would say I am very well, but such things aren't really relevant in the place where I am.'

'You're not – alone, are you?' Somehow it would have hurt very much, to think of her all by herself.

She laughed softly. 'Oh, no. There are many of us. We watch, you see; sometimes, at places such as here, we can get through to those we love. At other times, we can view you as from a far shore, where very often there is a sort of mist.'

'Was it you who called Ninian home?'

She laughed again. 'Of course.'

There was another, longer, silence. He had the sense that he was drinking her in, this woman he had loved so much, taking in every last moment of her to store up and keep in his heart for ever.

Again, she picked up what was in his mind. 'It's goodbye, my lovely Josse,' she whispered. 'I'll still be with you – I'll always be with you, even beyond death – but I don't think this – us being together – will happen again.'

He knew in his heart that she was right. He nodded, unable to speak.

He felt a warm touch against the flesh of his cheek, as if she had leaned close to him and brushed him with her soft hair. 'Do not waste the time that remains to you,' she said.

'What do you mean?'

'Oh, dearest Josse, you know what I mean! There is another who loves you as much as I do. You love her too, as you have always done, and it's high time you both acknowledged it.'

'I thought we had a chance,' he admitted. 'But I don't think she can ever leave the abbey behind her. She went back, you know, and she has been living in the little cell by the chapel.'

'Yes,' Joanna said softly. 'She *has* been.'

The emphasis was unmistakable. 'Might she come back home?' he asked. The moment the words were out, he understood how much he wanted the answer to be yes.

Joanna laughed again. 'If I were you, I'd ask her.'

He knew she was going. There wasn't very long. 'Joanna?'

'I'm still here.' He thought her voice was fainter now.

'Thank you,' he said. 'For your love; for the two children you bore me, and for your son, who feels equally my own.'

'Thank *you*,' she replied. 'No children could have a finer father.'

He stood there for some time. His left side – the side where she had stood; his heart side – felt cold. He knew she had gone.

Eventually, he turned, crossed the crypt, slowly ascended the steps and emerged into the cathedral. It was all but deserted. He made his way to the great north door, ducking down under some falsework holding up the roof. As he stepped out into the night, someone came out of the shadows and fell into step beside him.

'You must be cold,' he said gruffly.

'I didn't want you to be alone.'

He stopped, turning to look at her. Her face was anxious; did she think he wasn't pleased to see her?

He didn't want there to be any doubt.

'Thank you for being here,' he said. 'I – she was—' He didn't know how to explain. 'It's the last time I'll be able to reach her, I think,' he went on in a rush. 'She's done what she wanted to do, and the family is together again, or soon will be. I told her she's going to be a grandmother, but, naturally, she already knew.'

There was a short silence. He knew she had heard, and he guessed she was taking in everything that his remarks implied.

He turned and looked down at her. He smiled. 'Shall we set out for home tomorrow, if those nuns think Meggie is all right to travel?'

'I'd like that,' she replied. 'Tomorrow or in a few days; it doesn't really matter.'

She was right; it didn't. What mattered was that they went home together. 'I'll send word to Yves first thing in the morning,' he said, thinking ahead. 'We'll have something to celebrate, when we call in this time.'

She smiled. 'We will.'

He set off across the square, and Helewise walked beside him. After a few paces, he took her hand.

TWENTY-TWO

Meggie lay in her bed in the convent infirmary, wishing she could leap up and set out for home, yet recognizing that the nuns who had her in their care were quite right not to let her leave yet. The knife wound in her shoulder had turned red and angry, and it was only now – four days since the fight – that it was starting to heal. She had no fault to find with the nuns' nursing; on the contrary, they had used one or two methods which were new to her and undoubtedly efficacious. Such as putting maggots into the cut to eat out the pus and putrefaction; a tip which, according to Sister Marie-Joseph, they had learned from returning crusaders, who in turn had learned it from the Arab medicine men.

Efficacious or not, it had taken all her courage, not to mention her will to get well again, to tolerate the strange sensation of living creatures busy in her flesh. With a certain amount of pleasure, she imagined how it would be when she made a patient of her own endure the treatment.

The maggots had been removed now; the cut was clean and the flesh around it no longer hot to the touch. Meggie's brief bout of fever had also gone; in some ways a pity, she thought, because, in her delirium, her mother had come to tend her. Meggie had felt Joanna's cool, gentle hand on her fiery forehead, heard her soft voice murmuring the healing incantation, and even caught a glimpse of the familiar figure bending over her.

Meggie was well aware that such visions were a common symptom of delirium. Nevertheless, she knew that Joanna had been with her, in some form or another. If her welcome presence was a product of Meggie's memory and emotions, then that didn't make it any less valuable. And Joanna's magic touch, together with the nuns' skills, meant that Meggie was now almost well enough to leave.

She was restless. The nuns had put her in a little room apart from the main ward, which had been nice when she was sick and in pain and just wanted to be left alone, but was not so good now, when she was bored and would have welcomed the moving tapestry of a constantly busy infirmary.

To occupy herself, she thought about the others. Her father, she was all but sure, had had some encounter with her mother. Meggie hadn't asked him about it, nor would she. Josse had loved Joanna profoundly, and Meggie understood that a part of him always would. If Joanna had somehow appeared to him, reassured him of her love and persuaded him that the time had come for him to get on with his life, then that was wonderful. It was what Meggie suspected, for she had noticed a new gentleness between her father and Helewise. They, too, loved each other. Perhaps, at long last, Helewise was going to be able to forget she'd been a nun and remember she was also a woman.

Meggie's thoughts moved on to Jehan and Ninian. Josse had told her they were camping out in the place where Joanna and her people had once stayed; he'd also told her she had been there too, back then when she was a very small child, although Meggie had only a very vague memory of it. It had been wise of Josse to get both young men out of Chartres. Had there been any sort of enquiry into the deaths of King John's men, both of them would have been in danger.

She wondered how they were getting on. She hoped that the ferocity of their initial encounter would have formed a bond between them; they had, after all, been on the same side, and both had fought to the death, although fortunately not their own.

She had discovered, lying there, just how important it was that her brother – and her father – should like Jehan. Now that she was absent from him, for the first time in days, she had come to appreciate just how much he meant to her.

She was content, for now, to keep her tender new feelings for him locked away inside her, a delicious secret to take out and dwell on whenever she felt inclined. When she was with him again, she would be able to see whether he reciprocated her love. She smiled. She believed she already knew.

She thought back to the moment when she had rushed into the cathedral and the terrible frustration she had felt when the clerics, far from hurrying to help her, had been angry because her raised voice and frantic demeanour had been disrespectful and irreligious. *Irreligious!* She fumed all over again. Wouldn't anyone be irreligious, when someone they cared about was trying to fight off three tough men determined to kill him? Then, glory of glories, Ninian had come barging through the midst of them. Ninian, the one man she would have chosen to come to her aid, and there he was, tanned, slimmer than she remembered, his garments showing signs of hard wear but cleaner than she would have expected. No matter how he had looked, he'd been the answer to her prayer.

She was pretty sure her mother had had a hand in that, too.

She turned to plump up her pillows – the movement barely hurt her shoulder now – and, leaning back again, thought about her brother. She must speak to him, soon. He ought to know . . .

She closed her eyes and slipped into a doze. She was awakened by a gentle touch on her hand and Sister Marie-Joseph's soft voice telling her she had a visitor.

She knew who it would be even before he came in. 'I will leave you in peace,' Sister Marie-Joseph said with a smile. 'Don't tire her, now!'

'I won't,' Ninian said. He drew up the little stool set by the door and came to sit beside Meggie's bed. For some moments he said nothing, simply stared intently into her face, then he nodded. 'You're on the mend,' he said.

'I am.' She reached out and took his hand, holding it between her own.

'I'm so sorry you were hurt.'

She waved the apology away. 'It wasn't your fault. You and Jehan had your hands full.' She hesitated. 'What do you – er, how are you getting on, out in your camp?'

Ninian's quick grin indicated he knew perfectly well what she had almost said. 'We're getting on fine. He's a handy person to camp out with, I must say. Very skilled in all the useful crafts for keeping yourself fed, watered, warm and generally comfortable.' The grin was back. 'He's fine, Meggie. I like and admire him.'

She felt she ought to come clean. 'He came to England on a mission,' she said quietly. 'He and some other Bretons were going to—'

But Ninian put up a hand and stopped her. 'I know, Meggie. He told me.' Leaning closer, he said in a very soft voice, 'He felt he should explain about the men who were trying to kill the two of you. But we shouldn't speak of it again.'

'I think Father should know,' she protested.

'He already does,' Ninian replied. 'Jehan told him too.'

Oh no. Josse, Meggie knew, had long been a king's man, although, admittedly, that had been the previous one. Had Jehan been sufficiently diplomatic? 'How did he react?'

Ninian met her eyes. 'His response was, to sum it up: *I can't say I blame you, but don't tell me any more.* Nothing if not honest, dear old Josse, is he?'

'No.' Meggie thought about her big, strong, decent father. Honest he most certainly was, and, she realized, he was not the man to condemn another for an action he fully understood, even if he couldn't approve of it.

Ninian shifted on his seat, and she sensed he was about to speak again. 'I have something to tell you,' he began.

'No, wait.' Whatever it was, she felt she had to reveal her secret to him first. It was now or never, for she knew she must tell him while they were alone, and it might be ages before that happened again. Meeting his brilliant blue eyes, she said, 'Are you looking forward to seeing Little Helewise?'

A broad smile spread over his face. 'Meggie, if that's your delicate way of asking me if I've been faithful to her while I've been away and if I still love her, the answers are yes and yes.'

She was very surprised, for it had not even occurred to her that he could have fallen for someone else. She was, she realized, very, very glad he hadn't.

He was speaking: '. . . men I was with referred to her in their version of her name, which is Eloise, and I've begun to think of her in that way,' he said.

So Little Helewise had turned into Eloise, she thought, and wasn't Little any more. She found she was smiling. 'Perhaps that's just as well,' she said gently.

'What do you mean?'

'Referring to her as *little* isn't very appropriate at the moment and won't be for a while,' she said, still smiling.

'You're saying she's put on weight?' he asked. 'I shan't mind, she'll be lovely just as – *oh!*'

She gave him a few moments to absorb the news. Then, holding his hand again, she said, 'July, we believe. She is very well, and, once she had plucked up her courage and told us, also very happy.'

'I wish I'd been there,' he muttered. Then, as his face took on an expression of awe, he whispered, 'I've been seeing visions and images of mothers and babies all the way here! They've led me on and, when I've doubted myself, persuaded me I was on the right path. Do you think this is why, Meggie? Because I had to be brought north again, to meet my responsibilities?'

'I do,' she said gravely.

'But how—?'

She squeezed his hand. 'Don't think about it too much,' she advised. 'Some things we can't ever know, and it's probably better that way.'

There was silence in the little room, both of them occupied

with their own thoughts. Then, rousing herself, she said, 'You were about to tell me something?'

'I was.' He withdrew his hands and, reaching inside his tunic, took out a small, silk-wrapped package. He laid it on her bed, unwrapped it and spread out a set of images, beautifully painted on card.

She picked one up. It depicted an intricately-carved stone doorway, with a heavy wooden door set in it. The door was open just a crack, and a small figure was peering round it into a scene, just glimpsed, of beautiful countryside illuminated with shining light. She reached for another: a woman robed in the vestments of the church, her face stern, unforgiving; almost brutal. She picked up a third card, then, quickly now, two more, her heartbeat racing as she went swiftly from one to another until she had looked at each one. Then, stunned, shocked, she carefully put the cards on the white bedcover, the images facing downwards. They were just too powerful, and she did not think she could bear to look at them for long.

'I was given them by Alazaïs de Saint Gilles,' Ninian said. 'She's one of the elders of their religion, and a very revered woman. She asked me to bring this set of images out to safety – they all seem to carry similar sets, although few that I saw were as fine as these. They—' His brow creased in a frown. 'They're a sort of aid to memory, symbolizing the very basis of the bonshommes' beliefs. They tell the story of a journey,' he added, 'and, although Alazaïs explained it to me, I can't say I understand.'

Meggie felt ready to look at the images again. She picked them up, slowly arranging them until she was satisfied. 'I don't know if I've got it right,' she said, 'but it makes sense to me this way. The journey starts in fear and uncertainty, and the traveller has to face hardships and ordeals until he reaches his goal, which I suppose is paradise.'

He looked amazed. 'How can you possibly know that?' he demanded.

She smiled. 'You forget what I've been learning since I was small,' she said. 'All belief systems have a story at their heart – a journey of the soul, if you like – and the things I was taught, by our own mother and by the elders of her people, have similarities with these.' She placed a gentle, respectful hand on the images.

'I don't begin to understand.' He shook his head violently, as if to rid it of the puzzling things that perplexed him. She hid a smile; he was a man of logic and action, her dear brother, and he did not have all that much imagination. Even she, who loved him profoundly, had to admit it. 'I've got to hide them and keep them safe,' he went on. 'Alazaïs and her people fear, with justification, that the crusaders will destroy every last one of these precious images, and she asked me to bring this set out to safety. Where should I hide it, Meggie? I've thought about it endlessly all the way home, and I've come to no conclusion.'

She had tidied the images together into a neat rectangle, and now she wrapped them up in their silk. She was thinking; trying to decide if the idea that had sprung so abruptly into her head was the right thing to do.

She believed it was.

Looking up, she said, 'Ninian, do we know anyone who can draw well?'

'Er – there are probably nuns at Hawkenlye who copy manuscripts, and they are often illustrated.'

'Yes, and there's a beautiful Hawkenlye Herbal done by someone called Sister Phillipa,' she agreed, 'but I wasn't actually thinking of a nun.'

'Eloise draws very nicely,' he suggested. 'What about her?'

'Hm.'

'What do you want drawn?' he demanded. Then, as understanding dawned, he said quietly, 'Why?'

'Ninian, I agree that we should find a very secure place to hide these, for they are beautiful and beyond price. But I also think we ought to try, somehow, to perpetrate these images. They are too – too—' She tried to think how to explain. 'They depict the basic truths,' she said eventually, 'and are part of our very humanity. I believe we should keep them in the world.'

'But we only occupy a very small space in the world,' he pointed out.

She met his eyes, grinning. 'Well, we have to start somewhere.'

POSTSCRIPT

When Josse and Helewise led Ninian, Meggie and Jehan through the gates of Acquin, there was somebody waiting for them.

Josse felt the tears form in his eyes as, with a cry, Ninian leapt off his horse, ran across the yard and swooped up the young woman standing alone, staring at him. For a moment, Little Helewise was hidden, enfolded in Ninian's arms and his swirling cloak, but then, as if appreciating that he was handling a woman all at once as fragile as glass, he let her go and stepped abruptly away from her.

She burst out laughing. 'Idiot!' she said, swatting at him. 'I'm not going to break, and the baby's as strong as an ox, to judge by the way it keeps kicking me!' She threw herself back into his arms and, before them all, pulled down his head and kissed him, firmly and thoroughly, on the mouth.

Now Josse noticed Yves step forward, their brothers Patrice, Honoré and Acelin beside him, their wives a pace behind. 'Welcome, Josse! Welcome, my lady, and you youngsters, too!' Yves opened his arms as if to embrace them all. 'We received word that you were on your way and have had plenty of time to prepare the celebrations, as you see!' With a delighted smile, he indicated Little Helewise, now standing hand in hand with Ninian and looking slightly abashed.

'She didn't come all the way here to Acquin by herself, surely?' Josse demanded.

'Of course not,' a quiet, firm voice said, and Leofgar stepped out of the shadows. It was Helewise's turn to give a cry of delight; leaping down from Daisy's back, she ran to her son and into his arms.

The shortages which Josse and his family had been suffering for so long back in England apparently did not affect Acquin, and the feast which the brothers, their wives and servants had prepared was all the better for being such a welcome change.

The spring evening was warm and fine, and a trestle table had been set up in the courtyard, illuminated along its extensive length by candles and lanterns. Josse thought he counted twenty-five tucking into the endless succession of dishes, but Yves had a generous hand with the wine and he admitted to himself that he could have been wrong, especially since on a couple of occasions his count came to twenty-seven and once, well into the evening, thirty.

Before he lost the ability to stand up, he got himself to his feet, a hand on Helewise's shoulder to keep him steady, and raised his goblet in a toast. 'To my family,' he said, beaming round at them all. 'May God bless you all and keep safe those of you whom I see far less frequently than I should like.'

There was the sound of stools and benches scraping across the ground as everyone rose and echoed the words. Then, when they had all sat down again, Yves, on Josse's other side, said, 'You know, Josse, it took only three days for our message to be sent from Acquin to Leofgar's house, and for him and Eloise to arrive here.'

Josse tried to focus his fuddled wits. Then, appreciating what his brother was saying, he nodded. 'We must take the time, all of us, to make the journey,' he said solemnly. He turned to look into Yves's face, deep affection welling in him. 'The only times we have seen each other in the last twenty years have been when something dramatic has happened. Let's vow now, you and I, to change that, for none of us has unlimited years ahead, and in the time that remains, I wish to see more of those I love, on both sides of the narrow seas.'

There was a brief silence. Then Yves, emotion audible in his voice, said softly, 'Amen.'

Further down the table, Ninian and Eloise – delighted with the new version of her name, which, she decided, was more adult and therefore fitting for a mother-to-be – sat holding hands and trying to fill in for each other everything that had happened while they had been apart.

'You know I'd marry you as soon as we get home if I could,' he said to her, looking sadly into her eyes. 'Well, we'd have wed ages ago, had it been possible.'

She nodded. 'I know that.' Then she sighed. 'The only consolation is that we're by no means alone in our plight.' Leaning closer, she added in whisper, 'My father's accepted it now, although he was a bit shocked at first.'

'What about your mother?' Ninian whispered back.

Eloise sighed again. It was painful to think about her mother, for Rohaise, on finally hearing the news, had expressed her horror in no uncertain terms. 'That a daughter of mine should behave in that manner!' she had whispered, as if she could not bear to speak of it out loud. 'Mother is refusing to speak to me,' she admitted.

She felt a movement beside her, where Josse's sister-in-law Marie sat. 'I am sorry to interrupt and, indeed, to have listened to your private conversation,' she began.

'It's not really private,' Eloise said with a short laugh. 'My mother's attitude is no secret.' She turned to Marie, encouraged by the woman's warm smile. 'Maybe she'll change her mind once the baby's born,' she went on. 'People do, or so I'm told.'

'Would she forgive you, do you think, if you and Ninian married?'

'Probably, but we can't,' Eloise replied, slightly impatiently. 'The interdict, you know.'

Marie's smile broadened. 'There's no interdict here,' she murmured.

Meggie sat with Jehan, leaning back against a straw bale and watching the swirling dancers in Acquin's courtyard. It was early afternoon, a week after Josse and his party had arrived, and Ninian had just made Eloise his wife. Yves had found a band of musicians to come and play, and the Acquin household were trying to teach their guests the steps of a traditional wedding dance. Jehan had whirled Meggie round until she begged for a break, and now both of them were catching their breath and refreshing themselves from the trestles heavily laden with food and drink.

She knew now that she loved him. She had known from their first meeting that she trusted him, and that trust had been right. Throughout their journey, he had protected her and cared for her, while at the same time never treating her as less than his equal. She did not think she could have borne a man who tried to control or patronize her; she was far too used to her independence to accept that.

They had not spoken yet of the future. Now, watching Ninian and Eloise in their radiant happiness, seemed a good moment.

Leaning against him, Meggie said, 'What shall we do now?'

He bent to kiss the top of her head. 'I could fetch you another drink, and maybe we could dance again.'

She dug an elbow into his ribs. 'A proper answer, please.'

There was a pause, as if he were thinking of how to reply. Then he said, 'I do love it, Meggie, that you ask your question with such frankness. The matter of our future is undoubtedly uppermost in both our minds, and, typically, it is you who broaches the subject.'

She twisted round to look up at him. His head was uncovered, the long, black hair glossy and smooth. He looked extraordinary; still, sometimes, the very strangeness of his appearance took her breath away. 'I've never lived in the sort of world where women must act prim and proper, getting what they want from sly hints and little flirtatious glances,' she said. 'I prefer to be direct.'

He laughed. 'I do not know that sort of world, either,' he said. 'I'm a blacksmith, Meggie.'

'I know.' She grinned. 'I like a man who earns his crust with honest labour.'

There was a brief silence. Then he said, 'I will tell you, Meggie, how I see the future, and then you shall tell me if it is acceptable to you. I must return to my home in Brittany, for there I have family, friends and obligations. But I do not propose to remain there. If you agree, I will come to England.'

She tried to absorb what he had just said. Did he mean to go to Brittany on his own? Was he then intending to come to England to find her? *Ask him*, said a beloved voice in her head.

'Would you like me to go with you?' she asked. She wondered if he too heard the tremor in her voice.

He wrapped his arms round her; strong arms, in which she knew she would always feel loved and safe. 'I will not move from this spot unless you do,' he said softly. 'I do not wish ever to be parted from you.'

She turned her head so that they were face to face. 'I will come,' she whispered.

He stared into her eyes, his own deep and intent. Then, as if to seal their pact, he nodded.

It was late. The moon had risen over the fields and woods of Acquin, the revels were over, the guests had gone home and the household were in their beds. All except for two people, who walked in the long grass beside the little river that ran through the valley. Somewhere hidden in the willow trees, a nightingale sang.

Josse stopped to listen, and the sweet notes seemed to echo his happiness. As if Helewise picked up his thoughts – he would not have been at all surprised if she did – she said softly, 'The nightingale's song sounds like a comment on the day.'

He smiled. 'It all went well, didn't it?'

'Yes. I rarely saw a young couple that looked so very suited to each other.'

'Will Rohaise forget her distress and welcome Ninian into the family, do you think?'

'Oh, I expect so.'

Josse thought he detected a certain wryness in her tone. 'You don't care for her much, do you?'

'I believe she is a woman who faces her own devils every day,' Helewise replied. 'Ever since I've known her – remember, Josse, when Leofgar brought her to Hawkenlye when she was so unwell?'

He nodded.

'Ever since we met, I've sensed that Rohaise is a – a difficult woman, but she is my son's choice, and I must hope that he truly loves her, and that his love is a help and a support to her, as indeed a husband's love should be.'

'And now Little Helewise – Eloise – will have her own husband, child and home, and won't have to endure her mother any more,' Josse said with satisfaction.

Helewise's quiet laugh suggested he'd been rather more frank than he had intended.

They strolled on.

'You'll miss Meggie,' Helewise said presently.

'Aye, I shall, but she'll be back in the autumn. She has given her word, and her Jehan has too. I trust him,' he added, turning to look at Helewise.

'So do I,' she agreed. 'So the Brown Man will return to Hawkenlye. I wonder what people will make of him?'

'They'll stare at him at first, as they always do when something exotic and strange comes into their lives, and then they'll discover that he's a useful man to have around when their ploughshare breaks, or a horse needs a shoe, and they'll forget he looks any different from anybody else.' He paused, thinking of Jehan's beautiful sword. 'I hope he'll be content with such domestic work,' he said. 'He comes from a line of swordsmiths, and his own ability is very evident in that mini-ature sword he made for Meggie.'

'He'll be content with *her*,' Helewise said confidently. 'They'll settle down in some little house on the edge of the forest, close by the stream, and Meggie will produce beautiful babies with black hair, pale chestnut skin and eyes that hold the sunshine, like hers and her father's.'

'That sounds like a prediction,' he said with a smile. 'The sort of thing—' He stopped, shocked at what he had almost said.

'The sort of thing Joanna would have said,' Helewise finished for him. 'Yes, dear Josse, I was thinking just the same.'

They were on a small apron of land that jutted out inside a bow of the little river. The musical sound of its waters, rippling over stones, blended with the nightingale's song. Josse closed his eyes. For a moment, Joanna filled his mind and his heart. Then, with a soft sigh, she was gone.

He turned to Helewise. 'Will you come back to the House in the Woods?'

'Yes, Josse.'

'And will you . . . Shall we live there together, or will it be as it was before you returned to the cell by the chapel?'

'It won't be like that,' she said. She looked down at the river below them, then raised her head and met his eyes. 'I have changed, Josse. Going back there has taught me many things, most important of which is that the chapel, and the abbey, are now in my past.'

It was a vast relief to hear her say so. He wanted to speak, but sensed she had not finished.

'What I would like to do, with your agreement,' she said

after a moment, 'is to carry on giving the help we were giving up by the chapel, but from the House in the Woods. I would like people in need to know that they have friends to turn to when they are desperate. We may not have much, but we have more than many, Josse, and it is possible that the bowl of gruel, or the simple herbal remedy, or even the kindly word, that we give to someone will be crucial in saving them when they are at their lowest ebb.'

He did not immediately reply. She was right, and he knew it, in wanting to help. But the House in the Woods was isolated, and few knew where it was, and that was very precious; it was also, he believed, the reason why he and his household enjoyed the peace and the relative freedom that they did. 'I—' he began.

But she interrupted. 'I, too, treasure our seclusion, not least for the security it gives us,' she said, again reading his thoughts. 'Besides, we are well hidden there, and people would not find us easily. What I suggest is that we put up a simple structure on the edge of the forest, in that clearing up near the road close to where Ninian made his camp. It is not far from the house, yet far enough that we would manage to keep our seclusion.'

He turned to her. Her expression held such hope that his heart softened. He knew exactly what would happen: the new refuge would be built, then Helewise – probably helped by Tiphaine, Tilly, Little Helewise, Meggie, once she was back, and sundry others – would pour herself and everything she had into making it a success. She'd be out from dawn till dusk, he'd hardly ever see her, and—

Then, still staring down at her, he realized that there was more in her expression than the urgent hope that he would agree to her plan.

She would pour *everything* she had into making the refuge a success? No, he was wrong. She had just said that she had changed, and now, knowing her as he did, loving her as he had done for so long, he understood what she had not been able to put into words.

Aye, she'd work herself to a standstill, all day and every day, for the hungry, the sick and the needy who came looking for her, but that was because she was Helewise; she'd probably been put on earth to help people. But even the longest day came to an end, and, when it did, she would come home and he would be waiting.

It was enough.

'We'll build your refuge,' he said.

Her eyes filled with tears. She managed a nod and a watery smile. 'Thank you,' she whispered.

There was more to say, but he did not know how to begin. He thought for a moment, and then he believed he had it.

He said softly, 'You once told me that you were a wife before ever you were a nun,' he said. 'Do you remember?'

She smiled, moving closer. 'I do. I also recall saying that it wasn't the passion of the marriage bed I recalled with such fondness but the comfort and the companionship.'

He hesitated. Then, his voice gruff, he asked, 'Do you remember the passion with any fondness?'

'I think perhaps I do.'

He put his arms round her, and she moved against his body as if she'd been doing it all her life.

His lips closed on hers.

High in the willow tree, the nightingale sang its blessing.